AF486456

Also By Brenda Hasse

<u>An Afterlife Journey Trilogy</u>
On The Third Day
From Beyond The Grave
Until We Meet Again

<u>Non-Fiction</u>
Haunted Fenton
The Haunted Tours of Fenton
A Victim Of Desperation

<u>Young Adult</u>
The Cursed Witch
The Freelancer
The Healer's Apprentice
A Lady's Destiny
The Moment Of Trust
Wilkinshire

<u>Picture Books For Children</u>
My Horsy And Me, What Can We Be?
A Unicorn For My Birthday
Yes, I Am Loved

The Parade Of Souls

~

Brenda Hasse

To Karen

Chapter 1

Edinburgh, Scotland – April 24, 1829

The town witch's ebony cat crossed a vacant street in the squalor known as Old Town. He froze with a lifeless rodent dangling from his mouth and stared in the direction of an unfamiliar sound before blending in with the shadows of the night. Other than the homeless vagrants huddled around their warming fires, no one, not even those in upscale New Town, dared to venture out on the eerie night of Saint Mark's Eve.

In the Conway household, Marjorie, the eldest, took the poker from the stand and stirred the embers in the sitting room fireplace before adding a log to the budding flames. "The fire must be bright enough for us to see the faces of our future husbands in our chemises." Grinning, she turned toward her youngest pair of sisters,

Isobel and Grace, who sat beside each other on an elegant sofa. The two giggled while clutching their clean undergarments, eager to hold them before the firelight.

Tilting her head to the side, Isobel became dreamy-eyed. "I have several handsome men in mind. Of course, any will do, but I must admit, there is one I favor."

"I ken who you're hoping it will be." Grace, the youngest, teased.

Distracted from her reading while sitting on the opposite sofa, Sophie curled her lip in disgust at her sisters' naïve behavior, looked toward the ceiling, and snapped her book shut. "To believe the wrinkles in your chemise will sketch a man's face or the popping of a nut will predict who you will marry is nothing more than a fantasy, nonsense, a silly wives' tale."

Three distraught faces turned toward Sophie. Their smiles faded as they stared at their cynical sister.

"Sophie, it's been a Saint Mark's Eve tradition for nearly two hundred years." Grace justified as she set her chemise beside her, picked up the bowl of walnuts from the side table, and held it before Isobel.

Isobel selected a walnut. "Besides, what if it's true? What if we see the faces of our future husbands? Then we can begin planning our weddings tonight."

Grace held the bowl before her oldest sister, who returned the poker to its stand.

Marjorie stared at Sophie as she blindly selected a walnut from the bowl. "Wouldn't you like to ken who you will marry someday?"

Grace selected a walnut for herself. Scowling, she held the bowl before her disbelieving sister. "Come on, Soph, give it a go."

"No, thank you," Sophie began, "I firmly believe a gentleman should be the pursuer of a woman's heart. However, it's up to the woman to determine if his heart is true and if she feels the same toward him. Whispering a man's name into a nut doesn't make his love possible or even probable."

"Your loss." Grace returned to the sofa and put the bowl back in its place.

"I highly doubt it. It's the three of you who will suffer disappointment." Sophie watched her sisters place their walnuts in their hands, bring them to their lips, and whisper a man's name as if trapping his soul inside each shell.

The Conway's young maid, Flora, watched from the sitting room doorway. She smirked at the four sisters' merriment. Their prospect for a comfortable and luxurious future was bright. They were sure to marry well, own fancy coaches, expensive houses and furnishings, and countless dresses. The maid often dreamt of a life filled with such luxuries. Unfortunately, being born into the lower class gave her little hope in the fantasy, but that was about to change. She placed her hand on her abdomen and grinned. It was only a matter of time until she was pulled up from society's underclass and elevated in rank. No more would she be at another's beck and call, doing their hair, helping them dress, and serving their meals. She stepped from the lurking shadows of the hallway and into the sitting room. "I'm sorry to interrupt, but do you need anything before I retire?"

Everyone ignored the maid's offer except Sophie, who had come to know the young woman as her friend. "Nothing, thank you, Flora, goodnight."

"Goodnight." Flora curtsied before leaving the girls to fantasize about their future husbands. With the household settled in for the evening, her time was now her own. The tired maid glanced at the grandfather clock in the hallway as she opened the drawer in a small table and took out a candle. She lit the taper from the trio in the candelabra, illuminating the corridor, and climbed the stairs to the third-floor attic. Flora placed the taper in the holder on her narrow writing desk. She knelt, pulled aside the worn rug, and removed the interlocking floorboards to retrieve her journal and a folded cloth from the hidden compartment. Grinning as her heart skipped a beat, the maid unfolded the scrap of fabric like a flower opening its petals. Protected within the softness of the cloth was something very precious, something she would not wear while on duty in fear of Doctor and Missus Conway wondering how she could afford something so expensive on her small salary or accusing her of stealing it. She tied the translucent ribbon with its dainty gold Celtic knot and ruby pendant around her neck and tossed the cloth back into the secret vault. She looked down at the journal containing her innermost thoughts, grinned, and picked it up. Flora sat at her desk, dipped the pen in the inkwell, and began to scribble an entry. Unable to share her secret with others, especially her friend, Sophie, she quickly jotted down what she anticipated in the coming hours. The maid reread her entry while waiting for the ink to dry. Then, reverently closing the journal, she returned her recorded hopes and dreams to its hiding place where they would remain for her eyes only. Once the boards were replaced and the concealing rug straightened, she hurried downstairs, paused next to the sitting room, and peeked inside to see if the young women remained occupied.

One by one, each sister placed her walnut on the hearth as close to the flickering flames as possible. The clock on the mantel chimed half-past the hour of ten, drawing Sophie's attention. "It's a little early to place the nuts to cook, isn't it?"

"Only by half an hour. But who cares," Grace giggled, "this is so thrilling!"

"Grace, lower your voice. Mum and Dad are sleeping." Marjorie warned as she gathered her wrinkled chemise from the settee to sit with it in her lap.

Confident her absence would be undetected, Flora hurried to the kitchen, grabbed her coat from the peg near the backdoor, and left the house.

Even though Sophie scoffed at her sisters' silliness, a facet of Saint Mark's Eve fascinated her. She looked toward the hallway. Dare she sneak out of the house at this time of night? She could be banned from attending Mass at Saint Cuthbert if caught doing the unforgivable.

Glancing at her giggling sisters, who stared at the walnuts as if they expected them to move at any moment, Sophie placed her book on the end table, tiptoed to the hallway, and slipped her arms into her overcoat. Then, hastening her pace, she went to the kitchen, which she often visited to escape her annoying sisters, and left through the backdoor.

The breeze of the chilly spring night forced Sophie to shield herself by quickly fastening her coat. It was dangerous to leave the house on the Eve of Saint Mark, or so she had heard. Nevertheless, she was willing to risk her safety to satisfy her curiosity. As she stepped onto the sidewalk, Sophie scanned the street's golden illumination from the gas lamps for any stumbling drunkards or scavenging homeless. As luck would have it, the road was as silent as the grave. "No one else dares to venture out this evening except for me?"

Chapter 2

The aged trees of the kirkyard swayed in the wind with their new foliage on display after a winter slumber. A sliver of the moon peeked between the fast-moving clouds in the indigo sky, projecting its light between the branches like shifting spotlights on the headstones.

The gravedigger tossed another shovelful of dirt onto the growing mound between the two graves and watched a clod roll down the pile and collide with his lit lantern. Wiley wiped the sweat from his brow. "It's unfair one so young should die." He looked down at the small rectangle hole that awaited the baby's casket.

A spasm of violent coughing caused Davis to push the tip of his shovel into the grass and lean on the handle to catch his breath. The gravedigger inhaled, wheezing as it subsided, and looked at both graves waiting for the dead. "Angus said the woman died shortly after giving birth. Such a shame."

Taking pride in their work, the pair tidied the perimeter of each grave out of respect for the deceased and the guests attending the midafternoon funeral the next day.

"I think does it." Wiley picked up his lantern, put his shovel over his shoulder, and looked at the tower window where Angus, the nightwatchman, stood. "It must be getting close to the time."

Davis glanced at the silhouette of the night watchman. "Aye." He coughed, picked up his lantern, and dragged his shovel behind him as they passed the graves of the sleeping dead on their way to the kirk.

~

A wayward strand of Sophie's auburn hair fell over her eyes, which were the lightest blue. She pulled it aside to clear her line of vision as she grasped the iron bars of Saint Cuthbert's closed gate and watched two men, illuminated by their lanterns, walk toward the kirk. She needed to enter and sit on the kirk porch, but the gate was well-known to be locked after dusk. Taking a step backward; the wall was too high for her to climb in her ankle-length dress. Glancing at the tower, the dimly lit window indicated the night watchman was still awake. She wondered how many times he had witnessed the parade of souls. Sophie sighed, disappointed, as she placed her fisted hands on her hips and scanned the wall for another entrance. Without a way into the kirkyard, her effort to see if the legend was true would fail.

A rhythmic tapping and footsteps resonated from behind her. The hair on the back of Sophie's neck rose as she froze in place. She became saucer-eyed with fear as the sound grew nearer. Her heart began to race. Should she run or hope to remain unseen in the shadow of the trees that stood as sentinels by the barred gate?

The rhythmic sound stopped. All was silent except for the whispered secrets shared by the budding leaves as the tree branches swayed in the wind. Sophie was tempted to look over her shoulder but could not find the courage.

"Sophie Conway, why in heaven's name are you out and about unescorted at this late hour?"

Sophie squeezed her eyes shut as she cringed in recognition of the elderly crackled voice. Anticipating a lecture, she turned and stared into the steel-gray eyes of the town witch, Haggadah Blyth. The old woman's oversized rottweiler, Barret, stepped forward and nudged

Sophie's hand, encouraging her to greet him properly. She stroked the dog and patted his shoulder. "Hello, Barret."

"You didn't answer my question, or are you just trying to avoid it?" Haggadah pressed for an answer as she leaned on her cane, her long, thin gray hair moving with the wind.

"I was curious about the Eve of Saint Mark. I wanted to see if the parade of souls is true."

"I see." The town witch considered her options. She could have Barret escort the young woman home. Haggadah looked at the nearest close, where the inquisitive eyes of the homeless stared back at her. She determined it would be safer for Sophie to remain with her until the one o'clock hour. "Well, if you were interested in witnessing the procession, you should have sent word. We could have arranged to walk together." She scolded. "I assume your parents are unaware of your outing?"

Sophie saw no reason to lie. "Aye."

Haggadah shook her head as if perturbed by the admittance. "Come with me and close the gate behind you." The town witch pushed open the right side of the gate and entered. Barret obediently followed.

Sophie's mouth fell agape. "It's open?"

Haggadah turned toward the young lady, who looked like her sisters but was far more intelligent than them. "Aye, Angus leaves it open for me. I attend the foreboding of Saint Mark's Eve every year."

Sophie stepped onto the hallowed ground, turned, and shut the gate. "So, the legend is true?"

Haggadah saw the silhouettes of the gravediggers in the golden glow of their lanterns. They were sitting on the kirk porch, ready for the two-hour vigil. "Aye."

Sophie hurried her steps to peer into the eyes of the town witch. "And you come every year? Why?"

The town witch stopped walking and looked at her young friend. With her endless questions, she wondered if Sophie could remain quiet for the two hours. "Many of the poor seek my remedies when they are ill. I must ken who I can cure and who I cannot. For those I cannot make well again, I simply make the ailing person comfortable until they take their last breath. Nearly six months ago, I waited outside this kirkyard for my goddaughter, Anna Stewart. She had been declared dead. I knew she was alive because I did not see her soul in the parade."

Sophie interrupted. "If you knew she was alive, why didn't you have the gravediggers exhume her body sooner?"

"The killer was still at large and needed to believe she was indeed dead. For the time being, Anna was safe, resting peacefully within her casket. As luck would have it, the homeless body snatchers exhumed her body. Otherwise, I would have had to hire someone to do so." Haggadah chuckled. "Once the men dug her up and tossed her on the ground, she sneezed. They must have had their lives nearly scared out of them. They ran away, leaving Anna among the graves." Haggadah took a deep breath. "The men's true intention was to sell her body to Doctor Knox. He was the anatomy theater instructor who dissected the dead so medical students could learn and study."

"He was going to cut her up?"

"Aye. He was caught for buying the bodies and put on trial shortly after Anna's attempted murder."

"Burke and Hare, right?"

"Aye, William Burke, William Hare, and Doctor Robert Knox were involved in a scheme together. Burke and Hare killed sixteen people and sold the bodies to Knox. Knox and Hare were declared innocent, but Burke received a guilty verdict."

Sophie interrupted. "Aye! I remember the trial. Burke was hung, and his body was dissected publicly at the anatomy theater. Isn't his skeleton on display in the Anatomical Museum?"

"Aye, along with a book, a journal, bound with a cover made from Burke's skin." Haggadah looked up at the tower and waved her cane in silent gratitude to Angus. The nightwatchman nodded, turned away from the window, and cast his chamber into darkness as he extinguished the light. "Angus refuses to watch the parade." The town witch explained. "He fears he will see his soul."

"And learn he will die soon." Sophie whispered, completing Haggadah's thought. She was distracted as she saw a headstone embellished with an hourglass, a skull and crossbones, and a winged angel with a face like a cherub. How would she react if she saw her soul or a member of her family in the parade? It was a possibility, but Sophie brushed it off as highly improbable.

"Aye." The town witch confirmed as she and her canine continued forward.

A lifeless branch fell near Sophie's feet as if warning her to turn back, but she stood transfixed and looked from headstone to headstone, fearful of the shadows crawling between them. Pulling a strand of hair away from her eyes again, she turned to Haggadah for reassurance, but the town witch was several paces ahead of her. Finding herself alone amongst the dead sent a needle of panic into her heart. Sophie hurried to fall in step beside her friend and the protective canine.

Aware of the superstitious preparation to view the parade of souls, Sophie realized she had neglected the protocol. "Haggadah, wasn't I supposed to abstain from eating? Do I need to walk around the kirk before sitting on the porch? What about coming here for three years before I can see the spirits?"

Haggadah chuckled as she tapped her cane on the walkway and continued toward the kirk. "Silly superstitions, Lass." Nearing the porch, she looked at the two gravediggers awaiting her arrival.

Wiley stood to greet the renowned healer. "Hello, Haggadah, Barret. I see you have brought someone with you." He tipped his flat tweed cap respectfully.

"Good evening, Wiley, Davis." Haggadah greeted as she lowered her aging body to a stone step and pulled a lantern toward her. After receiving a welcoming patting on his head from both men, Barret lay by the town witch's feet. Haggadah motioned toward Sophie to properly introduce her. "This is Sophie Conway. I invited her to sit with us tonight. Sophie, this is Wiley and Davis. They are the gravediggers for Saint Cuthbert's kirkyard." She pointed to the empty step beside her.

"I'm pleased to meet you both." Sophie sat where Haggadah indicated.

Wiley nodded, acknowledging the young lady as he resumed his seat. He took his watch from his pants pocket, flipped open the scratched and dented cover, and checked the time before closing the protective lid.

"Nice to meet you too." Davis pulled a handkerchief from his pocket and coughed into it before blowing his dripping nose.

"Still have that cough, Davis?" Haggadah had tried several remedies but to no avail. She suspected the gravedigger would eventually succumb to his ailment.

"Aye, and still using your remedy as you told me." Davis confided, though he questioned if Haggadah should try something more potent.

The town witch leaned toward Sophie. "No matter what you see, you must remain seated and silent from eleven until one o'clock. Can you do so?"

Eager to see the parade of souls, Sophie nodded. She watched the town witch remove a leatherbound notebook, pen, and ink bottle from the oversized pocket of her tattered overcoat.

Haggadah placed the glass bottle on the step, uncorked the top, and dipped her pen as if ready to take dictation on the handmade paper. She looked at Sophie to emphasize the importance of her instructions. "We must remain vigilant for the two hours. The souls that appear near the eleventh hour will soon meet their maker. As time passes, the souls who appear near one o'clock will be the last to die, so sometime in the spring or just before the next Saint Mark's Eve."

Wiley flipped open his pocket watch again and read the time. "It's eleven." He handed the open-faced timepiece to the town witch.

Haggadah placed the watch beside the lantern, where she could easily read the time. She dipped her pen into the ink a second time and held it above the notebook as she scanned the headstones in the kirkyard.

Sophie was uncertain where to look among the countless graves. Would a doomed soul appear near a headstone or from a grave yet to be dug?

Rhythmic wheezing drew Haggadah's attention to Davis, who was leaning against the stone wall of the kirk, fast asleep. Wiley reached to wake his friend, but the town witch shook her hand and head, indicating to let the ill gravedigger sleep.

Believing Haggadah knew best, Wiley looked away from his ill friend, scanned the kirkyard, and pointed, drawing everyone's attention to a white mist.

Chapter 3

Sophie squinted as she leaned forward and watched a fog rise from the ground. The translucent mist floated upward and rotated as if the wind had a helping hand in sculpting the apparition like a bit of clay.

Haggadah glanced at Wiley's watch. It read one minute past eleven. The town witch jotted down the time and waited as the unfortunate soul continued to form.

Sophie's mouth dropped open as she watched the spirit of a young woman develop. The apparition was dressed in what resembled a maid's uniform. As the face materialized, Sophie's heart skipped a beat. It was Flora. She stared at her friend's soul as it floated past her and watched it disappear through the closed door of the kirk.

Her stomach twisted into a nauseous knot. Sophie tried to stand. She needed to warn her friend, but Haggadah's hand settled upon her knee, encouraging her to sit. Then, remembering the instructions, Sophie forced herself to remain in place on the step.

The sound of the town witch's pen scratching a notation in her notebook drew Sophie's attention. She wanted to know what Haggadah had written, but the spirit of an elderly man stepping out from behind a headstone squelched her curiosity. Mesmerized, she watched the soul as he seemed to limp toward the kirk.

Haggadah recognized the man. She scribbled the time and his name beneath her previous entry.

Sophie stared as the decrepit soul passed through the door of the kirk and disappeared. She wanted to speak, to ask questions. Instead, she leaned toward Haggadah and read the name she had written. Thankfully, it was unfamiliar to her.

Within minutes, another spirit arose from the hallowed ground. Unfortunately, those present and awake knew who it was. Wiley looked at his friend, peacefully sleeping. At that moment, Haggadah knew she had done all she could to help Davis.

A sullen heaviness overcame the small group as they watched Davis's spirit enter the kirk. Sighing,

Haggadah entered the gravedigger's information in her notebook.

After recognizing two doomed souls, Sophie wished she had not come. What if she saw her mother or father's spirit? Even though her sisters were annoying, Sophie wished them no ill will. If she watched any of their souls pass through the door of the kirk, would she wake every morning wondering if it was the day they would die? Unable to stop time, Sophie would wait helplessly, knowing she would soon bid them goodbye. She decided it would be better not to know who would die in the coming year. She wished she could leave the kirkyard but remained steadfast, silent, and covered her eyes with her hands to escape the foreboding predictions of Saint Mark's Eve.

Haggadah watched several spirits rise from the hallowed ground and recorded the information as they entered the kirk. She glanced at Sophie and placed her arthritic hand on her friend's knee. Sophie uncovered her eyes and looked at the town witch, who tilted her head toward the kirkyard to indicate she should continue watching.

The spirit of a small boy appeared. Sophie's heart became heavy with grief as she estimated the child's age to be six or seven. His clothes were ragged. He was thin and barefoot.

Haggadah's heart sank slightly in her chest as she recognized the child. He was an orphan living in the South Bridge Vaults. He had faced a terrible life thus far, but his fight would soon be over. Unable to look at his cherub face, she averted her eyes as the boy passed by her and entered the kirk. The town witch entered the name 'Jack' and the time in her notebook. She vowed to visit him soon and made a mental list of items she would take to comfort him until he took his last breath.

Curious, Sophie glanced at the entry in Haggadah's journal and read the child's name.

As time ticked by, the parade of souls continued. Sometimes, there was a large gap between appearances; other times, spirits came in clusters. When Haggadah recognized a doomed soul, she entered the person's name and time. Otherwise, she noted the individual's description and approximate age.

As the timepiece struck the hour of one, the town witch closed the protective cover of the pocket watch and handed it back to Wiley. "Thank you."

At the sound of Haggadah's voice, Barret opened his sleepy eyes and rose on all fours.

Tucking the timepiece in his pocket, Wiley posed the question burning in his mind. "Is there nothing you can do to save Davis?"

Haggadah corked the ink bottle and tucked it in her pocket with her pen and notebook. She used her cane to help her stand and turned toward the kind gravedigger. "Even though I'm a gifted healer, I'm not God. I've used every remedy I ken to cure him and have suspected his time would come soon. Tonight, my suspicion has been confirmed."

Wiley nodded his head in understanding, accepting his friend's fate. "Thank you for trying to make him well. You did your best. He's in the Lord's hands now."

"Aye, as we all are." Haggadah looked at the slumbering gravedigger. "Wake him and get him inside where it is warm."

"I will. Goodnight, Haggadah." Wiley turned to the young lady. "It was nice to meet you, Sophie."

Sophie sat transfixed, contemplating the number of souls she had witnessed enter the kirk.

"Sophie, we best be on our way." Haggadah and Barret began walking toward the kirkyard gate.

"It's nice to meet you too, Wiley." Sophie glanced at the slumbering gravedigger, casting his peaceful face to her mind. "Both of you. Goodnight." She decided her first order of business once she arrived home was to warn Flora of her impending doom. Could she prevent her friend's death?

Wiley tipped his hat as he watched the young lady rise and join the town witch and her canine. He gathered the shovels and paused momentarily to look at Davis, still sleeping against the kirk's wall. Wiley would keep his friend's approaching death a secret and make the most of his remaining days. Upon Davis's passing, Wiley would select a pleasant plot, dig the grave for his friend, and pray that his soul rested peacefully.

He watched Sophie scurry toward the gate. "Get yourself home safely, Lass." He whispered.

Chapter 4

With an urgency to warn Flora foremost in her mind, Sophie reached the gate before Haggadah. Clasping the iron handle, she pulled it open and waited for the town witch and Barret to pass through it. She glanced back at the headstones, curious to see if other spirits would make their presence known.

"Make sure the gate latches," the town witch said over her shoulder as she stepped off the hallowed ground onto the sidewalk. "We want others to believe it is locked."

Passing through the gate, Sophie pulled it closed until she heard the latch click and looked at the darkened tower window. "Since Angus is asleep, won't body snatchers try to go in the kirkyard?"

"The recently deceased have iron mortsafes protecting them. Even if they enter, there isn't anyone worth digging up. They're too decomposed."

Troubled by Haggadah's entry of the child in her journal, Sophie pressed. "The little boy, Jack. I assume you ken him."

"Aye, he lives in the vaults. It's a shame. There isn't much I can do for the child, but I will go and check on his condition soon."

Sophie had never been to the South Bridge Vaults. In fact, her father had forbidden her to go near them. "May I go with you?"

Haggadah thought of the horrid living conditions in which the orphan child existed. "Aye, if you are willing to face the squalor of the poorest of the poor. I'll send word before I go." She extended her gnarled hand toward Barret and patted him on the head. "Barret will see you home safely."

"I don't think that's necessary. I was able to walk here by myself." Sophie justified, confident she would arrive home unscathed.

"A drunkard may leave a pub with bad intentions. I insist Barret go with you. Send him home once you set foot on your doorstep." Haggadah looked at her dog, who stared at her with dark, sepia eyes. She pointed to Sophie and commanded her canine. "Be off with you now." The dog looked at Sophie.

"What about you?" Sophie inquired, concerned for the safety of the old woman.

Haggadah smiled, appreciating the young lady's thoughtfulness. "I'll be fine. Most people avoid crossing my pathway." She tapped her cane on the ground as she turned and began walking to her ancient cottage in Old Town.

Barret glanced at his owner before looking back at Sophie.

Sophie momentarily watched the retreating old woman before looking at the dog's askance eyes. "Let's be on our way, Barret."

The young woman and her canine escort followed the cobblestone street toward her home. Barret walked between Sophie and the buildings with their darkened windows. He often turned his head toward any unfamiliar sound.

Sophie thought she heard footsteps behind her. She turned and walked backward, scanning the street, and scowled as a shadow disappeared behind a tree trunk? But, after experiencing the traumatic event in the kirkyard, she assumed it was just her imagination. Sophie turned around and looked at Barret, who seemed unaware of the phantom footfalls.

Lost in thought from the evening's event, Sophie absentmindedly went to cross Princes Street and stepped in front of a trotting horse. The rider yanked the reins, causing his obsidian mount to sidestep. The gentleman struggled to control the animal as it shied away from Barret, who stood his ground and barked. The rider, dressed in equal darkness, resembled a grim reaper without a scythe. His face, shaded by the brim of his top hat, turned toward her.

"What in God's name?" He directed his horse back to the young woman, whose nearly gray eyes stared at him blankly.

A wayward strand of Sophie's hair was blown away from her face as the skittish horse's nose came within an inch of her forehead and exhaled. She noted the renowned crest on the leather nose strap embellishing the equine's bridle. Clenching her teeth, she watched as the rider adjusted his hat to illuminate his face in the streetlight, confirming her suspicion. It was indeed Laird Owen Ramsey. In closed circles of society, he was known as a womanizer and a wealthy snob who had recently inherited his deceased parent's vast estate. She stared at his ocean-blue eyes defiantly. "You are mistaken. My name is not God." Sophie turned and continued to cross the street with Barret by her side.

"No apology? I guess it's to be expected from a scabby whore."

Sophie turned to object to his false assumption, but Owen dug his heels into his horse's abdomen, and it darted away. She placed her fisted hands on her hips and yelled, "Pompous idiot!" She watched the despicable man disappear into the darkness. "Such a daft snob. No wonder he has such a horrid reputation." She patted Barret's head. "I'm glad we scared his horse. Although, I feel sorry for the beast. The poor animal has to deal with his nasty temperament." She looked up and down the vacant street, realizing she was standing dead center of the thoroughfare. "Let's be on our way, Barret."

Once safely across the street, the protective canine froze abruptly and stared into the distance. Barret lowered his head and resonated a guttural growl.

Upon hearing the canine's warning, Sophie froze and looked at the dog. She followed Barret's line of sight and stared in disbelief as a woman appeared out of the darkness and staggered toward her. Her face was battered and bloodied. She extended a trembling hand toward Sophie, silently asking for help before collapsing in the street's intersection.

"My god." Sophie thought of yelling for help, but at the late hour, she assumed no one would come to her aid. She hesitantly approached the woman, who lay unconscious. The maid's uniform and the woman's distinct blond hair caked with blood looked familiar. "Flora?" One of the maid's eyes was purple and swollen shut. Her jaw lay open, slightly askew, with several teeth broken and missing. Blood trickled from several lesions, making her face nearly unrecognizable. Sophie knelt next to her friend and shook her shoulder. "Flora, wake up."

Barret approached the body and sniffed.

"I doubt if she will," said a deep resonance voice from somewhere nearby.

Chapter 5

Sophie watched as a tall man stepped from the shadows, appearing like a disheveled guardian angel in the streetlight. His bearded face, long gray hair, and tattered clothing indicated he had been homeless for quite some time. She looked up into the kind chestnut eyes of the vagrant. "She must wake up. I can't carry her home." Sophie pleaded. "My dad is a physician. He can help her."

The stranger knelt and put his charcoal-covered fingers beneath the woman's disjointed nose. He felt her breath as she exhaled. "She's still alive and should be taken to Haggadah."

Barret approached the homeless man, who patted the dog's head gently. The canine sniffed the stranger's clothing and began to wag his tail.

It was clear to Sophie that Barret thought the man was of little threat. She looked at her unconscious friend. "To Haggadah? How?"

The man cautiously placed an arm under the shoulders and thighs of the woman, lifted her broken body, and held her against his chest as he stood. He stared at Sophie. "You should continue home with Barret. I'll see to her wellbeing."

"No, I'm coming with you." Sophie insisted as she stood.

He had managed to remain hidden as he followed the young lady. He admired her feistiness as she confronted the arrogant rider. The homeless man perceived Sophie's mind as steadfast and unwavering. "Suit yourself."

~

Haggadah opened the door of her old, thatched cottage, allowing Nero, her black cat, to enter before her. "By the way your belly moves back and forth, I assume you caught a mouse for dinner." She hung her overcoat on the peg near the door, took the notebook, pen, and ink from the pocket, and placed them on the table before adding a log to the fire.

Nero leaped onto the town witch's bed. He circled several times before curling himself tightly as he lay down and closed his eyes.

Hearing Barret's toenails scratching the front door, Haggadah grinned with pride, believing he had escorted Sophie safely home. With her cane in hand, the town witch opened the door, allowing her dog to enter, and stared at the abused woman presented to her. Haggadah looked up at the tall man staring back at her. His chestnut eyes looked familiar. He had aged, his hair had grayed, and his beard camouflaged his handsome features.

"Hello, Haggadah." Tavish greeted.

It had been forty years since Haggadah had last seen her betrothed. Haggadah knew he was alive, yet never expected him to walk back into her life. "Hello, Tavish." The town witch motioned for him to enter. "Lay her before the fire." She went to shut the door when Sophie entered and followed Tavish to the fireplace. "Sophie, why are you here? You should be home."

"I wanted to see if Flora is all right." She approached her friend.

"You ken this woman?" Haggadah questioned as she closed the door.

"Aye, she's my maid." Sophie looked at Flora. "And my friend. I wanted to take her to my dad, but," she nodded toward the vagrant, "he wanted to bring her to you."

Barret lay near the fireplace as Tavish placed the unconscious woman near the fire for warmth. He retrieved a blanket from the end of the bed and covered Flora's battered body.

Haggadah looked at the pathetic woman. Even in her abused state, she recognized the victim as the first spirit in the parade of souls. "I assume she must have a secret, or she is the secret her lover doesn't want others to ken."

Sophie stared at the town witch, offended at the insinuation. "Lover?"

"Aye. I doubt the lass's condition is the result of a robbery. Like most maids, she has minimal possessions or money. Why else would she be out of your house late at night, especially tonight." Haggadah took the short stool near the hearth, sat, and examined the woman. "There's nothing I can do for her."

Sophie scowled. "What do you mean there is nothing you can do for her? You're a healer."

"She is beyond healing."

"How do you ken if you don't try?" Sophie stressed.

Haggadah pointed at her notebook on the table.

Sophie understood the silent command and handed it to the town witch, who opened it, flipped to the appropriate page, and turned the book toward Sophie for her to see.

"She is the first soul."

Sophie stared at the entry. With her mind racing with worry to save her friend's life, she had forgotten Flora as the first apparition she had seen in the parade. She looked at the maid, knowing she would soon die. "Who could have done such a thing to her?" Sophie watched Flora's chest rise and fall. "Shouldn't the authorities be notified?"

Tavish glanced at Haggadah, awaiting her reply.

"I will send Tavish in the morning to retrieve the constable." Haggadah glanced at the maid's battered face. "Who ken how long she may linger." She tucked the unbound edge of the blanket under the young woman's chin. The town witch vowed to keep a vigilant watch over her dying patient until she took her last breath. "After we speak to the constable, I'll send him to your house to tell your parents of their maid's condition."

Sophie stared at Flora's contorted and battered face. "I'm a witness. I must tell him what I saw."

"Aye, you must. No matter the consequence." Haggadah warned.

Her parents? How would she explain to them her reason for sneaking out of the house at the late hour? She was almost sure her father would take her side. However, Sophie doubted her mother would be as forgiving and that her punishment would be severe.

The town witch read Sophie's mind. "Perhaps it would be best to speak with the constable out of earshot of your parents."

Sophie nodded. "Aye, that would be best."

"You must go home now. There will be a lot to answer for come morning." Haggadah looked at her slumbering canine and gave a command. "Barret, off with you now."

Barret lifted his head and looked at the town witch as if she had lost her mind. Then, the obedient dog lethargically rose from the floor and went to the door to wait for Sophie.

Tavish opened the door for Sophie and her escort to exit the humble house.

She paused at the threshold. "Thank you, Tavish, for your assistance tonight."

"Glad to be of help, Lass. Goodnight." He watched her step onto the flagstone walk. Barret looked up at Tavish. "You too, go." He ordered as he shut the door once the dog joined Sophie.

Barret walked with his head held low. He scanned the street as they headed toward the Conway residence.

Sophie remained silent. The picture of her friend's battered body haunted her mind. "A lover?" Tears welled in her eyes and cascaded down her cheeks like mournful raindrops. She was helpless, unable to save her friend. No longer could she confide her frustrations and secrets with Flora. "Barret, who could have hurt her so?"

The dog ignored her question as he walked loyally by her side. His toenails clicking on the cobblestone street resembled a tiny herald announcing their presence.

The evening entailed more than Sophie had imagined. In her bewildered state, she walked without thinking about where she was going. But thankfully, her feet knew the way.

Barret glanced at his ward as she paused before the front steps of the Conway house.

Sophie cupped the canine's head and kissed it in appreciation. "Good boy. Be off with you now." She watched the dog dart away before wiping the tears from her cheeks and entering the house. As quiet as a church mouse, Sophie took off her coat, hung it on the hallway hook, and entered the sitting room to find her sisters sprawled on the furniture, sleeping. She spied three walnuts on the hearth. "So much for the romance of Saint Mark's Eve." She added a log to the fire before randomly selecting a walnut from the bowl. "It's nothing but a silly wives' tale." She brought the walnut to her lips. "It's about as absurd as me marrying Laird Owen Ramsey." She taunted as she dropped the walnut on the hearth. She turned to leave the room when a pop echoed. Sophie rotated to face the fireplace and watched as the walnut she had dropped rolled and stopped before her foot. She looked at the clock on the mantel. It read three minutes before two o'clock.

~

Haggadah took a dampened rag and washed the blood from Flora's face. She saw a translucent ribbon peeking from beneath the maid's uniform. "What is this?" She pulled the ribbon to reveal an attached beautiful pendant. Haggadah untied the ribbon and examined the delicate gold Celtic knot. It was embellished with a single ruby, or perhaps the jewel was made of paste. She held it up for Tavish to see. "It may be wise to ask Sophie if she has seen this before."

He looked at the necklace and assumed it was expensive. "Do you think the maid stole it from Sophie's mum?"

"Not if she wanted to stay employed." Haggadah stood and placed it on the mantel. "It was probably a gift from her lover. I'll give it to the constable tomorrow. He can ask Sophie about it." She gazed at Tavish's weathered face. "Where have you been all of these years?"

Tavish looked away from her face. He saw his flat cap and their purple ribbon hanging on the peg on the wall. He grinned.

Haggadah followed his line of sight. "I found it in the gutter and cleaned it as best as I could. It's gotten dusty over the years, as has our handfasting ribbon."

Remaining silent, Tavish thought of the lost years they should have shared together.

"Where have you been?" Haggadah persisted.

Tavish thought back in time. "On a ship."

"A ship?"

"Aye. From what I can recall of that night, I was hit on the head and taken aboard a ship. By the time I woke and was discovered by the cook, the ship had set sail. I traveled the world. It was unpleasant loading dark-skinned people and watching them be sold as slaves in the West Indies and America. When the ship was sold, so was I as an indentured servant. I put in my time and worked to save money for my passage home. I returned to Edinburgh this past week."

"I knew someone was following me this evening."

A tenderness was conveyed in his weary eyes. "Aye. When I saw Sophie go her separate way with Barret, I wanted to make sure the young lass got home safely."

"Thank you for doing so." The town witch looked at her dying patient. "And for carrying the maid here." Haggadah grinned. It was a comfort to know he still cared for her welfare. "Thank you for caring for my welfare as well."

"I always will." He confessed.

After a few moments of silence, Haggadah exhaled. "I'll make some tea, and you can tell me more about your travels." She looked at her patient. "It's going to be a long night."

Chapter 6

An unladylike snore emanated from Grace. Sophie looked at her youngest sister and scoffed. She took a candle from the mantel, lit it from the flickering flames in the fireplace, and left the room. Climbing the staircase to the second floor, Sophie paused at the base of the third-floor staircase leading up to the attic where Lana, a middle-aged cleaning and washwoman, and Flora each had a small bedroom. A melancholy sadness settled within Sophie's heart as she placed her foot on the bottom step. Hesitating, she sighed, remembering how often she sat on the bed with Flora and taught her to read. Sophie tried to recall the number of times she isolated herself in her friend's bedroom to escape her family's evening drama after supper, or she would visit with the staff in the kitchen. Once a new maid was employed, the kitchen would be her only option to hide from her silly siblings.

The urge to visit Flora's bedroom in the dead of night pulled Sophie upward. She stood in the doorway of the maid's private quarters. It was modest with the barest of essentials – bed, nightstand, an unlit candle, chair, a small wardrobe, writing desk, and chamber pot. She stepped into the room and placed the candle on the nightstand. Wrinkling her nose, the distinct smell of urine indicated the chamber pot had not been emptied in several days. Sophie opened the wardrobe; it was nearly empty. After all, other than a uniform and nightgown, what else did a maid need to wear? She opened the nightstand drawer and picked up the book of poems she had given Flora for Christmas. Memories of helping the maid read beyond the common words she had learned flashed into Sophie's mind. She tried to keep her tears in check as she put the book back in its place. Pausing with her hand on the drawer knob, Sophie stared at the book, a symbol of their friendship that would always be a reminder of Flora. She picked up the book and held it close to her heart as she closed the drawer. Looking at the writing desk, she saw a pen, a bottle of ink, and a few pieces of stationary paper. A dirty uniform lay over the back of the chair. Sophie plopped down on the bed. "Oh, Flora. Who hurt you?"

Lana muttered something in the next room, causing Sophie to freeze. She listened to the mumbling, unable to decipher the rambling, and assumed the servant was talking in her sleep.

Without a sound, Sophie picked up the lit candle, tiptoed down the stairs, and went to her bedroom. She set the book of poems atop a stack of books on the small table next to her reading chair by the window. Placing the candle on her nightstand, Sophie stripped down to her chemise and snuggled beneath the covers of her bed. The candle sputtered as she lay motionless, recalling the events of the evening. When her eyelids threatened to close and sleep to overtake her, Sophie blew out the candle, hoping for a good night's rest before confessing the details of the horrid evening to the constable when he arrived.

~

Doctor Kendrick Conway sat at the head of the large oak dining room table and cut his breakfast sausage with the edge of his fork. He paused as he brought the meat to his mouth, realizing his favorite daughter was absent from the family breakfast. "Where's Sophie?"

His wife, Elspeth, ignored her husband's question as she sipped her morning tea.

He looked at his sleepy-eyed daughters, who ignored his question as they chatted about walnuts, chemises, and blamed the oldest for not building a fire properly. "Girls, where is Sophie?"

The trio looked at their father's inquisitive stare as he ate a bite of sausage. The girls then glanced at each other, exchanging silent pacts to not speak as they bowed their heads and remained quiet.

Kendrick suspected his daughters knew more than they were willing to reveal. "Well?" He pressed.

Marjorie shrugged her shoulder. Isobel shook her head in denial.

Grace, the youngest and his informant, nearly choked on her mouthful of buttered toast as she swallowed. "When we woke this morning, Sophie wasn't in the sitting room. As a matter of fact, she was absent for most of the night. She's probably in her bed sleeping."

Marjorie glared at her youngest sister, silently warning her to stop talking. Isobel, who sat next to Grace, kicked her sister's leg. Grace winced, quite certain she had incurred a bruise.

Kendrick looked at his wife, who returned her teacup to its saucer. "We need to rein in that one." He projected the façade of a patriarch who ruled with a heavy hand in raising his daughters. However, the opposite was true. As a physician, he understood the delicate balance between life and death. Even though he and his wife had not been blessed with a son, he knew each daughter was a blessing and a gift from God.

"I've tried, my dear. I've truly tried." Elspeth selected a slice of buttered toast from a serving plate and topped it with jam. "I've all but given up hope. She is as headstrong as you are."

"And I do admire her for it." Kendrick confessed as he scooped a forkful of scrambled eggs.

Lana entered the dining room carrying a platter of freshly baked currant scones. She placed it on the table and paused to examine the serving dishes to see if any needed refilling.

Kendrick looked at the unfamiliar woman. "Who are you?"

The servant addressed the master of the house. "Lana, Sir." Receiving a blank stare from Kendrick, she explained her responsibility within the household. "The housekeeper and washwoman."

"She does our laundry." Grace added.

Kendrick glared at his youngest daughter. "I ken what a washwoman does." He scowled at Lana. "Where is Flora?"

Lana shrugged her shoulders as she glanced at each member of the family. She was familiar with their undergarments but not their faces. "I don't ken. She was not in bed when I went by her room this morning. It looked like she hadn't slept in it at all."

"I don't recall giving her the day off." Kendrick persisted, glancing at his wife.

"She must be around here somewhere." Elspeth stabbed a fried potato wedge with her fork. "Lana, could you please go wake Sophie and have her come down to breakfast."

"Aye." Lana curtsied slightly before exiting the room. She hurried up the staircase and tapped on Sophie's closed bedroom door. "Miss Sophie, your parents request your presence at the breakfast table." There was no reply. She knocked harder a second time. "Miss Sophie?"

Sophie's sleep-covered eyes cracked open to see it was indeed daylight outside of her window. "Go away."

Lana heard mumbling but was unable to decipher what was being said. "Your parents request your presence at the breakfast table." Lana looked in the direction of the echoing knock on the front door. "Miss Sophie, you need to get up. I must go answer the front door." Lana scurried downstairs.

"The front door." Sophie mumbled as she wiped the drool from the corner of her mouth and rolled onto her back. Her eyes popped open, and her head sprang from her pillow as the housekeeper's words registered in the grogginess of her mind. Her heart skipped a beat as she stared at her bedroom door. "The constable." She jumped out of bed, dressed, and ran down the stairs. She caught her heel on the bottom step, stumbled, and grabbed the newel post to stop herself from falling to the floor. Catching a glimpse of herself in the hallway mirror, she skidded to a stop and stared at her disheveled hair. "Oh, no." She overheard Lana telling the constable to seat himself in the sitting room while she announced him. Sophie tried finger-combing her hair to make it presentable and examined it again in the mirror. "Good enough." Taking a deep breath to calm her racing heart, she entered the sitting room as her parents did from the dining room.

Elspeth glared at her daughter's unacceptable appearance as Kendrick extended his hand to their visitor.

The constable stood and shook the presented hand. "Good morning, Doctor Conway. I apologize for disrupting your morning meal."

"It's no bother at all. How can we help you?" Kendrick motioned for the constable to sit, as did he and his wife. Sophie sat in an upholstered chair.

The constable sat and took a small black notebook, pen, and a tiny ink bottle from his pocket. The officer pulled the cork from the bottle, set it on a side table, and dipped the pen into the vessel. He looked at the two women, hesitating to begin. "I have the unfortunate task of telling you that Flora, your maid, passed away early this morning."

Elspeth shook her head. "Nonsense, she is sleeping in her room. Lana."

The housekeeper appeared in the doorway. "Aye."

"Tell Flora to come and join us."

Lana glanced from Elspeth to the constable. "Aye."

Marjorie stepped into the room. Seeing the uniformed officer, she inquired. "Is something amiss?"

"Officer, would you like some tea while we wait?" Elspeth offered, always the perfect hostess.

"No, thank you." The constable watched as Isobel and Grace appeared behind their eldest sister. He assumed the youngest was nibbling on a slice of toast.

Sophie knew what the housekeeper would find. She saw the constable glance at her from the corner of his eye as if reading her mind. Knowing the officer had previously talked with Haggadah and Tavish, she hoped the town witch had advised him to speak to her privately.

Lana tried to catch her breath as she stepped into the sitting room.

"Well?" Kendrick inquired.

"Her bed is empty, never slept in." The woman informed.

"Thank you, Lana." Kendrick dismissed the servant as questions flooded his mind. "I would like some answers, Constable."

"She was beaten quite badly, found on the street approximately at one fifteen this morning. Her body was discovered by a homeless man. He carried Flora to Haggadah's house. The healer did her best, but the young woman expired just after sunrise."

Sophie sat quietly, thankful Flora's suffering had ended.

Kendrick was aware of Sophie's friendship with the maid. He noticed his daughter sat expressionless, unmoved by the news of Flora's death, as if she already knew. Looking back at the officer, he stated the obvious. "So, she must have left the house sometime last night."

"Aye." The constable nodded.

Without emotion, Kendrick stated the obvious. "Elspeth, we will have to employ another maid."

The constable stood. "I have been ordered to search her room for any evidence."

"Absolutely." Kendrick looked at his daughter, fully aware of her frequent visits to the maid's bedroom. "Sophie, please escort the constable to Flora's room."

Sophie led the way up the two flights of stairs. She entered the bedroom and closed the door after the constable entered.

The officer looked at Sophie. "I am particularly interested in hearing what you have to say."

Chapter 7

Sophie took a deep breath. "Flora and I were friends. Before retiring to her bedroom last night, she asked if my sisters and I needed anything. I didn't ken she had left the house."

"Aye, Haggadah confirmed as such. When did you last see her," the constable thought to clarify his question, "in the house?"

"About ten thirty. I can only assume Flora left shortly afterward, as did I."

"Go on." He jotted the information down in his small notebook.

"When I was walking home, Barret, Haggadah's dog, began to growl. That's when I saw a woman stumble from the darkness at an intersection." She paused for a moment. "She must have recognized me. Flora extended her hand toward me as if asking for help before she collapsed onto the street."

"Tavish has given me that information. Continue."

"Good." Sophie thought momentarily to recall where she left off in her story. "I didn't ken it was Flora until I got closer to her. She was so bloody. Her nose looked twisted to the side, her jaw was crooked, and her teeth broken." Sophie shuddered. "As I knelt beside her, Tavish stepped from the shadows. He picked up Flora, and we went to Haggadah for help. Afterward, I walked home with Barret by my side."

"Is there anything else you can remember? Did you see anyone along the way? Any other witnesses?" The constable hoped for additional information, any slight lead in the case.

"Wiley and Davis were with us at Saint Cuthbert, but they remained in the kirkyard when we left shortly after one o'clock. Angus was asleep in his tower. The homeless may have witnessed something."

"I see." The constable searched the nightstand, desk, and wardrobe and lifted the mattress. "She didn't have much, did she?"

"No, Sir."

"Haggadah insisted this was for your eyes only." The constable pulled the necklace from his pocket. "Have you ever seen this before?" He placed it in Sophie's outstretched hand.

She examined it closely. "It's beautiful."

"Haggadah discovered it around Flora's neck. She assumed the maid's admirer may have given it to her. But, by chance, could it have belonged to your mum?"

"No, I never noticed her wearing it." Sophie handed the necklace back to the officer. "Maybe it belonged to Flora's mum."

The constable returned it to his pocket. "Very well. If you think of anything else, please let me know."

As the constable opened the door for Sophie to exit before him, she stopped short of passing through it.

"Oh, I did see someone last night, Laird Owen Ramsey. He was riding a horse and nearly ran me down just before I saw Flora."

"Laird Owen Ramsey of Hilltop?"

"Aye."

They returned to the sitting room and rejoined Sophie's parents. The constable dipped his pen in the inkwell and noted the possible suspect. "I need the maid's personal belongings put in a box. I will collect it later as evidence. Do you ken if she had any family we should notify?"

Kendrick looked at his wife, who shook her head.

The constable put his notebook and pen into his pocket before placing the cork into the ink bottle. "Well, then the department will see to her burial. Usually, the generous parishioners of the kirk donate to a fund for the funerals of paupers." He slipped the ink into his pocket.

Kendrick withdrew his money from his suitcoat and extended his hand with a generous contribution. "Thank you for taking the time to inform us of Flora's passing."

The constable accepted the donation with a nod. "If any additional information is discovered, I'll contact you. Good day." He tipped his hat and passed through the front door as Lana held it open.

"I'll gather Flora's things." Sophie volunteered.

"After you have your breakfast." Elspeth insisted, scowling. "And please make yourself more presentable. Your hair resembles a rat's nest."

Sophie watched her parents return to the dining room table to finish eating their breakfast. She saw the housekeeper from the corner of her eye and made a request. "Lana, could you find a box for Flora's belongings?"

"Aye, Miss."

Out of spite, Sophie joined her family with her hair as is, caring little for the ridicule she would receive.

~

Sophie saw the empty wooden box outside Flora's bedroom door as she entered the third-floor hallway. Stepping inside the bedroom with the container, she stood momentarily and placed the box on the bed. "Oh, Flora, who killed you?" She opened the wardrobe and reverently folded its contents, added the hairbrush and a container of hairpins from the nightstand drawer, and removed the uniform from the back of the chair. Sophie assumed their next employee could use the candle, pen, ink, and paper and left them where they were. She wondered if she should strip the bed but decided the task and emptying the chamber pot was Lana's responsibility. Looking down at the pathetically tattered rug, she lifted the fringed edge and wondered if there was a replacement somewhere in the household. "Maybe there is one in storage we aren't using."

Sophie left the room, placed the box in the bottom of a hallway closet, and went to ask if there was an unused rug in the attic. Hearing the chattering of her sisters, she paused at the bottom of the stairs and eavesdropped on their conversation.

"If anyone knows anything about her death, it's Sophie. She knew Flora best." Grace moved her chess piece and waited for Isobel to make her move.

Sophie took a deep breath, brushed the imaginary wrinkles from her skirt, and entered the sitting room.

Elspeth looked up from her embroidery. "You have yet to fix your hair."

Tired of her mother's nagging, she tilted her head to one side and ignored the comment. "Where's dad?"

"He had a house call."

"I want to replace the rug in Flora's room. Do we have another we can spare?"

Elspeth stared at her daughter, ignoring her question. "Why do I suspect you ken more about Flora's death than you are letting on, Sophie?"

To help convey her honesty, she met her mother's penetrating stare with her own. "All I ken is Flora is dead. Since she was found outside of our house, she must have left sometime during the night. Unless she was killed within our home, and someone dumped her body?"

Marjorie looked back and forth between Sophie and her mother. She wondered who would break their challenging stare first. Isobel moved her chess piece absentmindedly. Grace, for once, was too stunned to say anything.

"Don't be absurd." Elspeth pulled her needle through the cloth. "There should be an old rug in the attic storage room."

The chime of the hallway clock rang twice, reminding Sophie that Flora's funeral would begin in an hour.

Racing to the attic, Sophie rummaged through the various items amongst the dust. She sneezed several times before seeing a rolled rug propped in the corner of the room. She grabbed the floor covering, which was heavier than it looked, carried it to the maid's bedroom, and set it near the bed. "I'll change the rugs later." Sophie hurried down the stairs, removed her overcoat from the hook, put it on, and tried to make her hair more presentable as she looked at her reflection in the mirror.

With a chess piece in her hand, Grace looked into the hallway. "Where are you going, Sophie?"

"To attend Flora's funeral." She looked at her sisters and mother, who stared at her blankly. Sophie shook her head and looked heavenward, disgusted by their lack of compassion for the loss of life. Sighing, she stormed out the front door, eager to be in the company of those who truly appreciated her.

Chapter 8

Uncertain which kirkyard would become Flora's eternal resting place, Sophie hurried to the town witch's house. As she wove her way through the streets of Old Town, the vision of Flora's battered body flashed in her mind. Sophie looked skyward at the cloudy sky and began mumbling a prayer asking for God's forgiveness of Flora's transgressions, pleading for her soul to be allowed into Heaven, and expressing her gratitude that her friend no longer suffered in pain.

Upon arriving at the gate of the old house, Sophie stared at the unfamiliar men standing outside the open front door. They turned toward her as she pulled the rickety gate open and walked cautiously along the flagstone pathway. The men respectfully bowed their heads in greeting.

"Good day, Miss Sophie." Tavish stepped forward and greeted her with a nod of respect.

"Hello, Tavish. Have I arrived in time for the funeral?"

"Aye, and a welcomed sight you are. Haggadah will be pleased to see you."

Sophie scanned the inquisitive men, many dressed in dirty, ragged clothing.

Perceiving her uneasiness, Tavish explained. "Haggadah asked me to gather friends to help with the maid's funeral."

Sophie politely smiled, conveying her appreciation to the homeless men. "It's very kind of all of you to attend."

A distant kirk bell rang three times.

"Best you get inside." Tavish encouraged.

Sophie stepped over the threshold to see a crudely made coffin supported on the seats of the four wooden chairs usually placed around the table. She stood silently as a priest performed a final blessing while Haggadah tucked a small brass bell beneath Flora's wrist.

The town witch smiled as she looked at Sophie. "Ah, you've arrived in time." She tapped her cane on the rag rug as she went to greet her friend.

A cluster of women turned and looked at Sophie, who smiled kindly, noting their disheveled clothing. She whispered to Haggadah as she joined her. "More of Tavish's friends?"

"Aye." The town witch confirmed.

Sophie glanced at the priest, keeping the volume of her voice at a whisper. "Does the church have enough funds for Flora's service and burial?"

"Not to worry. I gave the priest a remedy this past winter, so he is paying back the favor." Haggadah winked.

The priest put the casket top in place and nailed it shut. Then, he placed a mort cloth of black velvet over the casket and began to pray as he ceremoniously walked to the open door.

"I assume you wish to help with the first lift?" Haggadah suggested to Sophie.

"Aye." Sophie stepped into a vacant place between two women alongside the casket. She squatted, placed her shoulder beneath its edge, and lifted upward. It was much heavier than she anticipated. The women waited as the four chairs were turned upside down to prevent Flora's ghost from sitting on them and remaining in the house. The women shuffled toward the door, ensuring the body was carried out of the house feet first so the maid's soul could not find its way back inside the cottage. The casket was transferred to the awaiting men, and the procession began with a bellringer leading the solemn parade slowly and steadily toward the kirkyard.

The women remained inside the house and began preparing a feast. Sophie stood in the doorway, silently watching.

Haggadah joined her at the door as the men passed through the gate. "It may be against tradition, but I don't think you would be questioned if you wish to follow at a distance," the town witch said, offering her young friend closure. "Come back for something to eat when the burial is finished."

Sophie nodded as she joined the procession and followed a few paces behind the men.

Homeless men in the community offered to replace those who grew weary as they continued toward Flora's resting place. As the procession arrived at Saint Cuthbert's Kirkyard, Sophie imagined the speed at which Wiley and Davis had to dig Flora's grave. She stood a few steps away from the men and watched as the priest removed the mort cloth, said a few words, and the casket was lowered into the ground. Davis withdrew his handkerchief from his pocket and respectfully muffled his cough while the priest concluded the ceremony, folded the mort cloth over his arm, and scurried away. The pallbearers trickled from the rectangle hole in the ground, leaving Sophie alone near the grave. She stepped forward and looked at the casket in the shaded darkness.

Wiley and Davis went to her side.

"Would you like to add the first shovelful of dirt onto the grave?" Wiley offered. He presented his shovel.

Sophie looked at the gravedigger's sympathetic face. She nodded without replying, took the shovel, and dumped the first pile of dirt on the casket. "Thank you," she said, returning the shovel to Wiley.

Wiley nodded once. "You're welcome to stay for as long as you like."

Sophie watched until the grave was topped off with a mound of dirt. She hoped her father's donation would be used to purchase a small headstone to mark Flora's resting place.

Davis and Wiley put their shovels over their shoulders and walked away, leaving Sophie to mourn silently. She refused to think of Flora in her abused condition. Instead, she thought of her smiling face, their conversations, and their friendship. "I'm going to miss you." Sophie brushed a tear away from her cheek.

A movement to her left drew Sophie's attention. A man dressed in black stood before an elaborately gated mausoleum. Its stone walls, pillars, and decorative carvings were impressive. The person or persons lying at rest within the elegant tribute must have been either very important or very wealthy.

Sophie watched as the man turned and stared at her. His expressionless face sent a chill up her spine, for it was none other than the Laird of Hilltop.

Owen placed his walking stick in his left hand before touching his index finger to the brim of his top hat, acknowledging her.

Sophie glared at him, refusing to return his polite greeting, and watched the wealthy laird pass through the gate, leaving the kirkyard. She took one last look at the mound of dirt in which her friend's body lay beneath. "Goodbye, Flora." Sophie left the peacefulness of the kirkyard and walked back to Haggadah's house, thankful for those who participated in her friend's proper sendoff.

A small feast remained on the table when Sophie arrived at the humble dwelling. The wooden chairs had been returned to their proper place around the table. She hung her overcoat on a peg and remained unnoticed by the women washing dishes.

Barret rose from his usual spot and greeted Sophie with his tail wagging. She patted his head. "Hello, Barret."

Haggadah turned toward Sophie while drying a platter with a dishtowel. "We still have plenty for you to eat. Help yourself."

Sophie had little appetite, yet she wanted to be respectful of the effort made by the women. After all, this was a feast celebrating Flora's life. Picking up the chipped top plate from the few in a stack, she selected a wedge of cheese, a biscuit, and a slice of walnut and fruit bread before sitting on the bench by the fire. Barret sat before her. His pleading eyes conveyed his desire for a morsel of her food.

Haggadah made tea and placed a cup on the bench next to Sophie. "Did the burial go well at the kirkyard?"

"Aye." She bit into the bread. "This is very good."

Haggadah smiled. "I managed to find some dates and raisins and made two loaves. The men finished one off quickly and ate half of the second." She wrapped the remainder of the loaf in a cloth and placed it on the worktable. The town witch watched her suspiciously silent friend. She cleared what was left of the food from the table and put it away. Before long, she thanked the women and escorted them to the door. Once Haggadah was alone with Sophie, she pried, "I have a feeling there is something you wish to tell me."

Sophie sipped the delicious tea and returned the cup to the bench. "I told the constable everything I knew about last night."

Haggadah pulled a chair from the table and sat. "Good."

"I didn't recognize the necklace. As far as I ken, Mum never had one like it."

The admission enforced Haggadah's suspicion. "I see."

"I also put all of Flora's belongings in a box for the constable. Her bedroom is ready for the new maid whenever we employ one."

"I'm certain another woman will be hired soon."

"And I saw Laird Owen Ramsey in the kirkyard."

Haggadah's interest was piqued. "Did you?"

"He was visiting an elaborate grave." Sophie bit into the fruit bread.

"Most likely his parents. They passed away at sea, leaving him to manage his father's successful mercantile business and estate. It's a heavy responsibility for a young gentleman in his early twenties."

"I saw him last night, too, just before Flora collapsed onto the street." Sophie's eyes widened as she stared at Haggadah. "Do you think he could be Flora's assailant?"

Chapter 9

Owen entered the foyer of Hilltop Manor. His young maid, Phoebe, whose heels clicked on the marble floor, approached and curtsied before him. He handed her his walking stick.

"Laird Ramsey," the maid accepted his hat and overcoat, "a constable is waiting for you in the drawing room." She picked up the silver tray from the hallway table and presented the day's received posts. Her baby blue eyes stared at the estate owner, awaiting his reply.

Owen questioned, wondering if he had heard the maid correctly. "A constable?" He picked up the posted letters and began shuffling through them.

"Aye."

He glanced at the closed pocket doors before looking at the handwriting on another letter. "Did he indicate the reason for his visit?"

"No, Laird."

"Thank you, Phoebe."

The maid curtsied and left to resume her duties.

Owen opened the tall wooden paneled doors to see the officer sitting in an upholstered chair, looking about the room at the numerous oil paintings. He entered, closing the doors behind him. "Good day, Constable. You wish to see me." Owen tossed the unopened correspondence onto a side table near a sofa.

The constable looked at the young laird and stood. "Aye, Laird Ramsey. I hate to impose on your time, but I must ask you a few questions about last night."

Owen motioned for the officer to resume his seat. "Last night?" He sat on the sofa across from him. Years ago, his father advised him never to offer information, so Owen waited for the constable to direct his inquisition.

"I have a witness who places you in the area where a woman collapsed after being brutally beaten and eventually died."

Owen shrugged his shoulder. "A common occurrence in Old Town."

"The victim was not in Old Town."

"Who is this witness?" Owen pried.

"For her safety, I cannot say."

Recalling the long, tiring ride home after attending to business over several days, Owen's mind sifted through the people he saw at the pub where he had stopped for a late-night meal.

The constable continued. "Can you explain where you were last night and why you were out and about at a late hour?"

"Aye." Owen took a moment to compose his thoughts. "I was away on a business trip for the past few days. Eager to return to Hilltop, I left the last meeting just before dusk and rode through the night. I stopped at a pub in the city, had something to eat, and enjoyed a few glasses of whisky. Then I went directly home from the pub." He stated the name of the pub.

"Do you ken when you arrived and left the pub?"

Owen looked at the high ceiling as he recalled the timetable of his travel. "I rode into Edinburgh close to half past eleven and left at one." He stared at the constable, awaiting his next question.

The officer found the gentleman's excuse plausible but not an ironclad alibi until it was verified by the barkeeper, staff, or a guest. He stood. "I don't want to take up any more of your time. If I need additional information, I'll return."

Owen stood. "Very well." He escorted the officer to the front door before returning to the drawing room, snatching the letters from the table, and stepping into the foyer to see Phoebe with a feather duster and several candles in her hand.

"I'll be in my study," he said as he passed by the maid.

"Very well, Laird." She replaced the candelabra's burnt nubs with new candles and dusted the top of the table.

~

After hanging her overcoat on a hallway hook, Sophie climbed the stairs to Flora's room, which remained as she had left it. "I'll have to remind Lana to strip the bed and empty the chamber pot." She looked at the rug she had retrieved from the attic. "Probably dusty."

Sophie put the rug on her shoulder and carried it downstairs. Once she reached the foyer, she turned toward the kitchen. The rolled carpet knocked the candles from the table candelabra, sending them crashing to the wood floor. "Och." She whispered to herself. Sophie propped the rug against the wall, retrieved the wayward tapers, and inserted two candles, but the third was broken in the center. She opened the table drawer, exchanged the damaged candle for another, and inserted it in the vacant holder. Picking up the rug once again, Sophie went to the kitchen.

Olivia, the cook, paused with a jam-tipped knife over a cake, stared at Sophie as she passed by, and exited out the back door. "What in heaven's name?"

Even though the rug was small, it was well-made and heavy. Sophie dropped it on the ground, unrolled the carpet, and flung it over the clothesline, which had several lines stretching the length of the backyard. Returning to the kitchen, she opened the broom closet and stared. "Olivia, where is the rug beater?"

The cook smoothed the jam on the cake layer. "What are you intending to do with it?"

"Beat the rug for the new maid's room. It was in the attic and is quite dusty." Sophie spied the bamboo tool hanging on the backside of the door and lifted it from the hook.

"Don't fret yourself. Lana should do that."

Sophie firmly grasped the beater by the handle, paused at the back door, and looked at the cook. "How difficult can it be?"

Olivia's rounded belly jiggled up and down as she chuckled and shook her head as the back door closed. She traced her finger along the knife's blade, tasted the jam, and nodded satisfactorily. "Mmmm."

Sophie stood at the side of the rug, held the beater like a tennis racket, and wound up. She hit the floor covering with all the force she could muster, sending dust billowing into the air. Sophie gasped for breath. She dropped the beater and stepped away from the rug while waving her arms frantically to clear the dust from the air. "Oh, good lord." Sophie blinked her watering eyes to wash away the dirt and looked down at her muslin dress, which had dulled to a light shade of gray. Once catching her breath, she retrieved the beater, stood on the opposite side of the rug, and continued to hit it until it was dust-free. She pulled the small carpet from the line and rolled it before carrying it into the house.

Olivia was drying the freshly washed bowl when the back door opened. She watched Sophie enter with the rolled rug on her shoulder, noting her soiled dress and dirt-smudged face. The cook dared to ask, "How did it go?"

"I'm sure Lana is much more skilled than I am at beating a rug." She returned the beater to its proper place and left the kitchen.

"She's got gumption." Olivia smiled and shook her head.

Grace stepped into the hallway at the sound of disembodied footfalls and saw Sophie with the rolled carpet. "Soph, shouldn't Lana be doing that?"

"I prefer to do it myself." She disappeared from her inquisitive sister's sight as she climbed the stairs to Flora's room.

Sophie put the dust-free rug on the bed, knelt, and began rolling the tattered floor covering. She paused as she discovered two loosened floorboards. Curious, she lifted the pair of boards with some encouragement. Sophie stared at the journal within. She took it from its hiding place. "How long have you been here?" She opened the leather cover and saw Flora's name. The Conway family employed the maid for less than a handful of years. Flora's first entry was dated a year after becoming their maid. It contained several words that were horribly misspelled. Searching the compartment, Sophie found only one other item. It was a bit of soft fabric. She set the journal on the bed before replacing the boards on the floor. She finished rolling up the old rug, put it on the bed for Lana to throw away, and rolled out the new carpet to hide the secret of the floor safe. With her friend's journal in hand, Sophie went to her bedroom, hoping to remain undisturbed as she closed her door and leaned back against it. "Well, Flora, your secrets must have been too grievous to share with me. Let's hope you wrote them within the pages of your journal." Plopping down in her reading chair, she opened the cover. Flora's handwriting was neat, and the misspellings were easy to decipher.

"Perhaps your last entry is a good place to begin." She flipped to the back of the journal. The page was empty. She turned the pages until she came to the last entry and read.

> *It wasn't the reaction I had hoped for, but I ken, in time, he will adjust to the idea of fatherhood. I am to meet him tonight. He has promised a quick end to our predicament. Could he be hinting toward marriage?*

Sophie lowered the book to her lap. "She was with bairn."

A knock sounded upon her door. "Sophie?"

It was Marjorie. Sophie lunged from her chair and pushed the journal behind the pillow on her bed. She picked up a book from the stack on the table, returned to her seat, and opened it to a random page. "Come in." She looked down at the book. It was upside down. Sophie quickly rotated it as the door opened.

"How was Flora's funeral?" Marjorie sat on the bed and leaned against the pillow, dangling one leg off the side.

Sophie glanced at the pillow, hoping the journal would remain undetected. "Since she didn't have any family to notify, many of the homeless . . ."

"The homeless?" Marjorie interrupted.

"Aye. Haggadah's friend, Tavish, found Flora lying in the street. He gathered his friends, and they saw that Flora had a proper send-off. The men carried her casket to the grave, and the women made a lovely celebration feast."

Marjorie raised an eyebrow. "Feast?"

"Aye, it wasn't elaborate, but it was pleasant, thoughtful, and what they could do within their means."

"And how are you doing?"

Sophie looked out the window to gather her thoughts. Everything had happened so quickly. The events of Saint Mark's Eve seemed like a bad dream. She had yet to grieve. Finally, having time to think of her friend, she realized her heart had incurred a hollow spot. "I miss talking to Flora." Looking at Marjorie, Sophie's bottom lip quivered as she came to terms with her friend's final moments. "She was beaten to death. Her body was so battered and bloody."

Marjorie sensed her sister was on the verge of tears. "Her cruel death was undeserved, no matter her transgression. Please take comfort in knowing she is at peace and in a much better place." Coming off the bed, Marjorie hugged her sister. "I'll leave you to your reading."

As her bedroom door clicked shut, her sister's compassion pushed Sophie's welling tears to overflow. She set the book on the table, wiped the droplets from her cheeks, and took a deep breath before retrieving the journal and opening it. Anger crept into the void within her heart. "I pray you have written the name of the person who killed you."

~

"Phoebe!" Owen called from his study.

The maid stepped into the room. "Aye, Laird."

"Have Thomas drive you into the city and post this immediately." He handed her a sealed letter.

"Aye, Laird." With the letter in hand, Phoebe left the room grinning. A day away from Hilltop was always welcomed. In no time, she arrived in the city.

Unbeknownst to her, a pair of sapphire eyes had noticed her before. He was watching the maid's every move again.

Chapter 10

Phoebe counted the coins in her hand as she exited the building. She stepped to the wagon and grasped the seat to hoist herself upward but paused as someone spoke from behind her.

"If I may be so bold." The gentleman cupped his hands, offering his assistance. Sensing the young woman's hesitation, he added. "Or would you rather stay and have tea with me?"

The maid glanced at the stableman, Thomas, who was too distracted by an elegant passing coach to notice she had returned. "I'm needed elsewhere." Phoebe inserted her foot in his entwined hands and was lifted upward. Once in the seat beside the old stableman, she looked down into the bluest eyes she had ever seen. "Thank you." Phoebe heard the slap of the reins on the horse's rump as the gentleman touched the brim of his hat with his index finger, bidding her farewell.

~

Sophie failed to notice the afternoon sun peeking through the clouds as she began to read Flora's most profound thoughts. As the pages turned and shadows elongated on the bedroom floor with evening drawing near, she looked up from the journal as the hallway clock announced the dinner hour. Much to her dismay, Sophie had yet to discover the name of the man who won her friend's heart or perhaps tricked her into believing he was her true love. She had found several clues, such as his 'sapphire eyes,' 'tall and muscular,' and 'curly locks of the deepest auburn hair," which could be any man or frequent visitor to Edinburgh. Did Flora believe her pregnancy was her guarantee to rise in society's ranks once they wed? The wealthy and titled would still look down on her for entrapping the gentleman, who may resent her for doing so. Her marriage would have been loveless, leaving her as lonely as she was before meeting him.

"So, a gentleman, a family with money. But then again, even the lowest of the upper class has more money than a maid." Sophie snapped the journal shut and ran her hand over the leather cover. "If you truly loved him, then I sympathize with your misfortune. From what I gathered, you did. However, it appears as if he didn't feel the same." She hid the journal behind her pillow again, intending to read it after eating. "With the few details I have learned, maybe Haggadah can help me put the pieces of this puzzle together."

To avoid another conflict with her mother, Sophie changed her grungy dress, tidied her hair, and joined the family in the dining room for the evening meal.

Elspeth watched Sophie approach the table. "I see you have dressed for dinner and finally fixed your hair."

Marjorie glanced at her mother, appalled by her severe criticism. Did she not realize Sophie was grieving for her friend. "You look nice, Sophie." She countered.

Without a word, Sophie sat and looked at her father's empty chair. "Dad hasn't returned from his house call?"

"It must be a serious case that demands his time and attention." Elspeth placed a linen napkin in her lap. "The patient must be quite ill."

Lana brought a bowl of steaming boiled potatoes and a basket of freshly baked rolls into the room and placed them on the table. Grace and Isobel each grabbed a roll, split them in half, and smothered the bread with butter.

Before the housekeeper left the room, Sophie said, "Lana, Flora's room needs the bed stripped, the chamber pot emptied, and the rolled rug thrown away."

Lana stared at Sophie, wondering how she would continue doing her job as well as Flora's. So, she looked at the family's matriarch and dared to speak her mind. "Missus Conway, may I ask when a maid will be hired to fill Flora's position?"

Elspeth looked up from her plate, vexed by the interruption. She reached for her teacup. "I hope to begin interviewing tomorrow."

With a nod, Lana glared at Sophie before returning to the kitchen.

"Shall we go shopping tomorrow?" Grace suggested to her sisters. "It has been a while since we have done so."

Sophie groaned inwardly. Shopping was not her favorite pastime. Plus, being in the company of her younger sisters tested her patience.

"I think that is a wonderful suggestion." Isobel added as she bit into her buttered roll.

The four girls looked at their mother sitting opposite the vacant patriarch's chair. "Aye, go without me. I will be busy employing a new maid."

Sophie reached for a roll and remained silent while eating her meal under her mother's glaring stare. Once finished, she retired to her bedroom for the evening. She had no intention of going shopping with her sisters in the morning.

~

Kendrick returned home sometime during the night. With only a few hours of sleep, he sat at the head of the breakfast table with a sour expression, warning his mood was not to be tested.

The silence during the morning meal indicated everyone understood their father's intolerance for family bantering. Even Grace remained silent.

After eating quickly, Sophie retreated to her bedroom, hoping to avoid the day's agenda of shopping with her idiotic sisters. She sat in her reading chair with Flora's journal on her lap, gazing out the window at the sunny day.

Sophie had finished reading her friend's entries shortly after midnight and wanted to share what she had learned with Haggadah. However, she was disappointed the journal failed to reveal the name of the gentleman responsible for Flora's pregnancy and, most likely, her death.

Sophie's thoughts drifted to Owen Ramsey, the only person she saw shortly before watching Flora collapse. Could he have been involved with the maid?

An intrusive knock on her door pulled Sophie back to reality.

Grace pressed her ear against the wooden door. There was no reply, so she knocked again. "Come on, Soph. We're going shopping. We want you to come too."

Sighing, she looked at the closed door, knowing her annoying sister, if not all of them, stood on the other side. "You ken I don't like to go shopping. It's such a waste of time."

Grace opened the door and peeked around its edge. "Come anyway. It will be fun. I heard the dressmaker just got a new shipment of fabric."

Isobel's face appeared above Grace's. "Are you coming, Sophie?"

Exhaling with frustration at their persistence, Sophie stood and set the journal on her chair. Her visit with Haggadah would have to wait. "Very well. I could use some fresh air."

The three sisters, giddy with excitement, and Sophie set out for an afternoon of shopping. Since it was such a lovely day, they decided to walk instead of taking a coach.

"I hope I find fabric for a new gown." Isobel giggled as she walked beside Grace. "One never knows when we will be invited to a ball."

"I heard a rumor that several families will host a ball this summer." Marjorie shared as she followed her youngest sister. "Selecting a fabric for each of us before they get snatched up would be wise. We want to be unique in dress design too." She advised as she looked over her shoulder to ensure Sophie was still there.

Grace stopped and waited for Sophie to come in step beside her. She wrapped her arm around her sister's arm like a snake entrapping its prey. "I hope you choose a material that is bright and cheery. None of your usual drab colors."

"What if only drab colors are in stock?" Sophie reasoned with a smirk.

"Come now. Miss Jaymiee always has a variety of colors. Let me choose one for you for this season." Grace goaded, raising her eyebrows up and down.

Sophie had to admit Grace possessed an eye for fashion. "Very well, but I can refuse it if it is too bold."

"Fine. I will keep your taste in mind." Grace released her sister's arm and hurried to join Isobel and Marjorie.

Sophie shook her head. "I have a feeling I'm going to regret her choice in fabric."

The main street bustled with riders on horseback, wagons hauling goods, and coaches transporting people, making it difficult for anyone on foot to cross the street. Like the Conway sisters, many of the city's citizens were eager to enjoy the day's sunshine and crowded the sidewalks.

Grace pointed to a shop across the street. "Look, Miss Jaymiee is opening her store. We must hurry."

Sophie watched the dressmaker prop open the storefront door, a silent invitation to shoppers.

"Sophie, come on!" Isobel yelled over her shoulder as she began crossing the street with Grace and Marjorie while dodging horses, carts, and coaches.

Stepping onto the cobblestone road, a horse-drawn wagon with a load of lumber nearly ran Sophie down. Shying away, she stood on the sidewalk, staring as her sisters disappeared behind a passing coach. "They're going to get run over," she said as she watched their senseless foolishness.

"I agree; they should be more careful."

Sophie looked toward the resonant male voice and into the eager sapphire eyes staring down at her. Her face reddened. "I do apologize. I often talk to myself."

"No apology necessary. I hate to admit it, but I do the same." Carson glanced at the three women who made it safely across the street. "Since my destination is also on the opposite side of the street, may I assist you in crossing?"

Sophie looked at her sisters waiting on the sidewalk. Grace hopped up and down like a ninny, waving her hand over her head. It was her not-so-subtle way of signaling Sophie to join them. She looked at the bent arm the man presented. Feeling obligated, Sophie threaded her arm within his. "Thank you."

As they crossed the street, Sophie sidestepped a steaming pile of horse dung. She refrained from smiling as she looked across the street to see her three sisters staring in disbelief at the handsome man entwined with her arm.

When the pair reached the opposite side, Isobel boldly stepped forward. "Sophie, who have you picked up along the way?"

Sophie realized she had failed to introduce herself. She unthreaded her arm and opened her mouth to do so.

Carson bowed slightly. "Ladies, my name is Carson Hamilton. May I have your names as well?"

Marjorie took charge. "We are the Conway sisters. My name is Marjorie," she motioned to her sisters, "Grace, Isobel, and you kindly escorted our sister, Sophie."

"It is a pleasure to meet all of you." Carson displayed his straight, pearly white teeth as he smiled.

"Women as lovely as yourselves must be more cautious when crossing the street. Horses can be unpredictable."

Sophie stepped next to her sisters. "Thank you for your assistance, Mister Hamilton. We will heed your advice and be more cautious in the future."

"Good day." He tipped his top hat and walked away.

The Conway sisters watched the handsome gentleman disappear amongst the crowd of shoppers on the sidewalk.

"Oh, he is so handsome." Grace stated, glassy-eyed as her heartbeat quickened.

"He may be married." Sophie reasoned, hoping to dissuade any fantasy her youngest sister may have.

Marjorie interjected. "I didn't see a wedding band, but men often do not wear them."

Sophie shook her head. "Exactly, and why would you want to get involved with a married man. Other than his name, you ken little about him. So, get your head out of the clouds, and let's go to the dressmaker's shop."

For Sophie, her sisters were like herding cats as she tried to get them to refocus on the dreaded task.

They entered the shop and began scanning the bolts of fabric on the shelves.

"Ladies, if you find a fabric you like, just place it on the table, and I will be with you in a moment," Miss

Jaymiee advised before assisting a woman with measuring the length of a satin ribbon.

Isobel quickly chose three bolts of fabric and held them in her arms.

Marjorie shook her head. "Isobel, you can only have one new dress. Put two of them back."

"But I like all of them." Isobel put one bolt back on the shelf but could not decide between the remaining two.

Sophie ran her hand over a bolt of the finest muslin.

"Muslin again. Sophie, I think you should get this one." Grace held a bolt of the prettiest gold material Sophie had ever seen.

Taken back by the beauty of its color, Sophie confessed. "My goodness, I would look like a radiant Greek goddess in a dress of gold."

"Exactly, everyone will notice you." Grace smiled. "So, it's settled. This will be your dress." She went and placed it on the table. "Now to find embellishments." Grace withdrew a sheer golden fabric and held it before Sophie. "We can start with this. It will make the perfect overskirt." She looked at the spools of satin ribbon and selected one. "This one will do. Oh, Sophie, you will look like royalty." Grace placed the items on the table before choosing a fabric for her dress.

It was left up to Marjorie to select between the two fabric choices for Isobel's dress.

With their materials selected, the girls consulted with the dressmaker to determine a design, lace, ribbon, and any other decorative trim.

"I must admit, I think my dress will be the prettiest one I have ever owned." Grace boasted as she followed Sophie, who was eager and the first to leave the dress shop.

Sophie looked over her shoulder. "I thought you said mine would be the most eye-catching." She came to an abrupt stop as she collided with something that resembled a brick wall. Teetering backward, strong arms wrapped around her waist to prevent her from falling. She grabbed onto the muscular biceps that pulled her upright and stared into the ocean-blue eyes of Laird Owen Ramsey.

Owen stared into the nearly gray eyes of the woman he had seen in the kirkyard. He released her once he was confident she was steady on her feet. "I beg your pardon, Miss …"

"Her name is Sophie." Grace volunteered.

Sophie glared at her sister before turning back to her rescuer. She preferred not to speak, but out of politeness, she was obligated to admit she was at fault.

"It is I who must beg your pardon. I failed to look where I was going."

"Well, no damage done." He looked at the four women as he tipped his hat. "Good day."

The three women stood on the sidewalk and gawked at the gentleman as he walked away. Sophie clenched her teeth and glared.

"Who is he?" Marjorie looked at Sophie.

"Owen Ramsey." Sophie replied with a tint of disdain.

All three sisters turned their heads toward Sophie.

Grace was bold enough to comment. "Thee Owen Ramsey, the Laird of Hilltop?"

Sophie looked at her youngest sister. "Aye."

Isobel stood stunned. "Honestly, Sophie, how do you keep running into such gorgeous men?"

"Believe me, it's unintentional." Sophie watched Owen continue on his way with commanding strides, his walking stick firmly in his hand.

"Let's stop at the sweets shop." Grace suggested.

Three of the Conway sisters agreed a sweet treat was in order, turned toward the shop, and began walking.

Staring at Owen's retreating figure, Sophie shook her head. She turned to reply to Grace, but she was no longer there. Her sisters were several paces ahead, so Sophie hurried to follow them. Glancing across the street, she saw Haggadah standing on the corner. The town witch was staring, silently summoning her.

Chapter 11

Haggadah stood with her carpetbag in hand and Barret by her side. She was pleased Sophie had noticed her. The canine had seen his friend, too, and wagged his tail.

People on the busy sidewalk gave the town witch a wide birth as if she had a communicable disease.

Sophie glanced at Tavish as he crossed the street and came alongside her. He tilted his head toward Haggadah, indicating she needed to go with the town witch. She understood his unspoken communication and concocted a quick excuse to leave her sisters. "I'll meet you at home. I'm going to get a book from the bookshop." She lied. Her sisters, deep in conversation, failed to hear her.

With Tavish leading the way safely across the busy street, Sophie followed him without looking back to see if she was missed by the chattering trio.

Haggadah turned toward her destination, confident the pair would soon join her. She wove her way through the streets to the South Bridge.

An elderly man sitting on the steps of a building watched the town witch walk past. His weathered face, soiled clothes, and greasy hair labeled him homeless. Several people huddling around a warming fire peered from a close and watched the pair suspiciously, yet they knew of her reputation as a kind healer and one they could turn to when in need.

Haggadah looked toward the homeless group as the echo of a baby's cry reached her ears. The woman with the inconsolable infant stepped from the shadowed shelter and stared at her.

Tapping her cane on the cobblestone as she continued, the town witch stepped over a pile of dog dung and walked around the legs of a sleeping man who had propped himself between the stone wall of a building and a wooden barrel. The snap of a shaken rug caused Haggadah to look up several stories of a building to an open window. She watched the dirt and dust drift to the street as a transparent gray cloud and wished it would rain soon to wash the streets and rid Old Town of its offensive stench of sewage. Haggadah coughed as she inhaled the thick air heavy with fireplace smoke.

As she stepped beneath the South Bridge and waited, Haggadah scanned the inquisitive eyes of the poor and decrepit with nowhere to go and nothing to eat. She was thankful when Tavish and Sophie rounded the corner and joined her. Barret pranced toward Sophie, anticipating the affectionate greeting. She was more than willing to give him a good petting.

Sophie noticed the grungy people sitting against a stone wall staring at her. They were dressed in ragged clothing. She saw a little girl who itched her ratted hair, most likely infested with headlice. A woman, cradling a wee babe in a filthy blanket, looked at her with pleading eyes. An uncomfortable feeling, as if she did not belong in the retched place, made Sophie whisper to Haggadah. "What are we doing here?"

"We're going to visit Jack."

"Is he here?" Sophie looked about for the boy.

"He lives in the vaults. It isn't a pleasant place, but at least it's a roof over his head." Haggadah took a step toward the entrance. "Ever since seeing his spirit in the parade, my conscience has urged me to visit him." She paused before the open doorway of darkness. She took a pair of candles from her carpetbag and handed them to Tavish, who lit them from the dying embers of a warming fire under the South Bridge. "Once inside, we must stay together. It is easy to get disoriented in the labyrinth." Haggadah motioned for Tavish to lead the way.

Tavish handed a lit candle to Sophie before he entered the tunnel. Sophie followed, with Haggadah and Barret bringing up the rear.

Even with the candle to illuminate her way, Sophie's eyes took a moment to adjust to the inky darkness. She placed the sleeve of her overcoat to her nose, shielding it from the stench of urine and the distinct odor of mold. Her eyes burned from the smokey interior, making it seem like she was walking through an odorous fog. Sophie felt a drip of condensation on the top of her head. She looked over her shoulder. "I pictured this place to be much different."

"At one time, it was a marketplace containing craftsmen, taverns, and such. Shortly after it was built, it flooded, causing many merchants to leave. The homeless moved in. Burke and Hare used to store their murdered victims in one of the alcoves until they could take the body during the night to Doctor Knox at the anatomy theater."

Sophie stepped over a puddle and stared at a man who looked like he was sleeping or dead. She inhaled sharply as she saw a rat run across his body and disappear into the darkness.

A woman huddled on the damp ground reached toward Tavish. "Food, do you have any food?"

Tavish shook his head and kept walking.

The bleak living conditions made Sophie wonder how anyone could survive in the dank environment. Unable to help the pleading woman, she avoided eye contact and walked past her.

Heavy footsteps and the jingling of a ring of keys could be heard. There was a whistle. Someone whistled. Sophie tried to look past Tavish to see who was approaching but saw only darkness as the disembodied sounds drew nearer. She looked at the stone floor as the footsteps seemed to walk by her, but no one was there. Startled, Sophie looked over her shoulder at Haggadah. "What was that?"

"The spirit of the night watchman. He often whistled while he patrolled the shops. He collapsed and died one evening, never finishing his last shift. People have nicknamed him Mister Boots because of his heavy footfalls. He doesn't like strangers in the vaults and is sometimes known to be quite nasty."

"Nasty?" Sophie's eyebrows arched upward. "As in, able to harm us?"

"No, he likes to frighten people, though. Mister Boots is always angry, quite protective of his area." Haggadah reassured. "Jack should be just up ahead."

Tavish stopped walking, held his candle high, and searched the chamber for the child. He saw pairs of eyes staring back at him, but none belonged to Jack. "I don't see him." He looked at Haggadah, fearing the worst.

Haggadah scanned the pitiful souls peering at her, mostly women and children. She shook her head. "Try the next room."

"How many rooms are there?" Sophie stepped over another puddle.

"Someone once told me 120, but I may be wrong." Haggadah failed to see the puddle. Her stocking became sodden through her porous shoe as she stepped in it.

Sophie hoped they would find the child soon. She feared it would take an eternity if they had to search every room in the vaults.

They went deeper into the darkness to the next room, where a woman huddled in one corner. The opposite stone wall was sectioned into compartments, with four at floor level and one stacked above each. Curled into a ball was Jack. He was sleeping in an upper cubby.

Tavish held his candle over the boy as Haggadah went to the orphan and placed her hand upon his forehead. Thankfully, it was cool to the touch.

Jack opened his eyes, recognized the town witch, and smiled. "Hi, Haggadah."

She returned his contagious smile. "Hello, Jack. I've been thinking about you."

"It's nice to be thought of." He sat up and dangled his dirty, spidery legs over the cubicle's edge.

Standing on his hind legs, Barret placed his front paws near Jack and accepted a petting on his head.

"Hello, Barret." Jack giggled, pleased by the dog's affection.

Sophie stood to one side, trying not to stare at the child's pathetic state. "Hello, Jack. My name is Sophie. It's nice to make your acquaintance."

"Pleased to meet you, Sophie." The child looked at Tavish, who had visited once before. "Nice to see you again, Tavish."

He gave a single nod. "Hello, Jack."

"We can't stay long." Haggadah pulled something bulky from her carpetbag. "I brought you a blanket to keep you warm." She leaned closer to the child and whispered. "Inside, there is something for you to eat. It isn't much – some well-buttered bread, cheese, and biscuits. There is also a corked bottle of tea to drink. Keep it well hidden." She looked over her shoulder at the woman, hoping her comments had not been overheard.

"Thank you for the blanket, Haggadah." Jack winked in appreciation for what was hidden inside of it.

"You take care now. I'll try to come back soon and maybe stay longer then." The town witch's arthritic hand patted the child on the cheek.

Tavish dripped wax on the edge of the cubical and pressed the bottom of the candle into the puddle, allowing the child a bit of light for the duration of the taper's life.

Jack gave Barret one final pat on his head and waved farewell to his visitors as they left.

As they exited the vaults, Sophie filled her lungs with fresh air, lifting her empathetic heart in her chest. She blew out the candle and handed it to Haggadah. "Isn't there anything else we can do for him?"

"I've encouraged him to go to an orphanage, but he refused." Haggadah turned and stared at her friend. "You ken as well as I that his time is limited. He can at least spend it as he wishes."

Sophie looked at the darkened entrance. "Aye, he has a right to do as he pleases until he takes his last breath." She glanced at the unfortunate people who stared at her. "However, like many, being homeless was a choice he did not make."

As they left the South Bridge Vaults, Sophie confessed. "When I was cleaning out Flora's room, I discovered a journal hidden in the floor."

Haggadah glanced at her friend as she walked beside her. "And?"

"Flora was with child." She looked at the town witch's face to see her reaction to the news.

Haggadah's face remained placid. "I assumed as much, and more than likely, the father was a man of society who wished his galivanting remained a secret."

"Aye. Flora described him as tall, with sapphire eyes, muscular, curly auburn hair, and handsome."

The town witched grinned. "Flora was blinded by love. He could be the ugliest man in the world, and she would have considered him handsome."

Sophie surmised. "So, he could be anyone."

"Aye, and subtle in looks from what she described."

Chapter 12

Sophie's stomach grumbled as she entered her house and went directly to the kitchen. Even though frowned upon by her mother, she needed solitude and distance from Elspeth's scrutinizing stare and criticism.

She came to an abrupt halt as she stepped inside the room expecting to see her friend, then realized she was not there and never would be again.

Olivia turned toward the regular visitor to her domain. The young woman's face was void of expression. "Is there something you need, Miss Sophie?" The robust woman dumped the risen dough from a large bowl onto the worktable and began dividing it into loaves.

Sophie stood scanning the kitchen. "It's strange without Flora here." Her stomach grumbled again, reminding her of its emptiness. She crossed the room to the pantry.

"I ken what you mean. It's odd not having the maid in my way." Olivia cut the dough, dividing it into another loaf. "I warned her to be careful. Men with money don't like inconveniences."

Sophie paused with her hand on the door handle. Could Flora have confided in Olivia and not her best friend? She looked at the cook. "What inconvenience?"

"She was with bairn." The cook placed the rounded dough on a greased pan, covered it with a dishtowel, and set it near the cookstove to rise.

"She never told me." Sophie confessed.

"Nor me at first. I think I knew Flora was expecting before she did." The cook shaped the next loaf.

"How did you ken?" Sophie pried as she stepped closer to the cook, ignoring her complaining stomach.

It was apparent to Olivia that Sophie's mother had yet to educate her daughter on what to expect when a woman is with child. The cook knew it was not her place to do so, but she would rather Sophie know the signs than remain ignorant. "Her stomach was often unsettled. Sometimes, the smell of certain foods made her queasy.

When I confronted her, she told me she had missed two monthly courses."

"Did she ever tell you who the father was?"

"No, she would not tell me his name. She did say he is a man of wealth. She hoped to marry him and have a better life for herself and the bairn. But men don't like being trapped. I'm not saying he was the one who killed her, but it sure looks to be so."

"Did you ken she planned to leave the house on the Eve of Saint Mark?"

"No, but it makes sense. Nighttime was the only time Flora could be with him. Sometimes, she would stay all night and arrive home early the next morning." The cook placed another loaf with the first and covered it with a towel. "I'd go to wake her, and her bed would be empty. Flora must have loved him. She spent every minute she could spare with him, risking her employment. Blinded by love. Such a shame."

Sophie stood for a moment, transfixed by the cook's working hands. She wanted to go and tell Haggadah what she had learned, but other than the cook being aware of Flora's pregnancy, there was nothing new to tell.

"If Doctor Conway had discovered her condition, he most likely would have dismissed her. Most employers do so to avoid the embarrassment of their name and household. Then she would end up starving and cold on the street while caring for her bairn. Both may have become ill and died."

"So cruel."

The cook paused in her work. "Is there something you wanted?"

Sophie's stomach grumbled again, reminding her of the reason she had entered the room. "I need something to eat."

The cook tilted her head toward the pantry. "Help yourself."

"Thank you." Sophie pillaged the pantry and decided on a slice of date nut bread with butter before leaving the cook to continue her duties. She had placed her foot on the bottom step of the staircase when the front door flung open. Sophie turned to see her chattering sisters enter.

"Oh, Sophie, you missed the most delicious lunch." Isobel began.

"Aye, we had cherry-chip scones with hot chocolate, chocolate cake, and . . ." Grace added.

Marjorie interjected, glaring at her younger sisters. "And small sandwiches." She took off her overcoat and hung it with the others.

"Oh, you will never guess who joined us for lunch," Grace announced without giving Sophie a moment to speak, "Carson Hamilton."

"He promised to dance with us at the next ball." Isobel clapped her hands before scampering into the sitting room, with Grace following.

Sophie turned and ascended the staircase without sharing in the girls' excitement. She snagged her toe on the top step and caught herself before crashing to the floor.

Marjorie tilted her head to one side as she watched Sophie enter her bedroom and close the door. She had questions that needed answers, and she suspected Sophie knew them. She placed her foot on the bottom step.

Elspeth pulled her needle through her embroidery piece, which she was near finishing. "Marjorie, I need to speak to you."

Her inquisition of Sophie would have to wait. Marjorie went into the sitting room.

"I have employed a new maid. Her name is Vertie."

Hearing her name called, Vertie stepped into the room. "Is there something you need?"

Elspeth waved her hand dismissively. "No, I was just informing my daughters of your employment."

The maid nodded and returned to the kitchen.

Taken back by her mother's rudeness to the servant, Marjorie's voice had a hint of sarcasm as she spoke. "Shouldn't you have introduced us to her?"

Looking up from her embroidery, Elspeth huffed. "She's an employee, not family."

Disgusted by her mother's reply, Marjorie went to Sophie's room, knocked on the door, and entered without permission. "After leaving the dress shop, I turned to ask for your opinion of where we should eat lunch, and you had disappeared."

Startled by the intrusion, Sophie turned toward her older sister as she bit into the bread and sat on the far corner of her bed. She returned her sister's inquisitive stare as she chewed to avoid answering the question.

Closing the door behind her, Marjorie sat on the opposite corner of the bed and waited for a reply. Her lack of patience pushed her to prod her sister. "I believe you ken more about Flora's death than anyone in this household."

Sophie swallowed. "I knew Flora left the house sometime after she asked us if we needed anything before retiring for the night."

Marjorie scowled. "I don't remember her asking us anything."

"That's because you, Isobel, and Grace were babbling about your future husbands." Sophie mocked.

Guilty of the accusation, Marjorie folded her hands in her lap. "Go on."

"I looked at the clock around that time and noticed it was too early to put the walnuts on the hearth."

"Which was what time?"

"It was ten thirty."

"And then, when did you leave the sitting room?"

"A few minutes afterward."

"And went to your bedroom." Marjorie stated confidently.

Looking away from her sister, Sophie wondered if telling the truth was a good idea. Her misbehavior and misgivings tended to catch up with her, not in a good way. She bit into the bread to stall for time.

Marjorie leaned toward her sister. "Sophie, you went to your room, didn't you?"

"No." Her mouthful of bread muffled her reply.

"No?" Marjorie stared at her sister with her eyebrows raised, questioning if she had heard her correctly.

Sophie shook her head as she swallowed, silently confessing before meeting her sister's piercing stare. "I left the house and joined Haggadah in the kirkyard."

Marjorie's eyes widened as she inhaled. "Oh, you didn't. If anyone finds out, you will be confined to the house until the day you wed." She scolded. "And Mum will arrange your marriage too."

"Aye, and that's why you won't say a word of anything I have told you. Not to anyone, especially Isobel and Grace. Promise."

Marjorie looked toward the bedroom ceiling. She shook her head, realizing the situation Sophie had gotten herself into and the possible consequence. She nodded. "I promise."

"Give me your word." Sophie insisted.

"You have my word."

Sophie took a deep breath, confident she could trust her older sister. "After we left the kirkyard, I was walking home with Barret when I saw Flora staggering toward me." She took a moment to compose herself before continuing. "She was so badly beaten I could hardly recognize her. Her face was swollen, bruised, and bloody. She collapsed in the middle of the street." Tears welled in Sophie's eyes.

Marjorie placed her hand on her sister's as if giving her the strength to tell the gruesome tale. "Oh, I can only imagine your shock."

"Aye. Flora was still alive but unconscious. A friend of the town witch appeared and carried her to Haggadah's house, where she died the next morning."

"Do you ken why Flora left the house so late at night? She must have had an urgent reason."

Sophie shook her head and shrugged her shoulder. She would honor her friend and preserve her reputation by keeping her galivanting and condition a secret. "Maybe she went to a pub for a drink and offended the wrong person?" It was a plausible excuse and could have been where she met her lover for their tryst.

"It is a loss, nevertheless." Marjorie consoled, eager to change the subject. "Mum interviewed today and hired a maid. Her name is Vertie. The woman is middle-aged and quite stout. I doubt if she can keep up with Grace and Isobel."

Sophie chuckled as she wiped away a single tear from her cheek. She thought of her friend, who was her exact age and was more than capable of meeting their needs. "They ran Flora ragged."

"Well, I'm sorry for the loss of your friend. Maybe reading will help to distract your mind." Marjorie patted Sophie's hand before standing.

Sophie looked at the stack of books on her table as Marjorie closed the bedroom door behind her. Sighing, she stood and looked down at Flora's journal on the seat of her reading chair. "I ken someone who will want to read what you have written, even though there isn't much to share."

Chapter 13

Reading was the last thing Sophie intended to do. She ate the remainder of her makeshift lunch and picked up Flora's journal from the seat of her reading chair. Tiptoeing down the staircase, Sophie slipped the leather-bound diary into her overcoat pocket before taking it from the hallway hook. She went out the backdoor to remain undetected by her mother and sisters. Sophie walked briskly to the station house and entered. The sergeant sitting at the desk on the dais looked up from his paperwork.

"May I help you, Lass?"

"Aye, I have discovered a journal that was the property of my family's maid, who was murdered recently." Sophie handed the leatherbound book to the sergeant, who opened it and read the owner's name.

"We will need to record your statement. Step through the door." He pointed to his right and handed the journal to the constable behind him.

The officer opened the door and escorted Sophie down a hallway to a small room containing an oak rectangle table and two chairs. He motioned for her to sit in the chair behind the table. "I'll go and pull the file." He shut the door, isolating Sophie.

The echo of doors opening and closing, footfalls, and orders being given made Sophie thankful to be in the solitude of the tiny room. She scanned the bare white walls, focusing on a spider near the ceiling as it moved toward a corner.

Sophie looked at the door as it opened and saw the same constable who had visited her home to investigate Flora's murder.

"It's nice to see you again, Miss Sophie." He sat across from her and placed the folder and journal on the table. "How did you come by your maid's journal?"

"I volunteered to clear her room of her belongings and store them in a closet as you instructed. However, when I changed out her rug, I discovered a compartment within the floor. The journal was inside."

The constable noted her statement in the folder.

"I read Flora's journal." Sophie confessed.

His pen stilled as the officer looked at her. "Did you discover anything of importance?"

"She was seeing someone and described him as tall, muscular, with blue eyes and curly auburn hair. Also, quite wealthy. She did not reveal his name." She watched his pen scratching the details onto the paper and waited for the officer to stop writing. When Sophie had his undivided attention, she announced. "She was with bairn."

Desensitized over the years, the constable showed no emotion as he scribbled the revelation into the file. "Anything else?"

"There was a piece of wadded fabric with the journal but nothing else." Sophie was aware of the only lead in the case. "I'm curious, though. Have you spoken with Laird Ramsey?"

The officer detected a tinge of sarcasm in her voice as he made another entry and looked up from the file. "Aye. He returned from a business trip on the Eve of Saint Mark and stopped at a pub before riding home late at night. The owner of the pub confirmed his alibi." The constable closed the folder. "The journal will remain with us as evidence. Thank you for taking the time to submit it for our file. If you discover anything else of importance, please bring it to our attention." He stood and opened the door for his witness to exit.

Sophie was escorted from the room and through the hallway. Once outside the building, she looked in the general direction of Haggadah's house, up at the cloudless sky, and surmised she had enough time to visit her friend before the evening meal.

The late afternoon outing into Old Town calmed Sophie's soul. As Haggadah's cottage came into view, so did the poor woman who stood on her doorstep. Sophie waited outside the rickety gate as Haggadah handed a woman a remedy and explained its administration.

Spying Sophie patiently waiting as the woman left, Haggadah stood with the door open and watched her friend walk up the flagstone walkway. "This is an unexpected visit."

"Aye. I thought I would pop in." Sophie stepped inside.

At the sound of Sophie's voice, Barret lifted his head from where he was napping and stood with his tail wagging.

"Hello, Barret." She patted his head.

Nero, who lay curled on Haggadah's bed, opened his eyes briefly before going back to sleep. Sophie stroked his fur while the feline continued to ignore her.

Haggadah tidied the apothecary and closed its doors. "Do you have time for a cup of tea?"

"A quick one. I don't want to be late for supper." She chuckled. "But it wouldn't be the first time that I am." Sophie followed Haggadah to the cupboard and watched her take a pair of teacups, add tea from a tin into each, and place several biscuits onto a saucer.

"Put this on the table." Haggadah instructed Sophie as she placed the dish in her friend's hand. The town witch carried the cups to the fireplace, poured hot water from a hanging kettle into each, and placed a steaming cup before Sophie's chair.

"I just came from the station house. I gave the constable Flora's journal and told them what I read." Sophie sat at the table and blew on the tea before sipping.

"A good idea. After all, it is evidence." With her teacup in hand, Haggadah sat across from her friend.

Sophie selected a biscuit from the saucer and dunked it into her cup. "Not very good evidence. We still don't ken who killed her." She held the shortbread above her cup, allowing the excess tea to drip.

"Let's hope their investigation discovers the guilty culprit."

"The constable said Laird Ramsey was traveling home after a business meeting. He had stopped at a pub to eat, and the owner verified he was there." Dunking her biscuit again, she looked at Haggadah. "Do you think the constable truly cares who killed her? They may think of her as just a maid." She bit into the sodden biscuit.

"Let's hope they are diligent enough to discover the truth. If the murderer believes he can remain innocent, he may try to use another woman for the same purpose and eliminate her too."

A knock sounded. Barret went to the door.

"Another remedy is needed." Haggadah stood. "I shall return before my tea cools." The town witch opened the door to see Wiley. His face was sullen.

"Davis is asking for you."

Chapter 14

Tavish noticed his friends walk past the close opening. Curious about their urgency, he followed.

Haggadah sat in the chair before the bed of the dying gravedigger. "I'm here, Davis."

Sophie entered the small room beneath the stairs of the kirkyard tower. She stood near the door with Haggadah's carpetbag in hand and stared at the dancing dust particles in the sunbeams streaming through the only window in the room. She believed the good Lord sent the beam of light to guide Davis to Heaven.

Hearing murmured conversation drifted up from below, Angus descended the tower stairs and entered the room.

Tavish stepped inside and peeked over Wiley's shoulder. "Good to see you again."

The gravedigger nodded, but his concern was elsewhere.

Barret lay his head on the bed, offering his comfort. He looked from Haggadah to Davis, back and forth, when they spoke.

A cough rattled deep in Davis's chest. He gasped for air. "Time for me to go." His voice was barely audible.

Haggadah patted the man's hand. "Aye. We must all face our maker."

His eyelids closed as if he lacked the strength to keep them open. He nodded in agreement. Davis fought to open them again. "Thank you," he wheezed, "for trying to heal me." Closing his eyes, he took his last breath.

"Rest easy, my friend." Haggadah patted the gravedigger's hand one last time before standing and looking at Wiley. "He's in a better place now."

Wiley stared at his peaceful friend, who no longer struggled to breathe. "Aye. He picked out his grave. It's dug and waiting for him."

The town witch tilted her head to the side. "Will you have his burial tomorrow?"

"No, I'm to put him in the ground soon. No ceremony. No casket. Just wrapped him in a sheet. It's what he wanted." Wiley stated.

"No bell?" Sophie looked at the gravedigger before turning to Haggadah.

The town witch explained. "There's no need for a bell. The spirits in the parade of souls will not return."

"Then why did you give Flora a bell?"

"I didn't want the women or the priest to ken I was in the kirkyard on Saint Mark's Eve." Haggadah confessed.

Even though it was past the traditional time for a funeral, Wiley wrapped his friend's body in the bedsheet and carried him to the awaiting grave. Angus and Tavish helped the gravedigger lower Davis's body into its resting place.

"Would you like me to help shovel the dirt?" Tavish offered.

"Thank you, but I would like to do this myself." Davis pulled on the handle of the upright shovel in the mound of dirt and began shoveling while Angus, Haggadah, Sophie, Tavish, and Barret stood nearby. Compelled to offer the gravedigger her respect, Sophie bowed her head and said a silent prayer with each shovelful that fell onto the white sheet.

Wiley patted down the last shovelful with the back of his shovel to form a neat mound. He looked at his friends, steadfast during the burial. "Thank you for paying your respect to Davis. I'm sure he appreciated it."

Then, he looked heavenward, assuming his friend was watching from above.

"It's important to say goodbye." Haggadah looked at the mounded grave as a peacefulness settled within her heart, knowing Davis suffered no more.

"It's as he wanted it." Angus turned and went to his tower.

Haggadah leaned toward Tavish. "Have you heard who is responsible for the maid's death?"

Tavish shook his head. Since his return to Edinburgh, he spent his nights in closes and eavesdropped on conversations, hoping to discover who had beaten Flora.

Sophie saw a dark figure out of the corner of her eye and recognized Owen Ramsey, who was standing before the same elaborate grave. As he turned around, she looked away to avoid eye contact.

"Wiley, if you need anything, just send word." Haggadah knew the gravedigger would miss his friend but hoped memories would fill the void.

The trio bid farewell to Wiley. They were nearly at the gate entrance when Sophie heard someone call her name.

"Miss Sophie, it seems you and I come here often."

Sophie turned and stared at Owen. She remained silent.

The town witch looked from her friend to the handsome man who seemed to want a moment of her time. "Sophie," Haggadah gave an excuse to keep the discussion short, "please remember, you are expected at home. Barret and I will visit with you again soon." Haggadah reached for her carpetbag, and Sophie handed it to her.

"Aye, soon." She agreed.

The town witch tapped her cane on the walkway as she, Tavish, and her dog left the hallowed ground.

Once alone with Owen, Sophie glared at him, unsmiling. "Mister Ramsey, I agree. Unfortunately, we seem to share this common ground. After all, it is a morbid place filled with regret and memories."

Her coldness toward him was puzzling. He ignored her incorrect use of his title and opted to keep the topic of conversation light as he motioned toward the gate, indicating they should continue walking. "I try to visit my parents once a week. However, the demand on my time doesn't always allow me to do so."

"I'm sorry for your loss." She refused to look at him as they walked along the sidewalk, his walking stick tapping with each step. Their pace was more of a saunter, much too slow for Sophie's liking.

"Thank you." He searched for a topic of conversation to alleviate the awkwardness between them.

No longer able to withstand his company, Sophie abruptly stopped beside an awaiting coach. "Mister Ramsey, I must hurry along. My parents are expecting me for the evening meal."

Owen scowled. "Have I offended you in any way?"

Sophie stepped backward and stared at him as if he was totally daft. "Are you oblivious to our first encounter?"

He searched his mind. "I am not. It was here in the kirkyard. I acknowledged you, yet you did not return my greeting."

Sophie crossed her arms over her chest and struggled to retain her civility. "We have met three times before today."

Owen stood dumbfounded. He was confident, having only seen her twice before. "Ah, aye," he recalled, "when you bumped into me outside the dressmaker's shop."

Exasperated, Sophie placed her fisted hands upon her hips. Her face reddened. "Aye, that was my fault." She turned away and began walking home.

Unable to leave the conflict unresolved, Owen matched her gate. "And I forgave you for bumping into me. No harm done."

Sophie halted again, glaring.

Owen struggled to follow her train of thought. He refrained from grinning as he found her agitated state enthralling.

"Aye, I need to pay attention to where I am going." She looked heavenward. "Your infraction is another incident altogether."

"My infraction? Please, enlighten me." He tapped his walking stick on the sidewalk and glared defiantly.

Scowling, she announced, "I don't appreciate being called a, how did you put it, a scabby whore."

Stunned by her accusation, Owen opened his mouth to speak, hesitated, then admired Sophie's beautiful face as he argued in his defense. "I don't recall ever calling you such a name. In fact, it is not in my nature to insult a woman so."

"You deny calling me a scabby whore?"

"Aye, I do. I would not have done such a thing. Such an insult is beyond my character."

Sophie looked away, shook her head, and looked back at Owen. She scolded. "Then you have the shortest of memories. You nearly ran me over with your horse on the night of Saint Mark's Eve. No, it was in the early morning hours of the Feast of Saint Mark."

A vague memory flashed in Owen's mind. He had arrived in Edinburgh late, stopped at a pub to eat, and nearly ran down a woman. "Och! That was you? What in

God's name were you doing roaming the street at that time of night?"

"I don't need to justify an excuse to you." Sophie marched away, fearing she would be late for the evening meal if she delayed any longer.

Her retreating footsteps caused him to take a giant step and gently grasp her by the arm. "Let me explain."

She yanked her arm from his hand, causing him to splay his fingers as if he touched a hot iron. "No explanation needed. You judged me without knowing me. You assumed I was an uneducated lady of the night with low morals and rank just because I was walking in the dark." Sophie began walking away again.

Owen clasped her arm once again. "Wait, please."

Sophie glared at his hand on her forearm until he released it. Staring him dead in the eye, she said, "I don't have time to listen to you. I must go home."

He motioned to the elegant coach they had walked past. "I have a coach and can drop you off if you wish." His offer was sincere.

Sophie remained silent in thought. A scabby whore? Any gentleman would have apologized for such a grievous infraction, but the man standing before had failed to do so. Perhaps it was a true reflection of his character. "I doubt you would want to ruin your reputation by being seen with someone such as me. Good day, Mister Ramsey." Sophie mockingly curtsied before weaving between several horse-drawn wagons as she crossed the street.

Owen stared as she distanced herself from him. He had indeed offended her, perhaps beyond repair. Nevertheless, he admired her gumption and the way she spoke her mind. She was more than the silly females who went out of their way to impress him. He quickly detected their insincerity and read their true purpose – to elevate their social rank. "How am I going to make amends?" Unable to seek his mother's advice, he thought of the only person who may know Sophie well enough to ask. But unfortunately, it would have to wait. He had other matters to attend to for now.

Chapter 15

Looming clouds bellowed across the gray morning sky. Hearing the droplets falling onto the roof, Haggadah added another log to the fire, anticipating the dampness.

Barret raised his head. His ears perked as he listened.

"It's just the rain." Haggadah reassured.

A loud clap of thunder shook the house. Barret dove under Haggadah's bed.

"Barret, no harm will come to you." The town witch looked at Nero, who had yet to acknowledge it was raining as he slept on her bed. "And you continue to sleep like a bairn."

Three knocks sounded on the door.

"It must be serious if someone is willing to trudge through this storm for a remedy." Haggadah opened the door to see Owen standing in the pouring rain. She recognized him from the kirkyard. "I normally don't allow strangers into my house, but come out of the rain." The town witch motioned for her visitor to enter.

"Thank you." He removed his beaver top hat as he stepped inside. Scanning the tiny house's interior, he considered the meager items in the single room.

The stone fireplace was warm and inviting. Hanging over the fire was an iron kettle, a small cauldron perhaps. A lovely crafted bench and a small stool were near the hearth. Crudely made wooden candlesticks with unlit candles were on the mantel. A table with four chairs was in the center of the room, and a rag rug covered the stone floor for warmth. A single bed was to his left with an ebony cat sleeping upon it. A ladder leaned against the bottom of a loft. There was a small kitchen and a worktable. His head bumped into a dried herb hanging from a ceiling beam as he turned to watch the town witch walk away from the door as it clicked shut. A large cabinet was against the wall, which remained hidden from sight until Haggadah had closed the door. Tilting his head to the side, Owen saw a dog's rear end under the bed. His tail was tucked between his legs.

Haggadah chuckled. "He may look fierce, but he is afraid of storms." She anticipated her guest would remain for some time. "May I take your coat and hat?"

Owen took off his wet garment and handed both items to her. "Thank you."

"You look well enough." She hung his belongings on a peg. "How may I help you?" She went to the cupboard and gathered what she needed to make tea.

He stood respectfully, waiting for an invitation to sit. "I'm well. I have come on a more personal matter."

With her back to her visitor, Haggadah grinned. "Ah, Sophie. She has a mind of her own."

Taken back by the town witch's foresight, he recalled the rumors he had heard as a child. She had a black cat, read peoples' minds, and lived in a strange house. However, dead rats hanging by their tails and jars of dead men's fingers were nowhere in sight. "Aye, I've discovered as such."

"Please, sit." Haggadah went to the fireplace and added hot water to each teacup. She placed one before him, joined him at the table, and wrapped her arthritic fingers around the teacup to ease the ache in her hands.

"Thank you." He lifted the warm liquid to his mouth and took a sip.

"You were saying?" Haggadah prompted.

Setting the teacup on the saucer, he began. "At the kirkyard yesterday, I sensed Sophie was vexed with me, yet I could not understand why. She told me I mistook her for a loose woman and offended her the night of Saint Mark's Eve. I'm not making excuses for myself, but I had ridden most of the night and enjoyed a few drams of whisky at a pub. It was a logical assumption in the early morning hour. As we left the kirkyard together, our discussion did not go well. I fear I may have made matters worse."

The town witch's kind gray eyes scanned Owen's handsome face. She estimated his age to be just over twenty. Haggadah empathized with his loss, burdensome responsibilities, and besotted heart. "I've no remedy to force her to listen to you." Haggadah sipped her tea.

"I imagine not." He stared into his teacup before taking another sip.

The town witch perceived his frustration. "Her name is Sophie Conway. She is a doctor's daughter and one of four. She likes to read and is quite intelligent. I think Sophie is the prettiest of the sisters, although she doesn't quite fit in with their silliness. Some refer to her as the misfit of the family." Haggadah continued. "She has empathy for others, especially the less fortunate, and, as you have discovered, quite headstrong and opinionated."

"Aye." Owen chuckled. "Thank you for your insight." He took a deep breath. "Would it be too bold for me to call on her?"

"Unannounced? She would most likely refuse to see you."

"A note?" He pressed.

"No, a happenchance meeting would be best. On sunny days, Sophie often sits on a Princes Street Gardens bench and reads. Bide your time and rehearse your apology."

Owen weighed the town witch's advice.

Haggadah tilted her head to one side. "She must see something in you she dislikes."

"She doesn't ken me."

"Nor do you ken her. I'm the last to give advice for the heart. But, I ken this - forgiveness and trust are necessary for any relationship to work." She reached across the table and patted his arm reassuringly. "May God be with you in your desired conquest."

He wondered if the town witch was warning him of what may lie ahead.

~

The rain continued to fall over the next three days, entrapping the Conway sisters within their home. Sophie buried her nose in book after book while her sisters embroidered, played cards or chess, and practiced playing the pianoforte.

The sisters woke the following morning to sunshine streaming through their bedroom windows. Elspeth listened to her daughter's breakfast conversation while she ate. Since the indecisive sisters could not agree on how to spend their day, the discussion continued as they dismissed themselves from the table.

"Shall we go shopping today?" Grace suggested as they went to the sitting room to plan their day.

"I need a new book to read." Sophie added, picking up her book from the end table. She removed the ribbon bookmark where she had left off and continued to read the last few pages.

A knock summoned Vertie to the front door. She moved her stocky legs quickly and paused to tidy her gray hair in the hallway mirror. She took a moment to catch her breath before opening the door. "Aye."

The young man stood on the stoop with four rectangular boxes in his arms. "I have a delivery from Miss Jaymiee for the Conway sisters."

Grace sprang off the sofa and raced to the front door. "Our dresses are here!"

"Our dresses!" Isobel followed her younger sister.

Elspeth looked up from her embroidery and smiled at her daughter's excitement. She was eager to see their choice of fabric and design.

Sophie turned the page, ignoring her idiotic sisters and their excitement.

Marjorie stared at her preoccupied sister as she stood from the sofa. "Aren't you the least bit excited to see what your new dress looks like?" She lowered her face to Sophie's and stared her in the eye until Sophie looked up from her book. "Close your book and come. We shall try them on together."

Begrudgingly, Sophie placed the ribbon bookmark between the open pages, snapped the book shut, and set it on the settee next to her before standing.

Grace grabbed two boxes while Isobel took the remaining pair from the delivery boy. The girls climbed the staircase, with Marjorie and Sophie following.

Vertie thanked the lad, closed the door, and stared at the girls as they went to the second floor. "Do you need me to help you dress?"

Marjorie looked over her shoulder. "No, we can do it ourselves."

"Thank goodness. I've no energy to race up those stairs." Vertie returned to the kitchen.

Sophie entered the shared bedroom of her younger sisters and discovered Grace had already stripped down to her chemise while Isobel opened all the boxes.

"Here's mine." Isobel held her new dress before her as she stood in front of a full-length mirror. "Oh, isn't it pretty?" She turned toward her sisters for their approval.

Marjorie glanced up and down the entire length of the gown. "It's lovely, Isobel. Miss Jaymiee and her staff are experts with a needle and thread."

"Very pretty." Grace agreed as she pulled her dress from a box.

Sophie tilted her head and admired the design of Isobel's dress. "Some of their best work, indeed."

Encouraged by her sister's comments, Grace slipped into her dress and turned toward the full-length mirror, presenting her back for Marjorie to fasten it closed. She ran the palms of her hands over the skirt and touched the delicate pleats of the empire bodice. "Now, how shall I embellish it?"

"That can wait. Me next." Isobel laid her dress on her bed, stripped down to her undergarment, and held her arms over her head. Marjorie picked up the gown and waited for Isobel to insert her arms into the short sleeves.

Sophie was drawn to the box containing her golden dress. She touched the material, the dainty puffed sleeve, and admired the detail of the design. A pair of matching gloves lay vertically in the box.

Marjorie stepped beside her sister. "It's exquisite, Sophie. And she thought to include a matching pair of gloves too."

Grace peeked over Sophie's shoulder. "You got matching gloves?"

"Who got matching gloves?" Isobel stood before the mirror and smoothed the wrinkles from her skirt.

"Sophie." Grace held them up for Isobel to see.

"Lovely." Isobel turned and admired the reflection of the back of her dress in the mirror. "Sophie, you'll surely draw the men's attention when you enter the ball."

"Well, let's hope not all of them." Marjorie downplayed Isobel's teasing. "There are four eligible Conway sisters for them to consider."

Once Isobel stepped away from the mirror, she peeked at Sophie's dress lying in the box. "Put it on, Soph." She thought it would be wise to offer a logical reason for her to do so. "We need to ken if it fits you properly."

Even though fashion was unimportant to Sophie, she thought it was the most beautiful dress she had ever seen. Almost afraid to touch it, she lifted the elegant gown from the box.

"I'll hold it while you undress." Isobel offered as she took the gown and pressed it against her body. She turned from side to side, admiring the garment in the mirror. She hoped Sophie would allow her to borrow it someday. Isobel saw her sister's reflection behind her, dressed only in undergarments. Between the three sisters, they helped Sophie put on the dress.

Sophie looked at her sisters for their approval. They remained silent, too stunned by the gown's beauty.

Grace handed her the gloves. "Put these on."

Sophie did so, admiring their perfect fit. Then, she stepped before the mirror and turned to the right and left to take in the full beauty of the skirt.

"You look beautiful, Soph." Isobel smiled, pleased to see a glimpse of a proud grin on her sister's face.

"Breathtaking." Marjorie added.

"I told you it was the right color for you." Grace beamed with pride.

"How are the dresses?" Elspeth called from the bottom of the staircase.

Grace went to the top of the stairs and nearly flung herself over the railing. "Wait till you see Sophie's dress. I picked out the fabric, and it's . . . come and see for yourself."

Marjorie was slipping into her dress as Elspeth entered the room. She inspected Grace's dress, admiring its fine stitching and design. "Ah, very pretty." She turned next to Isobel. "Well made, a fine fabric."

Sophie turned away from the mirror and stepped forward. She waited for an unkind word often spoken by her mother, but none came. The silence was deafening.

"Well, Mum, what do you think? Isn't Sophie's dress breathtaking?" Grace prompted.

Elspeth motioned for Sophie to rotate in a circle. "Nice design." She touched the pleating of the bodice. "Impressive." Placing the sheer fabric between her index finger and thumb, Elspeth inspected the sparkling fabric. "Lovely." She lifted the overskirt to view the quality of the golden material beneath, let it fall from her hand, and took a step backward. "The color suits you." She touched the puffed short sleeves made of sheer fabric.

Grace beamed with pride. She had chosen the most beautiful fabric that even her mother could not find an unkind word to describe it. The youngest sister stood behind her mother and mouthed the words 'told you' to Sophie. "Mum, are you going to get a new dress too?"

"There is no need for the expense, for I'm not trying to catch a husband." Elspeth turned and winked at her youngest daughter.

Sophie stared at her mother as her words struck true. She was not in the market for a spouse and had no intention of marrying any time soon.

After inspecting Marjorie's dress, Elspeth returned downstairs.

While the girls helped each other out of their dresses, Sophie remained before the mirror, staring at her reflection. She stood taller and more confident, or was it her imagination? For the first time in her life, she did not think of herself as plain but saw herself as beautiful. Was it the rich golden color of the dress that complimented her auburn hair and enhanced her nearly gray eyes that made her feel so? Never had she owned a garment that affected her in such a positive way. She removed her gloves and placed them in the box reverently.

"I wonder who will host the next ball?" Isobel draped her dress over the foot of her bed. She turned toward Sophie to unfasten her dress.

A soft tickle on Sophie's back indicated Marjorie was unfastening her gown. She would shed the coverings of the beautiful golden butterfly she had become and return to the dull and unnoticed moth. Sophie raised her arms as her dress was lifted over her head and placed in the garment box while she put on her boring everyday muslin dress.

The chattering of her sisters was more than she could take. She picked up her box and retreated to the solitude of her bedroom. Kicking the door closed, she placed the box on her bed, lifted the garment, and held it to her body to view it again in her mirror.

A knock sounded upon her door. "Sophie, we must go shopping for accessories!"

Sophie groaned at the sound of her sister's footfalls, stomping down the stairs like a herd of elephants. She admired her reflection in the mirror one last time. "It's unfortunate that I detest attending balls." Sophie reluctantly returned her dress to the box and joined her sisters.

Chapter 16

Grace tapped her index finger on her chin as she walked down the sidewalk arm-in-arm with Isobel. "I'll need something to put in my hair to accompany my new dress. Maybe a ribbon. Oh, and a necklace with earrings too."

"Gloves, we need new gloves. Lana can no longer get the dirty grayness out of my white pair." Isobel added.

Sophie trailed behind her younger sisters with Marjorie by her side. She listened to Grace and Isobel's chatter and admitted their excitement over buying accessories for their new dresses was contagious. She considered decorative clips for pinning up her hair. A dainty necklace may look nice too. She hoped to find what she needed quickly, for what she looked forward to most was purchasing a new book.

The girls crossed the busy street, entered the shop, and scanned the many ribbons hanging from a dowel.

"Oh, this one is pretty." Isobel selected a satin mint green ribbon.

"That won't match your dress." Grace scolded.

"Who said I was looking for a ribbon to match my dress?"

Sophie shook her head at her youngest sister's bantering and selected a pair of golden-brown slippers in her size. "Perfect." Spying an off-white cashmere shawl, her heart nearly skipped a beat. It had a long fringe on each end and was embellished with intricate gold, beige, and brown embroidering. Sophie placed it over her head, draping it between her arms and behind her back like a suspension bridge. She admired its softness as she ran the palm of her hand over the wool.

"It's perfect, Sophie."

Sophie looked at Marjorie, who was smiling. "I agree." After finding decorative clips for her hair, she made her purchase, picked up the wrapped items from the counter, and announced to her sisters, "I'm going to the bookstore. I'll meet you at home."

Marjorie pulled a glove over her elbow, flexed her fingers, and rotated her arm to admire the fit. She looked at Sophie as she turned toward the door. "Aye." As usual, Isobel and Grace argued, ignorant of their sister's departure.

Sophie tilted her face skyward, soaking up the sun's warming rays as she stepped onto the sidewalk. She strolled three doors down to the bookstore. The bell above the door rang as she entered and inhaled the familiar fragrance of ink on paper. "I could spend the rest of the day in here."

"May I help you, Miss Sophie?" The bookstore owner, an elderly man with wire-rimmed glasses, came out from behind the counter. He pushed the bridge of his glasses upward from the end of his nose.

"Hello, Mister Edwards. It's always a pleasure to visit your store." She glanced at the books on the shelves.

"As you often do. I assume you are looking for a book to read."

"Aye."

"Another romance?" He grinned.

"You ken me well." Sophie began scanning the books on the shelves.

"I have something for you." The bookstore owner went behind the counter and retrieved a book he had tucked away. "I set it aside, knowing you may enjoy reading it. The author is anonymous."

Sophie went to the counter. "Anonymous?"

"Authors are usually male. But, more than likely, the author of this book is female and wanted to keep it a secret." He placed the three volumes in her extended hand. "From what I hear, the author writes quite well."

Sophie read the spine. "Pride and Prejudice?" She opened the cover to the title page and read 'BY THE AUTHOR OF "SENSE AND SENSIBILITY."' Sophie looked at the bookshop owner. "So, the author has written other books."

"Aye, several. I can hardly keep the novels on the shelf for long," Mister Edwards adjusted his glasses on his nose again, "that is, when I get one."

"If I like this one, you can be sure I'll want to read more by this author, whoever she may be." Sophie smiled and raised her eyebrows, privileged to know the secret of the author's gender.

"Since you are such a regular customer, I will set aside any of her books for you as I receive them."

"Thank you, Mister Edwards. That is so very kind of you." Sophie paid for her book.

"Would you like me to wrap them for you?" He offered.

"Just these two." Sophie handed him volumes II and III. "I plan to begin reading the first volume right away." Sophie put the novel on top of the packages she carried and watched as her purchase was wrapped.

"See you again soon, Miss Sophie." Mister Edwards handed her the wrapped books.

"Maybe sooner than you think. Good day."

~

Owen stood before his parents' grave. He wondered if they were looking down on him from above. Did they approve of his management of the family estate? Did they agree with the business decisions he had recently made? Had he treated a tenant too harshly or too leniently? Was he living up to his father's strict standards? Owen received no guidance other than the opinions of his staff. He was doing his best, but no matter how he fought it, self-doubt often crept into his mind.

It was comforting for Owen to be alone with his thoughts. However, no matter how frequently he stepped onto the hallowed ground, his questions remained unanswered.

Owen turned and looked at the newly dug graves where he had seen Sophie during his last few visits. She was angry. Her negative opinion of him was troublesome and weighed heavily on his mind.

Why should he care what she thought or assumed of his character?

Owen left the kirkyard and strolled along the West Princes Street Gardens pathway, admiring its beauty. The grass was plush and green, a few of the bushes still had a hint of color, and the budding trees were giving way to display their foliage and offer shade. He inhaled the fragrance of lilacs carried by the gentle breeze. He looked for its source and saw the tall white, lilac, and purple bushes in full bloom.

People sat on blankets on the plush green grass, making the park resemble an abstract patchwork quilt. Many were enjoying something to eat while conversing. "Happenchance." Owen scanned the benches along the pathway, paying particular attention to any female reading a book. She was not there.

Continuing his walk, he crossed The Mound and stood on a terrace overlooking the East Gardens. People dotted the slight incline of the ground and basked in the sunshine. Benches lined two parallel pathways above. He did not see Sophie seated on the lower path. The trees shaded the upper path from his view.

Determined, Owen left his perch and followed the upper pathway. A beam of sunlight peeked between the canopy of trees, making her appear as if she were glowing. He slowed his pace as he approached and stopped before her.

As a shadow darkened the page Sophie was reading, she looked up from her book to see Owen standing before her.

"Hello, Miss Sophie."

"Mister Ramsey." Her greeting was stern. Wishing he would be on his way, she returned to her book and continued reading.

A twinge of hesitation caused him to pause, but he needed to apologize for his mistake. He pressed. "Do you mind if I sit with you?"

Forcing herself to be polite, she shook her head, mentally noted the page she was on, and closed her book. Sophie placed it in her lap and rested her clasped hands on the cover.

Owen sat at the opposite end with her packages between them. "I have been troubled since our last meeting and want to express my sincerest apology for mistaking you for a lady of the night."

His apology seemed sincere, but Sophie saw deeper into his character. "You are very quick to judge someone when you ken nothing about them." Sophie was direct. Her words cut deeply.

"I admit, it's a fault of mine. But under the circumstances, my assumption was a logical conclusion. However, I'll be more mindful of it in the future." Owen realized she had not accepted his apology. "I am truly sorry." He watched as she looked at the book in her lap. He thought it best to change the subject. "What are you reading?"

Wishing to be rid of him, she handed him the book and remained silent.

He read the title and author. "Pride and Prejudice. The author is anonymous?"

"The bookstore owner believes the author is female and wishes to avoid any criticism of her sex."

He opened the book to the first page and read aloud. *"It is a truth universally acknowledged, that a single man in possession of a good fortune, must be in want of a wife."* Owen stared into the distance, not focusing on anything as he thought. He closed the book and stared at the cover before looking at Sophie. "Do you believe the author's sentence is a true statement?"

Sophie met his stare. "You should ken better than anyone."

Owen grinned. "In my defense, the statement is from a woman's perspective."

"And isn't a woman's assessment and opinion usually correct?" She remained unsmiling.

Owen chuckled. "Something tells me I should agree with you." He watched as each end of Sophie's mouth turned upward slightly. It pleased him. He handed the book back to her. "I would like to read it when you are finished. You have my word; I'll take the greatest care of your possession and return it once I am done."

His request surprised her. Sophie placed the book back in her lap. "Aye, you may borrow it."

Owen glanced at the packages on the seat between them. He was not curious about what she had purchased but wanted to extend their conversation and remain in her company. "I see you have been shopping. Did you find what you needed?"

Sophie glanced at her packages. "Aye. My sisters and I shopped for embellishments to match our new dresses."

"Aye, a new dress for this season's balls. Do you often attend balls?"

"Only when I'm forced. I have two left feet, so I'm not fond of dancing." She confessed, wondering why she had done so. Perhaps it was because he appeared to have some intellect despite his faults.

"Then we have something in common. Perhaps you can reserve a dance for me at the next ball, and we can stumble through it together."

"Perhaps." Sophie had no intention of dancing with him and hoped to conceal herself in an alcove to remain undetected if he were in attendance.

Silence stretched between them as Owen became mesmerized by her nearly gray eyes in contrast to her auburn hair. He stood. "I've kept you from enjoying your book. Until we meet again, good day." He touched his index finger to his hat, bowed slightly, and left.

Sophie stared at Owen as he walked away, his walking stick keeping in time with his gait. She became aware of several women on the surrounding benches staring at her. She opened her book and continued to read.

Chapter 17

Three days later, on a misty afternoon, a messenger knocked on the door of the Conway house.

Sophie sat in her favorite chair beside her bedroom window and read the last line of VOLUME III. She smiled as the emotion of the novel penetrated her heart. She ignored the squeals of her sisters downstairs, closed the book reverently, and held it against her heart before placing it in her lap and running her palm over the cover. "Ah, if only men were more like Mister Darcy."

Grace and Isobel raced up the staircase. Their heavy footfalls forewarned Sophie of the approaching pair before her bedroom door flew open.

"Sophie, we've been invited to a ball!" Grace jumped up and down, unable to contain her excitement.

The romantic spell of the book was broken, bringing Sophie back to reality. She exhaled and stared at her idiotic sisters.

"It's in two weeks." Isobel added as she clasped her sister's hands and jumped in unison. "We can wear our new dresses!"

"Who is hosting the ball?" Sophie placed her book on the table next to her chair and waited for her sisters to compose themselves.

They stopped jumping and stared at her. "The Pringles." They said simultaneously and began jumping again.

Sophie looked heavenward. The Pringle family's only son, Archie, was sure to ask her to dance. Her feet would be bruised by the evening's end, for he was a worse dancer than she. He lacked intellect and humor and thought of himself as superior to most. As excited as she was to wear her new dress, she vowed to put on last year's gown, hoping to give him less of a reason to pursue her.

"Let's go try on our dresses again." Grace pulled Isobel out of the room.

Sophie took last year's dress from the wardrobe. She held it against her body as she looked at herself in the mirror. "Aye, this dress will do fine. Of course, Mum will disapprove, but I hope I can devise a way to leave the house wearing it."

~

As a blanket of darkness fell upon the city, coaches lined the street to transport guests to the evening ball.

Sophie had spent the past two weeks creating an alibi for wearing the previous season's gown.

"Come on, Sophie! We're waiting for you!" Grace called up the staircase.

Sophie took a deep breath as she emerged from her bedroom and saw Vertie holding the front door open. She hurried down the stairs, ordered the coachman to depart for the ball as she entered the coach, and plopped down on the crowded seat between Grace and Isobel. She was jerked forward as the driver slapped the reins on the horses' rumps, setting the wheels in motion.

Doctor Kendrick had failed to return from a house call, leaving his wife to escort their daughters for the evening. Elspeth looked away from the window and stared at Sophie. "Why aren't you wearing your new gown?"

"Aye, why?" Grace's mouth hung agape.

Growing uncomfortable under their glaring stares, Sophie focused on her skirt and brushed away imaginary wrinkles. "I'm saving it for a special occasion." She defended and returned her mother's piercing stare. "A ball at the Pringles is not a special occasion. They host several every season."

Since she stated the truth, no one could argue with her logic.

The silent ride to the Pringle house was filled with excitement by most of the passengers in the coach. As the driver reined the horses before the front steps of the impressive house, a footman opened the carriage door and offered his hand to help the Conway women disembark.

Grace was the first to escape the confinement of the coach and place her foot on the loose gravel. She gazed at the granite pillars supporting the entrance's protective roof and noticed nearly every window aglow with candlelight. She could hear music and good conversation echoing from within. "Oh, I love attending balls."

The last woman to be helped exit the coach was the matriarch. Elspeth led her four daughters up the stairs toward the open doorway of the foyer. Distracted by the evening's numerous coaches, guests, and ambiance, Sophie tripped up the last step. Marjorie pulled her upright before she could fall and make a fool of herself.

As they entered the foyer, a silver tray with fluted crystal glasses of bubbling beverages was presented.

Elspeth, Marjorie, and Sophie selected a drink. When the youngest two reached for a glass, Elspeth scolded, "You're too young." Grace and Isobel withdrew their hands and devilishly grinned at each other, knowing they would partake in the beverage when their mother was not watching.

The Conway women entered the candlelit ballroom. Its candelabras and chandeliers illuminated the room in a subdued golden glow. The fragrant flower arrangements on tabletops and numerous plants created a natural ambiance. Guests were dressed in their finest garments with embellishments of their tartan colors proudly on display. The single men in the room looked toward the doorway as additional female guests entered.

Carson set his drink aside as he recognized the Conway sisters.

"I feel like a cow being selected for slaughter," Sophie said under her breath.

Marjorie scowled. "Hush, Sophie. Don't be so melodramatic. You're much too thin to be a cow." She grinned, trying to improve her sister's sour disposition.

Elspeth led her daughters to one side of the dance floor and watched the twirling couples finish with a bow and curtsey as the music waned. Marjorie placed her empty glass on the silver tray of a passing servant.

"Good evening," Carson said as he bowed before the sisters and their matriarch. "As promised, I hope to dance with all of you tonight. Who shall be first?" He gazed at Marjorie.

"Me." Grace stepped forward and placed her hand within his offered palm. He smiled and escorted her to the dance floor.

Sophie tipped her glass upward, hoping to avoid the request of a gentleman who approached next. She was relieved when he asked Marjorie to dance instead. Isobel, along with her partner, took to the floor too.

"Now, if we can only find a suitable partner for you, Sophie." Elspeth took Sophie's empty glass and placed it on a servant's tray as he walked by.

"I prefer not to dance." She took a half step behind her mother, hoping to shield herself.

Elspeth grabbed her daughter's elbow, pulled Sophie beside her, and smiled as a gentleman approached them. "Here is your opportunity whether you want it or not."

Sophie groaned inwardly as Archie Pringle walked toward them. He had gained weight since last year, and his lips were grossly wet like a hungry lion who licked them before eating his prey.

Archie bowed. His auburn curly hair seemed to bounce back in place like coiled springs. "Miss Sophie, would you care to dance?" His sapphire eyes pierced her soul, anticipating her reply.

Sophie glared at her mother. "I would be happy to." She curtsied.

They joined the other couples standing in two lines on the dance floor. Sophie wedged herself between Isobel and a somewhat robust young lady. She looked across the floor at Archie as the music began at a fast tempo. Sophie had difficulty keeping in step with the rather lively dance. However, she was pleased to keep her distance from Archie as most of the dance was done separately. When they came together and clasped hands, Sophie turned her face away from his rancid breath.

"Och!" She paused in dancing as the heavy oaf stomped on her foot.

"My apologies. I'm not the best of dancers." He smiled.

"You don't say." Sophie limped through the remainder of the dance and quickly curtsied as the song ended. She sought an alcove and hoped to remain hidden until it was time to go home.

~

Owen ascended the stairs of the Pringle house. It paled in comparison to Hilltop, but he thought it adequate for the event.

He stood in the doorway of the ballroom and scanned its guests.

As the musicians chose their next song to play, the room grew quiet with murmured conversations, and everyone looked toward the newest arrival. Mister Pringle rushed forward.

"Laird Ramsey, it's so good of you to come." He bowed before the laird, dressed in a black jacket, pants, and a Ramsey tartan vest.

Owen stared at the man, unsmiling. "Thank you."

"I hope you enjoy your evening."

"I intend to."

A servant presented a tray of drinks. Owen shook his head, declining.

Women eager to see their daughters wed to such a wealthy laird quickly got in line to meet the most eligible bachelor in the room. The matriarchs introduced their daughters individually, hoping Laird Ramsey would ask them to dance. Instead, Owen scanned the room as if ignoring the line of women before him. He was polite and bowed to each young lady as they curtsied but made no offer to dance with any of them.

Feeling bombarded by the on-slot of females, he questioned his reason for attending the ball. He needed to escape. As a woman stepped forward to introduce her three daughters, he recognized the silly girl at the fabric shop.

Elspeth smiled. "Laird Ramsey, may I introduce my daughters, Grace, Isobel, and Marjorie." They curtsied. "I have a fourth daughter, Sophie, who is currently absent."

"Hello, Laird Ramsey. It's nice to see you again." Grace giggled.

Owen bowed slightly. "If you will excuse me." He walked away, leaving Elspeth and her daughters staring blankly.

"See what you did, Grace. You scared him off." Isobel accused. "When are you going to learn to keep your mouth shut."

"I was trying to engage him in conversation." Grace defended but wondered if she had somehow offended Laird Ramsey.

~

Sophie sat on the cushioned bench by the open window in the small three-sided room illuminated with a single candelabra of five tapers. The partial moon offered enough light for couples to walk in the torchlit garden below. She watched them wander through the pathways and could hear their whispered conversations as they cooled from dancing or attempted to form a relationship.

Removing her slipper from her throbbing foot, Sophie saw it was swollen and bruised. If she were discovered by a gentleman wanting to twirl her about the dance floor, the injury gave her the viable excuse to refuse his invitation.

"May I hide in here with you?"

Startled by his voice, she forced her dainty foot into her shoe.

Owen watched as she concealed her swollen foot beneath the hem of her dress.

Sophie looked up to see Owen standing in the shadowed doorway. "Mister Ramsey, I thought you didn't attend balls?" Her voice was again stern, distrusting.

Owen stepped into the solitude of the alcove. "I don't, but since I have declined the invitation from the Pringles several times, to refuse it again would appear rude."

An awkward silence stretched between them.

Owen chose a topic that Sophie was sure she would engage in. "Did you finish your book? The one by the female author. What was it called?" He approached her hesitantly and stood before the window to gaze into the garden below. Owen clasped his hands behind his back.

His closeness was unnerving. "Aye, Pride and Prejudice. The rain over the past few days allowed me to read it twice."

He looked down at her. "Twice? You must have enjoyed it then."

Sophie became lost in the memory of the fictional couple's romance, and a serene smile appeared on her face. "Very much so."

Owen motioned toward the vacancy on the window seat. "Do you mind if I sit?"

Her smile faded as if the spell was broken. She shook her head and watched as he sat.

"So, you agree with the female author's perspective?" He continued.

"I found her to be the most intuitive of writers. Her point of view is one that I agree with wholeheartedly." A smile spread across her face as she nodded. "It is by far one of my favorite reads. I'm quite eager to read all of her books."

"If you don't mind, I would love to stop by tomorrow and borrow it. I'm most intrigued to see what has captivated you so. Once I have read it, we can have a real discussion, which includes a male perspective."

Sophie looked down at her gloved hands in her lap. "Aye, I look forward to your opinion." A giggle drifted in from the garden, causing Sophie to look out the window for its source.

"Would you care for a stroll in the garden?" He offered.

Shaking her head, she declined. "I was forced to dance with Archie Pringle earlier. He stomped on my foot, causing a rather painful bruise. He is heavier on his feet than I am, especially since he's gained nearly two stones over the winter. I've been hiding in this alcove ever since to avoid anyone asking me to dance."

Owen shook his head, displaying a slight frown. "That is unfortunate." He paused, hesitant to make his offer. "Would you like to go home? I can have my coachman take you."

Sophie desired nothing more but knew it would be frowned upon. "My mum would have my head if I left early."

He liked the sound of her voice. It soothed him. Owen prompted. "Tell me, what else do you like to read?"

"I have read many topics, too many to recall. However, I'm not very fond of philosophy. It's so dry."

"Hilltop has a good-sized library. You are welcome to borrow any book you wish." Owen grinned. "I doubt it contains one written by your favorite anonymous author." He jested.

"How can you call it a proper library without one of her books?" She teased.

He laughed. "I agree. Then I will have to add one of the author's novels to complete it." Owen sensed the tension between them had lightened and stated what weighed heavily on his mind. "Have you forgiven my transgression and accepted my apology?"

"There you are!"

Sophie and Owen looked toward Carson as he joined them in the alcove.

"I have danced with all your sisters. And as promised, I must dance with you before the night is finished." He held out his hand to help Sophie stand.

"I'm honored by your request, Mister Hamilton. Unfortunately, my foot was bruised by my previous partner. Perhaps another time?"

Disappointment masked Carson's face as he let his hand fall to his side. "Very well. The next ball, then." He bowed and left to find another partner.

"How badly is it hurt?" Owen looked to where he assumed her foot was beneath her gown.

"It throbs but will most likely be fine in the morning. For now, it gives me an excuse not to dance." She confessed.

Elspeth stepped into the alcove. She glanced from Sophie to Owen. "I see you found my wayward daughter, Laird Ramsey."

Owen stood. "Aye, I thought to keep her company since she cannot dance."

Elspeth glared at Sophie. "Why can't you dance?"

"Archie stomped on my foot. It's quite inflamed."

Elspeth opened her mouth to speak.

Owen interrupted to save Sophie from a foreseeable tongue-lashing. "We were just discussing a stroll in the garden." He stood, turned his back toward Elspeth, and offered his hand for her to rise. Owen winked and grinned to encourage Sophie to stand.

With a defiant glance at her mother, Sophie lifted her chin. Aware of the man's rumored galivanting with women, she placed her gloved hand within his palm and stood.

To offer Sophie his support for her injury, he threaded her arm through his and placed his hand on hers to ensure it remained in place.

Sophie fought the urge to pull her hand away as its warmth seemed to sear her skin through her glove.

As they stepped forward, Elspeth saw her daughter walk with a slight limp as they passed by her. She turned and stared at the retreating pair, both puzzled and intrigued.

Many noticed the entwined couple's exit from the ballroom. Heads tilted together as whispered assumptions were shared.

Once outside, Sophie pulled her hand away and unthreaded her arm. "Thank you. She can be most persistent." She used the sculptured stone handrail for support as she descended the steps.

He clasped his hands behind his back as they stepped onto the loose gravel. "Most mums are. I assume she only wants the best for you."

"Unfortunately, her idea and my idea of what is best for me differ greatly."

They entered the torchlit garden with its winding grassy walkways bordered by various bushes, trimmed hedges, and decorative plants.

Considering Sophie's injury, Owen motioned for her to sit on the first bench they came upon. She sat and placed her gloved hands in her lap. Sophie thought it awkward for him to remain standing, so she scooted to the end of the bench and motioned for him to sit for ease of conversation.

Owen sat at the far end and remained silent as a couple walked past them. Their intrusion gave him time to think of a topic of discussion. However, only one topic of discussion invaded his peace of mind. He turned his body toward her. "I have yet to receive an answer to my last question."

Sophie could not recall the question. "Which was?"

"Your forgiveness of my transgression." His voice conveyed sincerity.

"I have given it some thought. Even though it was hurtful, your assumption was logical. There is nothing to forgive." She looked skyward, wishing to talk of it no more. "Your loose reputation is renowned. Trusting you as a friend is another matter altogether." She began to stand. "My reputation may be ruined while remaining in your company."

He recalled the town witch saying the same. It was true. Before his parents' deaths, he enjoyed the company of women, many women. His hand reached out and boldly clasped hers as he stood. "Then I will have to earn your friendship. Please stay. Let me explain."

They stood, facing each other. Owen released Sophie's hand. She stared up into his ocean-blue eyes. The soft curls of his auburn locks swayed like feathers in the breeze. She returned to her seat, willing to listen to what he had to say.

Owen sat, silent and reflective as another couple passed by them. "I'm aware of what people say. Some of it is true. However, since many consider me the most eligible bachelor, it is easy to get caught up in the flattery of women." He paused. "The veil has been removed from my eyes, and I now see their motives. I'm no longer that person since acquiring my father's responsibilities."

"Ah, responsibility. Always lurking over your shoulder, much like the night is to the day." Sophie had nothing else to relate to in his confession. She thought of her face as plain, not beautiful, with no suitors for her affection. She could only imagine being pursued by someone with ulterior motives and tangled in a loveless relationship. "You've shared an interesting perspective of your life. Unlike you, I have never been pursued and don't share your burden." She looked skyward once again.

The cloudless sky dotted with countless stars resembled indigo velvet sprinkled with diamonds. Serenaded by the music from within the ballroom, couples wandered the garden arm in arm in conversation. A flirtatious comment invoked an occasional giggle within the shelter of the foliage.

Sophie exhaled. "So many stars. It's beautiful."

"Aye, beautiful." Owen was not looking at the sky. He was looking at Sophie.

Chapter 18

Kendrick paused with a forkful of fried potatoes midway to his mouth. "How unusual." He sat alone at the table, enjoying his breakfast. His only company was the ticking of the hallway clock. The doctor was thankful for the peace and quiet while reflecting on the treatment of his last patient.

Vertie brought a fresh pot of coffee from the kitchen. "A second cup?"

"Aye, thank you."

Thunderous footfalls resounded from the staircase. Kendrick scowled, realizing his solitude was coming to an end.

"Good morning, Dad." Grace sat in the chair nearest her patriarch. "Oh, guess who Sophie spent most of the evening with?" She gave him no time to answer. "The Laird of Hilltop."

Drawing his eyebrows together, Kendrick looked at his youngest daughter, assuming he had misheard her. "Laird Owen Ramsey?"

"Aye, the very one." Grace scooped fried potatoes onto her plate.

A knock sounded on the front door. Vertie looked toward the hallway, set the coffee pot on the table, and left the room.

Isobel came bounding into the room. "Wasn't last night wonderful! We danced all night. Well, until Mum forced us to leave the ball. In my opinion, we left far too early."

"It was so nice of Carson to ask us to dance too." Grace selected a slice of toast and smothered it with jam.

Kendrick's curiosity pulled him into the conversation. "Who's Carson?"

"Carson Hamilton. We met him, or should I say, Sophie met him one day when we were shopping." Grace shoveled potatoes into her mouth before placing an over-easy egg from a platter onto her plate.

"He's so handsome." Isobel poured herself a cup of coffee and added cream and sugar.

Marjorie, sleepy-eyed, joined the table. "Good morning, Dad."

"Morning." He sipped his coffee as the chattering of his daughters continued.

Kendrick watched as his wife joined the gaggle of women. He heard footsteps descending the staircase, announcing his last daughter had risen.

Vertie shut the door, turned, and handed Sophie a message as she descended the last step. "This just arrived for you."

"Thank you, Vertie." Sophie stood in the hallway to avoid her family's inquisition and read the message. She glanced at the clock. "No time to waste." She put on her overcoat, stuffed the note into her pocket, and hurried into the dining room. "Good morning." Grabbing a slice of buttered toast in one hand and sausage between her thumb and index finger in the other, she left the room.

Kendrick paused with his coffee cup halfway to his mouth. "Where are you going?"

"Out!" Sophie put the toast in her mouth and opened the door to see Owen standing on the stoop with his fisted hand raised to knock.

Owen tried not to laugh as he watched her eyes widen, knowing she had been caught with the toast clamped between her lips. "Good morning, Miss Sophie."

A muttered sound passed through the toast as she held up one finger and slammed the door in his face.

Owen blinked as he took a step backward. "I'll try not to take that personally." He heard stomping footsteps fade to silence. Moments later, they returned with intensity. The door flew open.

Sophie shoved the three volumes toward him. She slammed the door behind her, stepped onto the stoop, and removed the slice of toast still clenched between her teeth. "Sorry, I must run. Pardon me." Sophie stepped forward, squeezing her body between her visitor and the railing.

Owen stepped aside, allowing her to pass. He glanced at the books in his hand and then watched her descend the steps, racing down the sidewalk. "Where are you going in such a hurry?"

"To Haggadah's." She yelled over her shoulder before biting into her toast once again.

A strong desire to be in her company forced him to speak. "If you are constrained for time, I can take you there in my coach."

Skidding to a stop, she turned abruptly and stared at him. "Very well." Sophie nearly ran to the coach and entered as Owen opened the door. He gave the driver instructions before sitting in the seat opposite her.

"I'm sorry. I didn't mean to be rude." Sophie put the sausage in the center of the toast and folded it in half. She ate a healthy bite and glanced out the coach to see her mother's stern face staring at her from the sitting room picture window.

"If I recall correctly, we agreed I would stop by today to borrow your book. However, we didn't agree on the time. Perhaps I'm too early?" He saw she was unable to reply. "I should have sent word of my arrival."

Sophie simply shook her head as she chewed. She reached into her pocket and handed Owen the note. Forcing the mouthful of food down her throat, she explained. "I received this a few minutes ago."

Owen's eyes widened as he read the note. "Who is Jack?" He stared at the scribbled handwriting, guessing it belonged to the town witch.

"He is an orphan who lives in the South Bridge Vaults."

Concern masked his face as he looked at her from beneath the brim of his hat. "You're going into the vaults?"

"Aye, with Haggadah and Barret. She knows the lad's time is growing near."

He stared into her gray eyes as he handed the note back to her. "His time? As in, his death?"

Sophie ate another bite of her sausage sandwich, nodded, and tucked the note back in her overcoat pocket.

Old Town was well known for its homeless vagrants and rampant crime. The vaults housed the worst of the worst and poorest of the poor, or so Owen had heard. He voiced his concern. "I don't think you should go into the vaults. It's dangerous."

She swallowed. "I've already been there once. We're returning to merely check on the child."

"Where are his parents?"

"Dead."

"Why isn't he in an orphanage?"

"He refuses to go." She ate the last of her makeshift sandwich as the coach halted before the town witch's cottage. Sophie did not wait for the coachman to open the door, nor did she wait for Owen to do so either. "Thank you for the ride." She burst forth from the coach, leaving the bewildered laird alone inside.

Owen stopped the door from slamming shut. "Another door closing in my face. This is becoming a habit." He emerged from the coach and followed her with commanding strides. "Even I have never ventured into the vaults. I've heard the conditions are retched. They're too dangerous for you to enter."

Sophie stopped before the cottage door. "Nonsense. I'll be perfectly safe. If you would like to see for yourself,

I'm certain Haggadah won't mind if you tag along." She knocked.

The town witch opened the door. "Good morning, Sophie, Laird Ramsey." She saw the exquisite coach on the street.

Barret pushed his head between Haggadah and the doorframe, anticipating an affectionate greeting from Sophie, who patted the canine's head as she accepted the carpetbag from Haggadah.

Owen took the worn satchel from Sophie's hand. "If it pleases you, Haggadah, I would like to accompany you and Miss Sophie to the vaults. My coach can take us there."

The town witch sized up the man of luxury, uncertain if he could stomach the wretched conditions of the poor. "As you wish."

He escorted the women and Barret to the awaiting transportation and offered his hand to help them inside. Sophie and Haggadah sat together while Owen gave their destination to the coachman. He sat on the vacant seat opposite the women and placed the carpetbag beside him.

Barret sat before Owen, staring. Finally, the canine placed his paw on the man's knee, demanding his attention.

Grinning, Sophie looked from Owen to Barret and back to Owen, who sat as still as a statue with his eyes glancing at the dog occasionally. She began to laugh. "Barret expects you to greet him."

Owen looked at Barret, who began wagging his tail. "Hello, Barret." He patted the dog's head. "You're a good boy." The dog seemed to smile as he was showered with affection.

Haggadah remained silent. She knew Owen was accompanying them for Sophie's protection, even though it was unwarranted. The town witch had known Laird Hector Ramsey, Owen's father, who was renowned for his strict policies with his son's upbringing, treatment of his tenants, and lack of empathy for the poor. Sheltered in a luxurious lifestyle, she hoped Owen's conditioned prejudice would give way. Would he have an open mind and empathetic heart to those who lived in and around the squalor of the vaults? Would his heart soften? Would he rise and help to alleviate their suffering? He had the means to do so.

Haggadah's mother once explained to her that there would always be those who are poor. It was unkind for society to shun them, for those who were destitute through no fault of their own simply needed a chance for a better life.

The town witch knew many people thought of her as poor, but she believed she was more prosperous than most. Her healing knowledge gave her a purpose and made her feel valued as a community member. She prided herself on helping others.

Studying the young laird, Haggadah watched as the wealthy man seemed to warm to her dog. She hoped he treated the less fortunate the same way. She would soon find out.

Chapter 19

The coachman directed the horses into the most destitute area of the city. It was littered with the homeless sleeping and loitering on the sidewalks. Several onlookers gawked in question at the rarely-seen expensive coach as it passed by, making the coachman nervous. "Laird, where would you like me to stop?" He called from the driver's seat.

Owen looked at the town witch, uncertain of the answer to give the servant.

Haggadah sensed the uneasiness of the man's voice. She looked out the window, recognizing her surroundings. "He may stop here, and we will walk to the entrance. It is not far. Have him return in an hour to this spot."

Owen relayed the request.

As the coach came to a stop, Laird Ramsey stepped onto the crumbling sidewalk with the carpetbag in his hand. He peered at the homeless from beneath the brim of his hat. Their clothing was filthy, tattered, and threadbare. Many were shoeless. He assumed it had been years since they bathed. He watched a runny-nosed child scratch his head from an infestation of lice. The smell of sewage and smoke from warming fires lingered in the air.

Glad to have his walking stick in hand, apprehension tied Owen's stomach in a knot. He feared for Sophie's safety. He turned to see her appear in the coach's doorway and presented his hand for assistance. "Are you sure you want to do this?"

Sophie scowled, failing to understand his apprehension. "Aye." She placed her hand within his, stepped onto the sidewalk, and relieved him of the burdensome carpetbag.

Owen helped Haggadah from the coach and waited for Barret to join them before closing the door and telling the servant to return in an hour.

The town witch and her canine led the way to the entrance with Owen protectively by Sophie's side.

Haggadah paused near the opening to the vaults. "Sophie, the candles."

Sophie searched inside the carpetbag, took out a pair of candles, and touched their wicks to the flames of a nearby warming fire. She handed one to Owen and gave one to Haggadah.

Passing through the entrance, the town witch and her faithful dog disappeared into the darkness. The tapping of her cane echoed her progress as she walked.

Owen glanced at the homeless lingering about. Their eyes conveyed a resentment as they scanned his expensive clothing. Even though he was born into wealth, his father's success resulted from hard work and common sense. Laird Ramsey had heard of wealthy men who lived frivolously and lost their fortune. Owen wondered what circumstances or decisions the curious onlookers had made that led to their downfall in society.

Dismissing his thoughts, he entered the vaults behind Sophie and wrinkled his nose at the odorous conditions. With each step he took into the dank darkness, the odors became more pungent, the dampness thicker, and the plight of the people increasingly dire. Owen held the candle near Sophie to help her see where she was walking. His foot splashed into a puddle, and he prayed it was not urine. He looked into an alcove to see pairs of tiny glowing eyes staring back at him. He assumed they were rats. A baby's cry echoed in the passage. He was unsure of which direction it came from. Owen stared at an unwell man who sat on the damp floor coughing. Owen leaned toward Sophie. "How far must we walk?"

"Assuming Jack is in the same location, he should be just ahead."

A grungy woman reached toward Owen. "Food, do you have any food?"

He reached into his pocket and tossed her a few coins, hoping she would stay away from Sophie.

They finally reached the correct chamber and discovered Jack in the same cubby.

Haggadah affixed her candle to the stone cubical and assessed the child's health. Jack's skin had become paper thin. He had declined and weakened considerably. The town witch knew he was very near death.

Jack cracked open his eyes and saw Haggadah's wrinkled face illuminated by the candlelight. "Don't let Katherine get me." He pleaded.

Sophie went to the cubby and whispered to Haggadah. "Who is Katherine?"

"She is a nanny who was fired from her job. She comes into the vaults to harvest the dead children's bodies, takes them to the anatomy theater, and sells them to be dissected." The town witch explained.

"But Doctor Knox is no longer there to pay her."

"Aye, someone else will. The anatomy theater still needs bodies to educate the medical students."

Owen thought the child was delusional, a fever perhaps. He took a step closer and peered down at the boy. "Is he mad?"

Haggadah looked over her shoulder. "He speaks the truth. The nanny is well known within the vaults."

"I don't want to be cut up." Jack's voice faded.

Haggadah tucked the blanket beneath the child's chin. "You have my word. No one will cut you up. Rest now." She motioned for Sophie and Owen to accompany her to the opposite side of the chamber. "He hasn't got much time left. I'll stay here with him until he passes."

"Alone?" Owen looked about, concerned for the old woman's safety.

Haggadah patted his arm reassuringly. "Barret will be with me."

"And so will I," said a male voice.

Owen looked over the heads of the women standing before him to see an impoverished man in the opening of the chamber. He grew concerned, stepped forward, and pushed Sophie behind him. "Who are you?"

Haggadah recognized his voice before she turned around. "Hello, Tavish."

Tavish looked from Owen to Haggadah. "I saw you pass by in a fancy coach. It piqued my curiosity."

Sophie scowled at the back of the ebony overcoat before her. She stepped out from behind Owen. "It's nice to see you again, Tavish."

Owen glared at Sophie, shocked by her association with the vagrant.

"Hello, Miss Sophie." Tavish grinned, displaying his smile, which appeared crooked because of several broken front teeth on one side. He looked at Owen, who stared at him.

"Tavish, this is Laird Owen Ramsey." Sophie watched as Tavish extended his hand. Owen hesitated to accept it.

"Nice to meet you." Tavish waited.

Obligated, Owen shook the man's hand. "My pleasure."

Soothing whispers echoed within the chamber as Haggadah comforted the dying lad. She described the beautiful place he would be traveling to soon, how he would rejoin his mother and father and never be cold and hungry again.

The town witch turned toward Sophie and pulled her out of earshot of Jack. "I need you and," she nodded to Owen, "Laird Ramsey to go to Wiley. Have him prepare a grave. Tavish and I will take the child there once he passes."

Sophie nodded, accepting the child's fate. She approached the dying boy. "I must go now, Jack. Goodbye." As she looked at his face one last time, helplessness settled within her heart. She bent down and patted Barret's head, who sat at the base of Jack's cubby. His tail remained still. Even Barret understood the despairful situation within the chamber.

Owen went to the town witch. "Who is Wiley?"

"Wiley is the gravedigger at Saint Cuthbert's Kirkyard. He needs to prepare a grave for the boy."

"That's a great distance from here. How do you intend to get the boy's body there?"

"Jack is nothing but skin and bones. I doubt he weighs much. Tavish will carry him the distance." She looked to Tavish, who nodded in confirmation.

Sophie handed Haggadah her carpetbag before looking at Owen. She assumed he was ready to leave the vaults. She cupped the angelic face of the boy in a final farewell. Her eyes began to well with tears.

Laird Ramsey offered an option. "Sophie and I will take my coach to Saint Cuthbert. It will return for you to bring the lad." He glanced at the dying boy. "My coachman will be ordered to circle until you, Tavish, and Barret appear with the boy."

"Thank you, Laird Ramsey. That is very kind of you." The town witch bowed her head.

Owen stepped toward the chamber opening, wishing to escape the pungent and filthy environment as quickly as possible. Tavish stepped aside from the doorway to allow him to pass. Owen stopped and turned to ensure Sophie was following closely behind him before entering the next chamber.

She tried to see through the tears that blurred her vision, making navigating a challenge. Sophie nearly collided with Owen's chest.

He held the candle aloft, basking them in a golden glow, and recognized Sophie's emotional state. Owen wanted to ensure she made her way through the vaults safely. He feared she would become lost and cross paths with an assailant. "Hang onto my coat until we breach sunlight." Owen's suggestion sounded absurd, but he needed one hand to carry the candle while the other held his walking stick, which he would use for defense if necessary. Assured she had the back of his coat in her hand, Owen turned and led the way, hoping they would remain unscathed.

Emerging from the dank darkness, he blew out the candle and tossed it aside. Owen took a deep breath to cleanse his lungs with fresh air.

A woman sitting against a stone wall with a baby in her arms watched the nicely dressed man emerge from the entrance. She glanced at the discarded taper lying on the ground and struggled to her feet. Careful not to disturb her sleeping child, she retrieved the snuffed-out candle and tucked it in her ragged coat pocket.

Sophie stepped into the light. She numbly stood in silence, haunted by the impending death of someone so young. "It's unfair. It's incredibly unfair." She mumbled.

Owen stared at her blankly as she brushed a cascading tear away from her cheek. He shifted his weight from one foot to the other, uncertain of how he should comfort her. He finally withdrew his handkerchief from his pocket and held it before her.

Seeing the folded white cloth through her blurred vision, Sophie took it from his extended hand. "Thank you." She dabbed the dampness from her eyes.

His coach rounded the corner at that very moment and stopped before them. Owen opened the door and gave the driver their destination before joining Sophie inside. She stared at the handkerchief as she fiddled with it in her lap.

Owen prided himself in giving his parents a unique and elegant resting place in Saint Cuthbert's Kirkyard. The thought of the filthy orphan's body buried in the same hallowed ground as his parents disturbed him. "Shouldn't the lad be buried in a pauper's field?"

Appalled by his question, Sophie looked up and into his stern face. "If Haggadah did not have a connection with the gravedigger, he probably would be." She watched as Owen clenched his fist several times and rolled his lips inward as if suppressing his true feelings about the child's resting place. "Does it trouble you that Jack will be buried in the kirkyard?" She pried.

"A wee bit, aye." He admitted. "More specifically, he will be buried in the same ground as my parents."

"What resides in the graves are only the vessels that the souls once occupied." Uncertain of his beliefs, she watched his reaction to her statement. There was none. "Either wealthy or poor, aren't we all the same once we're dead?" She reasoned, yet he did not reply. Displeased and disappointed by his lack of empathy, sarcasm crept into her voice. "Mister Ramsey, it is rumored you possess vast wealth. Have you ever considered helping the poor escape their dire situation?"

He tried to relay the lecture he received from his father years ago. "There will always be poor people, no matter where one travels. Even if I spent every pound my dad and I have worked for, I could not help them all. At any given time, a bad decision can cause a person, including me, to become just like them, destitute and homeless. I strongly believe the homeless made a choice, possibly many bad choices, and their dire situation is a result of their decisions." He reasoned.

Sophie clenched her teeth and lifted her chin. "I disagree. Some choices are made for a person. You, for example, were born into wealth, a life of privilege. Did you have a choice, or was it made for you? Jack had little choice in his situation, of his parents dying and leaving him alone to fend for himself." She continued. "I often ask myself why God takes little pity on the poor. The only conclusion I can surmise is that they are among us to teach us compassion, something you have never given any of them."

Her words were like an arrow piercing his consciousness. He recognized anger in her eyes, or was it disappointment?

Sophie looked out the coach window, unable to withstand the selfishness that blackened his heart.

~

Haggadah held Jack's hand and brushed his hair away from his eyes as he took his last breath. "He's gone. May his soul rest in peace."

"Poor lad never had a chance." Tavish shook his head. He thought of the child's short life and its unfairness and questioned why he was blessed to become an old man.

Haggadah laid Jack's blanket on the floor. Tavish placed the deceased child's body in the center and bound it as best he could. They left the chamber, leaving the candle burning on the edge of the cubby, a gentle reminder of his departed soul. With Jack's body cradled in his arms and his knowledge of the vaults, Tavish carried the deceased child into the filtered sunlight of the overcast day. Haggadah sighed as she stood just outside of the entrance.

The coach stopped before them, and the coachman stepped down to the street. "Laird Ramsey said I'm to give you a lift to the kirkyard."

"Thank you." Haggadah handed the coachman her carpetbag as he opened the door and offered his hand to help her inside. Barret hopped in. Tavish laid the lad's body on the vacant seat, sat beside the town witch, and admired the plush upholstered interior. The coachman placed the carpetbag on the floor before the door was closed. Their bodies jerked as the coach began the journey to Saint Cuthbert's Kirkyard to lay Jack to rest.

"Have you overheard anything else of the maid's murder?" Haggadah patted Barret on the head.

Tavish shook his head. "No. My gut feeling is he likes to beat women."

"Aye. I think so too."

~

Sophie found Wiley in the kirkyard, tidying the lawn with a rake. "Haggadah needs a grave dug for a boy."

The gravedigger stilled his tool as he looked at Sophie and the well-dressed gentleman, who he recognized from his frequent visits to the kirkyard. The request from the town witch was not unusual but not often received. "A lad? Is he big or wee?"

"He's not a babe. Frail, thin, about the age of six." Recalling the boy's lack of food, Sophie went on to clarify. "Small for his age."

Wiley scanned the kirkyard in thought, looking at the paupers' graves. He focused on an empty plot, the perfect resting place for the boy. "When does she need the grave dug?"

"Immediately, I'm afraid." Sophie empathized with Wiley, knowing he was expected to dig the grave alone, yet time may not allow it.

The gravedigger went to the tower where his tools were stored. "Angus, get up," he yelled up the stairway, "I need your help."

The night watchman opened his eyes a crack, rolled over, and went back to sleep.

Wiley grabbed his shovel, turned to leave the tower, and nearly bumped into Sophie and Owen, who had followed the gravedigger and stood directly behind him.

"I don't ken how soon Haggadah and Tavish will arrive. She said the child had little time left, so his grave must be dug quickly. When Davis was alive, there were no quicker gravediggers in Edinburgh than the two of you." Sophie made an offer. "Laird Ramsey and I will help you." She grabbed a pair of shovels that were leaning against the wall.

Sophie and Owen followed Wiley, who walked to the area of the kirkyard where several of the poor were buried. He outlined a grave with the handle of his shovel. "Will this suit the lad?"

Both Sophie and Owen stared at the rectangle etched in the grass. Having little knowledge of the child, Owen shrugged his shoulders and looked at Sophie, who nodded. "It should do." She presented a shovel before Owen, who glanced at it as if her suggestion to help was mad, yet the expression on her face was insistent. He grasped the wooden handle.

Wiley began to dig at one end of the grave and Sophie at the other. Owen stood transfixed. He watched the gravedigger attack the task with determination. Being a man of superior birth, it was beneath Owen to perform such manual labor, let alone dig a grave for an orphan. He watched Sophie jump onto the shovel's blade, forcing it into the ground, a task beneath her social rank too. A sense of guilt nagged at his conscience. He dropped his walking stick and top hat on the ground before removing his overcoat and placing it with his other items. He lined the shovel blade on the grave's edge and pushed it into the grass.

The few visitors touring the kirkyard stopped and stared at the trio. They questioned why two nicely dressed visitors were helping the gravedigger and were quite appalled that one was a young woman.

The grave was nearly halfway dug when Barret came scampering around the corner of the kirk and rushed toward Sophie, who placed the tip of her shovel on the grassy edge of the grave to greet the canine. She looked toward the kirk and saw Haggadah and Tavish walking toward her with Jack's body wrapped in a blanket. Her smile faded.

Owen and Wiley stopped digging as they watched Tavish lay the boy's body on the ground before taking the shovel from Sophie's hand and joining the men in preparing Jack's eternal resting place.

The three men worked until the grave was the proper depth.

Wiley went into the hole and tidied the loose soil. When he was satisfied it was perfect, the gravedigger leaned on the handle of his shovel and announced, "It's done." Tossing his shovel onto the grassy ground, he reached up to Owen and Tavish, who helped him out of the grave. Wiley looked at Haggadah. "Do I need to get the priest?"

The town witch shook her head. "No, a simple burial is best. It's the way Jack would have wanted it."

Tavish and Wiley reverently laid the boy's body in the grave. The small group of mourners bowed their heads while the gravedigger mimicked the words the priest had recited during most funerals. The trio of men worked together to shovel the dirt into the grave, leaving a slight mound that would settle over time.

Haggadah looked at the weary gravedigger. "Thank you, Wiley."

He nodded once before collecting the shovels. "No reason to thank me. You do so much for me and everyone who can't afford remedies. I'm just returning the favor." He extended his hand toward Tavish and Owen and shook their hands. "Thank you for your help in digging the lad's grave." Wiley touched the rim of his flat cap as a farewell to Sophie and Haggadah before taking the shovels to the tower.

The town witch looked at the tiny grave. "Thank you, everyone, for helping me keep my promise to Jack." Even though she had seen the child's spirit in the parade of souls, his death was still unsettling. However, she took solace in knowing the lad was no longer suffering. She had also honored his last request by preventing Katherine from selling his body to the anatomy theater for dissection.

Owen picked up his overcoat and hat and put them on. Grabbing his walking stick, he wandered toward his parent's grave while Sophie visited with the town witch and Tavish. His father had prepared him for a lot in life, but nothing like what the young laird experienced today. He thought of the wretched living conditions in the vaults, the woman's pleading eyes holding her babe, and Jack. The care Haggadah unselfishly gave to the boy and others in desperate need of help and did so unconditionally. Owen saw a side of Sophie that astonished him. She was fearless. It bothered her little to be among the poor, with no concern for her safety. Had his father's teachings been wrong?

Time ticked by. What seemed like a few minutes became an hour. When Owen turned toward Jack's grave to rejoin the group, no one was there. Scanning the graves in the kirkyard, he discovered they had left him there with his thoughts. Perhaps Sophie knew he needed time to be alone and reflect. He indeed had a lot to think about, especially her.

Chapter 20

The images of the innocent child's suffering and his final moments haunted Sophie's mind. Tears threatened to well in her eyes once again. She hung her overcoat on the hook in the hallway and turned to see her mother standing in the sitting room doorway with her arms crossed over her chest.

"Are you deliberately trying to cause a scandal?" Elspeth accused.

Sophie fought through the grief in her mind, searching for her transgression while keeping her tears in check. She decided to remain silent and shook her head.

"How dare you get into a coach unescorted. Do you ken the possible rumors tattling tongues would circulate throughout the city?" Elspeth placed her fisted hands on her hips. "Sometimes, I think you deliberately try to embarrass this family."

"That was not my intention." Sophie defended as she watched her mother's scowl intensify until her eyebrows were nearly touching.

"Your intention or not, you are forbidden to get into a coach alone with a gentleman, or I will see that you never leave this house again without your sisters or myself to accompany you." Elspeth turned abruptly, leaving Sophie to stare at her mother's flaring skirt as it disappeared into the sitting room.

Sophie took a deep breath and ascended the staircase to her bedroom. The only book she could bury herself in was one she had read many times before. Safely isolated behind her closed door, Sophie plopped down in her upholstered chair and chose a book at random from the stack on the table. As she turned to the first page, the handle of her bedroom door twisted, and the door opened.

Grace bounced onto the bed and sat with her legs over the edge, swinging them back and forth. "I saw you get into the coach too. Mum is angry, but she will get over it. So, is he nice?"

Marjorie and Isobel tiptoed into the room.

"Do tell." Isobel sat next to Grace while Marjorie leaned against the bedpost.

Sophie ignored her sisters and attempted to read.

Marjorie stepped forward and snatched the novel from her hands. "No reading until you answer our questions."

Sophie knew her nosy sisters would continue to pester her until they received some tidbit of information, or in their case, gossip. She sighed and relented. "There isn't much to tell. He offered to give me a lift to Haggadah's house. Since I was cramped for time, I accepted his offer. My actions were innocent."

"And," Grace prompted.

"Yes, he appears nice and polite but possesses a cold heart. I hate stereotypes, but some wealthy people think only of themselves. I don't see a future with him."

Marjorie's mouth dropped open. "How can you judge him so quickly? You have only spent a few hours with him."

"He's so handsome," Grace added, touching her heart and looking skyward.

"Did he kiss you?" Isobel giggled.

Sophie made a face as if she had just drunk sour milk. "No, no, he did not kiss me. And I have no intention of letting him do so." She stated adamantly as she extended her palm toward her entrapped novel in Marjorie's hand.

Marjorie pulled the book away from the askant hand, which dropped to Sophie's lap. "Oh, don't make promises you won't be able to keep." She warned. "Men have a way of wearing us down and wiggling into our hearts."

Sophie chuckled. "And how would you know?"

Marjorie grinned. "I'll never tell."

Grace and Isobel touched their foreheads and laughed.

Marjorie blushed, making Sophie wonder when her sister had encountered someone of interest. "Who is he?"

"He made me promise not to tell," Marjorie confessed, her face reddening even more.

Isobel leaned toward Grace and twisted her mouth to her sister's ear before concluding, "It must be someone she danced with at the ball."

"Oh, not horrid, Archie, is it?" Grace scrunched her face to look like a prune.

Marjorie shuddered. "Heaven's no."

Recalling the evening of the ball, Sophie wondered if her sister had been so bold as to accompany a gentleman to a secluded area in the garden. She would have to keep a closer watch over Marjorie, in truth, after all her nonsensical sisters, at future gatherings. They tend to lose their sense of logical thinking whenever a gentleman is present.

"Sophie, didn't you have the urge to kiss him?" Grace persisted. "Didn't your heart skip a beat or your stomach flutter like butterflies were in it when you were near him?"

Sophie was reaching the end of her patience with her sister's immaturity and wished to be left alone to read her book. "Grace, I don't think I'll ever experience such silly emotions." Sophie admitted. "I think you believe in something that is just an obscure fantasy about love."

The smile on Isobel's face became a straight line. "Oh, Sophie. What else is there if a woman doesn't believe in love?" She shook her head, appalled by her sister's negative perspective.

Resenting her sisters' insinuation, Sophie looked at each of them as they nodded in agreement. "Perhaps I'm a realist who questions if love truly exists?"

"I believe the day will come when you discover it does." Marjorie returned the book to Sophie and herded her sisters out of the bedroom.

Alone again, Sophie replied to no one. "I doubt it." She opened the book, read the same paragraph three times, and still did not know what it said. Frustrated by her lack of concentration, Sophie snapped the novel shut, stood, and tossed it on the seat of her chair. Crossing her arms, she began to pace. Her sister's insinuation bothered her more than she was willing to admit. "Laird

Ramsey is the last person I would ever fall in love with. From what I saw today, he has few redeeming qualities."

~

Relaxing after dinner, Owen sat in an upholstered chair before the crackling fireplace in his study at Hilltop. He turned the page of the book he was reading when Phoebe entered with a letter on a silver tray.

"Laird, this just arrived." The maid curtsied.

He looked up from his book. "Thank you, Phoebe." He broke the seal and read the hastily written message. "I'm needed elsewhere and will leave at sunrise. Have my horse saddled by then. More than likely, I'll be away for a few days, maybe more."

"I'll have your bag packed and readied as well."

"While I'm gone, accompany the cook to the market. She may need help carrying what she purchases." He returned the letter to its folded size.

"Aye." Phoebe curtsied and left the room. She smiled as she imagined a day away from Hilltop and hoped she could purchase a few items for herself.

Owen looked down at the open book in his lap. He put the letter inside, closed it, and set the novel on the small table between the pair of chairs. Going to his desk, he rapidly wrote a letter, sealed it, and put it on the silver tray on the foyer table, knowing Phoebe would see it was posted.

~

After the Laird of Hilltop departed on business the following morning, Phoebe and Isla, the cook, climbed onto the seat of a flatbed wagon. Thomas slapped the reins on the horse's rump and set a leisurely pace to the local grocers.

Isla handed Phoebe a list of items to purchase as Thomas reined the horse to a stop. "I'll be at the butcher's shop. Don't forget to negotiate for a better price. Even though our laird is wealthy, it doesn't mean we should squander his money. Be quick about it," the cook looked skyward, "I fear we have rain coming."

"Aye." With her basket in her hand, Phoebe hopped down from the wagon and went to the first shop. As instructed, she dickered with the owner and was proud of her ability to negotiate a reasonable price. Phoebe went from shop to shop, filling her basket to the top. She stared at the shopping list in her hand and hurried to the next store with only one item left to purchase. A gentleman on the sidewalk bumped her arm. The impact knocked the basket from her hand, sending it and its contents tumbling to the sidewalk. Phoebe stood dumbfounded as she watched the man gather the scattered items from the sidewalk. She stuffed the list into her pocket. "My apologies, Sir. I didn't see you there." Phoebe squatted and began gathering the wayward items.

He picked up the last item. "It was entirely my fault. My mind was elsewhere." They stood face to face. His smile was apologetic and genuine as he placed the item in the basket and handed it to Phoebe. "Ah, we meet again." He ran his tongue over his lips, leaving them moistened.

The maid looked up into his eyes. They appeared kind and were the deepest shade of blue she had fantasized about in her dreams. He was tall and nicely dressed. "Aye."

"Since I'm at fault, let me make it up to you. Join me for dinner tonight? Shall we say seven o'clock?"

Phoebe blushed, intrigued by his ability to easily engage in conversation. It was odd for a man, who appeared to be a gentleman, to invite a woman from a lower class to dine. Flattered, Phoebe grinned. With Laird Owen away for the night, sneaking out for an evening meal would be easy. "Aye."

"Meet me here, and we'll decide on a place to eat." He turned away, hesitated to step, and turned back around. "What is your name?"

"Phoebe."

"I'll see you at seven o'clock, Phoebe."

She stood transfixed for a moment and watched him walk away. Phoebe realized she did not know the gentleman's name. "Until tonight, kind Sir." She whispered, confident there would be no objection to her leaving for the evening. If need be, she would simply sneak out of Hilltop without anyone knowing.

With a spring in her step, the maid purchased the last item on her list. Phoebe touched her apron pocket. It was empty. She had forgotten to bring Laird Ramsey's letter to post. "A day or two to have it delivered won't make much difference." She joined the cook at the butcher's shop.

~

Nestled comfortably at the end of the sofa and reading near the warmth of the fireplace, Sophie glanced up from her book, annoyed by her chattering sisters. With the crackling fire as background music, she turned the page and tried to focus on the novel once again.

A flash of lightning illuminated the room, outshining the many lit candles that donned various side tables.

Thunder shook the panes of glass in the windows, drawing Grace's attention. "My, it's a blustery night." She paused to listen to the rain.

Elspeth pulled a needle through the embroidery piece, nearing the last of its remaining stitches. She glanced at the window. "Aye." Turning to her husband, who was reading the broadsheet newspaper while he puffed on his pipe. "Thankfully, dear, you aren't running out on a call in the middle of this horrid night."

"The night is still young." Kendrick continued to read.

As Sophie finished the novel, she snapped it shut. "Goodnight." She climbed the staircase, dressed in her nightgown, and gazed out the window at Mother Nature's light show of jagged bolts streaking across the night sky.

~

Phoebe reined the horse before their meeting place. She stepped down from the wagon and into a puddle of water. The maid shook her foot, trying to remove the excess filthy water. She pulled the hood of her cloak down over her forehead to shelter her hair from the rain. The extra time she had spent pinning it in place was wasted. For now, Phoebe was pretty sure it was ruined, and she resembled a drowned rat.

The gentleman stepped out from beneath an awning. "Rotten night. I wasn't sure if you were coming."

"Despite the bad weather, I'm looking forward to a night out." She grinned. "Where are we going to eat?"

"I've arranged for a room above the pub. That way, we can escape the noise of the patrons, enjoy our meal, and get to ken each other." He motioned toward the door with more on his mind than eating and talking.

Chapter 21

The rain continued for several days, making Sophie feel like a caged animal. Other than retreating to her bedroom to get away from her sisters, her only other option was to hide in the kitchen.

Olivia stepped out of the pantry and saw Sophie sitting on a stool at the worktable. "Hiding again?" She carried a tin canister of flour.

Tilting her head to one side while listening to the rain splash against the window, Sophie never thought of her time in the kitchen as 'hiding.' "Aye." She agreed as she looked at the large canister. "What are you going to bake?"

"With the dreary weather sticking around, it's a good day to make bread." The cook returned to the pantry to gather more ingredients.

"Bread?" Sophie did not know how to make something so basic, something she ate during most meals. When Olivia returned to the worktable and placed several containers on its top, she ventured an idea. "Can you teach me how to make bread?"

The cook looked at her as if she had lost her mind. "Are you planning to take over my job?"

Sophie scoffed. "No. Dad has always advised me to take advantage of knowledge, especially when offered for free."

Olivia smirked. "Who said I would teach you for free?" She chuckled before grabbing an apron from a peg on the wall. "Better cover your bonnie dress so you don't get flour all over it."

Sophie bounced off the stool, joined the cook on the opposite side of the worktable, and slipped the apron over her head. The cook rotated the young apprentice's body and tied the apron behind Sophie's back.

Olivia was patient and quite flattered that a person in the household took an interest in her job. Her instructions were explicit as she guided Sophie through the process of mixing the dough, kneading, and shaping.

As was expected, Sophie had flour on the apron and several places on her face when the loaf was set to rise.

"The dampness of today's rain helps the dough rise. When it is placed near the stove's warmth, that helps too." Olivia covered the loaf with a towel.

Sophie stood like a surgeon, her hands covered in flour, ready to slip into sterilized gloves. "Now what?"

"We form the next loaf. Then, when all the dough is shaped, we wait for the bread to rise again."

"How long does that take?"

"Depends on the weather conditions. Usually an hour or so." Olivia cut away another section of the dough to shape it into a loaf.

Imitating the cook, Sophie did the same.

When all the loaves were set to rise, Olivia made tea and placed two cups and the pot on the small table near the back door. "We can enjoy a cup or two while we wait for the bread to rise." She retrieved a tin of biscuits from the pantry, opened it, set it before Sophie, and sat across from her. Her young friend remained silent. "Now, I feel there's something on your mind that you've been keeping inside. Out with it, or it will make you ill."

There was a lot on her mind – the death of Flora, her annoying sisters, and her nagging mother. The question was, where should she begin? Sophie dunked a biscuit in her tea. "I don't seem to fit in."

Olivia raised her eyebrows, uncertain of the young woman's meaning. "In what? Your clothes?"

Sighing, Sophie shook her head. "No, into everything. This family, especially my mum, and society. I would rather sit at home than attend a ball, read a book than converse, and I detest shopping. I'm not like my sisters. I'm just different."

The cook smiled. "Thank God." She sipped her tea.

Sophie bent over her cup and bit the portion of the sodden biscuit. With her mouthful, she went on to explain. "My sisters come across as silly and nonsensical. I believe my mother encourages their behavior."

"I think it's a matter of maturity. However, for some, it may be instilled at birth." Olivia took a sip of her tea. "But on the other hand, some women have loose morals because of their parents. I blame their fathers who took little interest in their daughters when they were little, so they seek the company of men to discover why their father ignored them."

"My sisters are so fixated on men, who each will marry, and when. I have yet to meet one with enough wit and intelligence to carry on a decent conversation."

"Perhaps you've set your expectations too high?" Olivia selected a biscuit. "I must admit, what you describe sounds like your father."

Sophie wrinkled her nose. "I'll admit he is intelligent and possesses wit, but I don't need a father figure as a husband."

"You're young. You have plenty of time to find a husband. But if you're looking for perfection, you won't find it. No one is perfect."

"Aye. No one is perfect, but those I have encountered are far from it."

"It's a matter of tolerance, overlooking things you can't change and admiring the gentleman's redeeming qualities. You need to look deeper than the surface." The cook winked before dipping her biscuit in her teacup and taking a bite.

Uncertain of what Olivia meant, Sophie sighed and dipped another biscuit in her tea.

~

Sophie stared at the freshly baked bread sliced on the platter as Vertie placed it on the table for the evening meal. Pride swelled within her heart, knowing she had a hand in making it. Sophie selected a slice, smothered it with butter, and bit into the crisp crust and soft center. Closing her eyes, she savored the flavor. For some reason, it tasted better than any bread she had ever eaten.

A knock sounded on the front door.

Everyone at the dining room table looked toward the knock, curious about the visitor.

Elspeth looked at her husband. "Dear, I hope you can finish your supper, but I fear it may be another house call." She used the side of her fork to cut a small potato.

"It will depend on the severity of the patient. I may be able to delay until I'm done eating."

Vertie entered the room with a letter on a tray. "It's for you, Miss Sophie."

Knives stopped cutting, mouths stopped chewing, and everyone at the table looked at Sophie.

Sophie's eyes popped wide. She nearly choked on the bread in her mouth. She quickly swallowed and looked at Vertie, uncertain if she had heard the maid correctly. "Me?"

Vertie read the name on the letter a second time. "Aye."

Sophie took the letter from the tray, glanced at the unfamiliar handwriting, and tucked it under her plate.

Grace's mouth dropped open as curiosity got the better of her. "Soph, aren't you going to open it?"

Even though Sophie was eager to learn who had sent the letter, she knew if she opened it, her family would want to know what it said and who sent it. "It's probably nothing. But truly, who would send me a letter?" She bit into the slice of buttered bread, ignoring her family's inquisitive stares.

"Some handsome man calling on you?" Isobel teased.

"What if the note is from Archie Pringle? He may be requesting to dance with you at the next ball." Marjorie added.

Grace began to giggle.

"Girls." Kendrick scolded. "I believe Sophie would like to read the letter in private. It's her decision to share its contents with you or not." He smiled slightly at his favorite daughter.

"Thank you, Dad." Sophie ignored her sisters' scowling faces and continued to eat her meal.

Curious, Elspeth wanted to know who sent the letter, but she gave no hint of her piqued interest as she continued with her meal.

The tension in the room was as thick as molasses. Even though the girls had finished their meal, they remained at the table, hoping Sophie would open the mysterious letter and reveal who had sent it. To convey her lack of interest in the correspondence, Sophie selected another slice of bread to top off her meal. When she finished, she wiped her mouth with a linen napkin, stood, and took the letter from beneath her plate.

As dusk covered the city, warning of the darkness to come, Sophie climbed the stairs to her bedroom. Much to her surprise, Vertie had anticipated her retreat and thoughtfully lit the candle on her nightstand. Sophie closed the door and locked it to ensure her privacy. She sat on the edge of her bed and stared at the unfamiliar handwriting. "So very strange. I rarely receive a post." Unable to withstand the suspense any longer, she broke the seal, unfolded the letter, and read.

> *Miss Sophie,*
>
> *I began reading your book but have been called away on business. Unfortunately, our discussion of the novel must be delayed. I will return by week's end and call on you once I have read it in its entirety.*
>
> *Owen Ramsey*

Lowering the letter to her lap, Sophie stared at the blank wall in front of her. "Why would he feel the need to tell me of his delay in reading my book? I trust he will keep it in good condition, no matter how long it takes him to finish it." She put the letter in the drawer of her nightstand.

A knock sounded on her door, the handle twisted, followed by a whispered voice. "Sophie, let me in." It was Marjorie.

By telling her older sister who the letter was from and its contents, Marjorie's waggling tongue would soon spread the information to everyone in the household. As far as Sophie was concerned, what was insignificantly communicated between two friends should be of little importance to others.

Taking the lit candle with her, Sophie opened the door to not only find Marjorie staring at her but Grace and Isobel too.

Grace pushed her sisters out of the way and stepped forward. "Well? Who sent the letter?"

"It's nothing. I lent my book to a friend, and it's taking longer for them to read it than they planned. It was a polite and considerate letter to ease my worry of its prompt return." Sophie closed her bedroom door, walked past her sisters, and descended the staircase.

Isobel looked at Grace. "What friend?" A devilish smile spread across her face. The pair turned to enter Sophie's bedroom, but Marjorie stood in their way.

"Downstairs, both of you. Your lack of respect for Sophie's or anyone else's privacy is unwelcomed in this household."

The girls descended the stairs. Marjorie looked at the closed bedroom door, tempted to find out for herself. "Perhaps later." She followed her sisters down the staircase and joined the family in the sitting room.

Chapter 22

The day's spring weather was pleasant, with the sun shining brightly. It gave the Conway sisters the perfect excuse to leave the house to shop. Of course, they needed nothing, but, like most young ladies, they loved to look and imagine the possibilities. If their hearts became set on a particular item, convincing their father to allow the purchase took little effort.

They visited Miss Jaymiee's shop to see the newest fabric and stopped by the sweet shop to indulge in the decadent creations made by the candymaker. Sophie insisted on going to the bookstore, caring little if her sisters tagged along. However, they did.

Mister Edwards looked toward the bookstore door as the bell above it rang. He peeked over his wire-rimmed glasses at his favorite customer. "Hello, Miss Sophie." With her sisters in tow, he addressed them as well. "Lasses."

"Hello, Mister Edwards." Sophie greeted the kind man and went directly to the shelves containing a selection of novels.

"Have you finished your newest book already?" He came from behind the counter and stood before her.

"Aye. I must confess, I've read it several times. Do you have any more by the same author?"

The bookstore owner shook his head. "Her books are difficult to come by. Quite popular, but I put in an order. It should be here any day. Until then, there are plenty of other books to choose from." Mister Edwards motioned toward the bookshelf.

"Aye, you do have a lot in stock." Sophie took her time reading the titles on the spines of the books.

Isobel stepped beside her sister and whispered. "Soph, how long is this going to take?"

Sophie continued to read, refusing to make eye contact with her pestering sister. "You may leave if you wish." She brushed her away with a swish of her hand.

"We can't. Mum lectured us last time for not staying together." She confessed.

Sophie discovered several titles of interest, so she selected two of them.

"We'll wait outside for you." Marjorie ushered her younger sisters out the door while Sophie approached the counter to make her purchase.

"Ah, both are excellent novels." The bookstore owner accepted her payment. "Shall I wrap them for you?"

"Aye, please." She turned and looked out the bookstore window at her sisters. They were huddled together like conspiring thieves, ready to pounce on the next gentleman who walked past them, hoping to steal his heart. She recognized the poor, unfortunate soul who had made the mistake of stopping to talk with them.

"Thanks again, Miss Sophie." Mister Edwards handed her the wrapped books. "I'll let you ken when I receive the novels you are interested in reading."

"Thank you." Tucking her purchase in the crook of her arm, Sophie joined her sisters on the sidewalk. "Good day, Mister Hamilton. It's nice to see you again." She greeted the handsome gentleman.

"Hello, Miss Sophie, the lass who refused to dance with me." Carson teased, his blue eyes sparkling with mischief as he touched his index finger to the brim of his hat.

"The lass with the good excuse of having a swollen foot from my previous dance partner." Sophie defended.

Marjorie stopped their bantering. "Mister Hamilton has offered to accompany us to the Princes Street Gardens for a stroll."

"Has he now. I think that sounds like a lovely idea." Sophie wondered if her suspicion would soon be confirmed.

They walked to the open green space in the heart of the city and strolled its pathways. The head gardener had laid out several bushes and trees to be planted. A crew of men armed with shovels was busy digging each hole to the correct depth and size and securing a plant within them.

Carson offered his arm to Marjorie, who threaded hers within his. Grace and Isobel followed, often walking with their heads nearly touching and giggling. As usual, Sophie brought up the rear.

Their afternoon stroll was lengthened by walking both the East and West Gardens. Then, as the hour for the evening meal neared, they gathered on the sidewalk to part ways.

"Miss Sophie, I hope you save me a dance at the next ball." Carson insisted.

"Mister Hamilton, you won't want to dance with me. I seem to have two left feet."

"Then I shall look forward to suffering through our dance. Have a pleasant evening, everyone." Carson nodded his head before turning and walking away.

Marjorie threaded her arm through Sophie's as they walked home. "He's so handsome, polite, and nice. He wants to court me, but I told him he must ask permission from Dad first."

Having her suspicion confirmed, Sophie looked heavenward. "Och! Dad would have his head if he didn't."

"Isn't it such a wonderful day?" Marjorie sighed as she stared into the distance.

Groaning inwardly, Sophie shook her head, knowing her oldest sister had fallen in love, or at least Marjorie believed she was so.

Tired from their outing, the sisters remained silent as they walked home, with one of them lovestruck and her head in the clouds.

~

Doctor Kendrick sipped his black coffee, thankful it was extra strong after returning home in the early morning hour from a late-evening house call.

Elspeth entered the dining room and sat at the table. "Did all go well with your patient?" She inhaled the aroma of the freshly brewed beverage, poured herself a cup from the pot, and added sugar and cream.

"Aye, I'm pleased with his rebound, as is his family." He watched as Grace and Isobel entered the room.

"Good morning." Grace greeted, sitting in her place at the table and filling her plate with food. Grumpy upon rising, Isobel remained silent and poured herself a cup of coffee to begin her day.

Sophie emerged from her bedroom as a knock sounded on the front door. Curious, she descended the stairs as Vertie opened the door and greeted Carson.

"I wish to speak with Doctor Conway." He announced.

"Please come in, and I will see if he is available." Vertie allowed the guest to stand in the foyer while she went to the dining room.

"Good morning, Mister Hamilton." Sophie stepped onto the hallway floor.

He removed his hat and nervously rotated its rim with both hands. "Miss Sophie. It's nice to see you again."

She noted his voice wavered. "Are you well?"

"Aye, quite."

Kendrick wiped his mouth with his napkin, placed it on the table, and rose from his chair, assuming the gentleman needed medical attention. He entered the hallway.

Sophie grinned at him and left to join the remainder of the family in the dining room.

Kendrick addressed the visitor. "May I help you?"

"Aye, indirectly, Sir. My name is Carson Hamilton. I would like your permission to court your daughter, Marjorie." He blurted.

Kendrick paused to surmise the caller's character. The young man was polite and appeared nervous as he continued to rotate his hat in his hands. "Does she ken of your intention?"

"Aye, I believe so."

A door closed from above. Marjorie appeared at the railing overlooking the hallway. Stunned to see Carson, she looked from him to her father and back.

Kendrick turned toward his daughter. "Marjorie, do you ken this young man?"

Marjorie descended the stairs. She struggled to keep the smile off her face. "Aye."

"From where?" He persisted.

"We have the uncanny ability of bumping into each other while shopping, and we danced together at Pringle's ball."

"He has asked my permission to court you. Are you in agreement?" Kendrick's face was stern.

Marjorie smiled, conveying her silent approval. She looked at Carson. "Aye."

"Go and eat your breakfast while I talk to Mister Hamilton." He waited until Marjorie was out of earshot before he began his lecture on the 'dos' and 'don'ts' of courting his oldest daughter.

Grace looked at Marjorie as she entered the dining room. "Sophie told us Mister Hamilton is here."

"Aye, he is asking for permission to court me." Unable to contain her excitement, Marjorie smiled from ear to ear and clapped her hands without making a sound.

"It's so exciting." Grace giggled.

"Dad will most likely give his permission." Isobel added.

Elspeth picked up her teacup and stared at Sophie, expecting her to react to the news. "Sophie, what do you think?"

Sophie looked up from spreading jam on her toast. She looked at Marjorie as she sat next to her. "I'm happy for you, Marjorie."

The front door clicked shut. Everyone looked at Kendrick as he entered the room. To keep them in suspense, he returned to his seat, placed his napkin in his lap, and poured coffee into his cup to warm it.

Grace leaned forward, unable to withstand the wait. "Well?"

He returned the pot to the table. "I have given Mister Hamilton my permission to court Marjorie."

Three of his daughters squealed with delight. Sophie bit into her toast and savored the delicious jam.

Chapter 23

Elspeth ensured the courtship of her eldest daughter was under strict supervision. Grace accused her mother of being too protective and set in her old-fashioned ways. However, Isobel knew to keep her mouth shut while Sophie refused to get involved.

Carson willingly accepted the terms of the courtship and visited Marjorie in the Conway sitting room while in the company of her family members. When the couple went for a stroll or on a picnic, Elspeth sent Sophie to tag along behind them.

To Sophie, the pair seemed well-suited for each other. Marjorie seemed happy, with an ever-present grin on her face.

~

Owen rode his horse into the city as the sun sank below the horizon. He had been away longer than he expected. Tired and hungry, he reined his horse before a pub. Once inside, it took a moment for Owen's eyes to adjust to the darker interior. A few patrons looked in his direction, curious about his arrival. Others ignored him.

He sat in the nearest empty seat at the bar and ordered a meal and whiskey. Conversations drifted around him as he sipped his drink.

The barmaid set a plate of food before him. "Need a refill?"

He drank the last mouthful of the caramel-colored liquid and handed her the empty glass. Owen cut his meat pie with the side of his fork, thankful to see steam rising like a translucent cloud. "At least it isn't cold." He mumbled to himself as the barmaid put another whiskey before him. He shoveled a forkful of savory beef dripping with thick gravy and waited for it to cool before putting it in his mouth. A boastful comment drifted down from the bar, drawing Owen's attention.

"Aye, I've got a lovely lass I'm seeing and a gullible maid on the side to satisfy my needs."

"Don't we all!" Remarked another, which sent laughter echoing off the quaint walls of the pub.

Owen assumed the arrogant gentleman was deep into a bottle of whiskey and must be close to its bottom. His stomach grumbled, urging Owen to no longer allow the meat to cool. The beef was indeed rich in flavor, but it was still quite hot. He exhaled to cool the mouthful before grabbing his whiskey to extinguish the heat.

Owen kept to himself while eating, not interested in socializing nor having the energy to do so. With his appetite satisfied at the finish of his meal, he pushed his plate away, drank the last of his whiskey, paid the bar owner, and rode home.

The Laird of Hilltop looked into the distance at his estate as he approached the open gates. The windows were absent of light, indicating his staff had retired for the night. They would have greeted him at the door if he had sent word ahead of his arrival.

He rode to the stable, dismounted, and pulled open the door before leading his horse inside.

Stirred by the noise, Thomas woke and rose from his cot. Even though Owen's father had offered the stableman better sleeping accommodations, he insisted on sleeping with the horses. So, a room was built to accommodate his request. "Laird Ramsey, your arrival is unexpected." The elderly man put on his cap and took the reins from his laird's hand.

"Sorry to wake you, Thomas. I was eager to get home." Owen removed the saddlebag and placed it over his shoulder. Noticing the flatbed wagon was missing from its usual spot, he assumed Thomas had left it outside for the night. "Goodnight."

"Goodnight, Laird."

The distance to the manor was a short walk in the brisk night air. Owen entered the back door of the kitchen, stepping into the darkness. He took a candle from the wooden box on the wall, opened the iron door of the cookstove, and lit the taper from the dying embers.

With her bedroom just off the kitchen, Isla rose from her bed and slipped her arms into her robe. "Phoebe, what are you..." She stopped short, seeing Owen's face within the glowing glow of the candle. He stood staring at her. "Oh, Laird, I didn't expect you this evening."

"My apologies, Isla. I didn't mean to wake you."

"Is there anything you need? Tea, perhaps?" She offered as he took off his overcoat and handed it to the cook.

"No, thank you. Goodnight."

"Goodnight, Laird." Staring at the garment, she placed it over the back of a kitchen chair for Phoebe to take care of whenever she arrived home.

The Laird of Hilltop went to his study and placed the candle in an empty holder. Owen sat in the elegant oak desk chair that once belonged to his father and began removing the paperwork from the saddlebag. Sitting back in the chair, he ran his hand over the stubbled whiskers and pulled his loose auburn curls toward the back of his head. He stared at the pile of documents on the desk's blotter with little desire to sort and file them into the drawer.

Even though the hour was late, business issues continued to rattle within his mind. Hoping to find a way to calm his thoughts before retiring to bed, Owen rose, went to the fireplace, and placed the candle on the table between the two chairs. To take the chill from the room, he took kindling and a log from the decorative brass log holder on the hearth, stacked it within the fireplace, and used the candle to set it aflame. As Owen picked up the book from the table and sat in an upholstered chair, he watched the flames feather over the curvature of the log. Pleased by the warmth, he opened the book. Enthralled by the novel, he fell into the author's imaginary world. Only the crackle of embers remained as Owen closed the book reverently and stared at the finished novel in his hand. "Miss Sophie, this should be an interesting discussion." He returned the book to the table before rising. Owen went to his desk, scribbled, sealed a letter, and placed it by the tray in the hallway for delivery at sunrise. With the candle in hand and his mind at ease, he retired to his bedroom.

~

Vertie disrupted the Conway breakfast by bringing a letter into the dining room. "It's for you, Miss Sophie."

Everyone at the table stopped eating as they watched Sophie glance at the handwriting and tuck the folded paper beneath her plate.

"Oh, another mystery letter." Grace teased as she cut a sausage with her knife.

"Enough." Kendrick ordered. He looked over the rim of his coffee cup at Sophie, suspecting the correspondence was from the town witch.

Perceiving their patriarch's sour mood, Grace diverted the topic of conversation to Marjorie and her courtship.

Sophie refrained from grinning. Keeping the secret of the correspondence from her sisters was most satisfying. She finished her breakfast, took the letter from beneath her plate, and stared at the familiar handwriting as she climbed the staircase to read it privately. Sophie closed her bedroom door, broke the seal as she sat in her reading chair, and unfolded the letter.

Miss Sophie,

I have returned from my business trip and finished reading your novel. I will stop by at noon, and I hope you will join me for a picnic to discuss each other's perspectives on the book. I am most eager to listen to your opinion.

Owen Ramsey

"He must believe I have nothing else to occupy my time today." Sophie smirked, lowering the letter to her lap. She shrugged her shoulder. "He assumed correctly." She stood and put his note with his first letter in the nightstand drawer. Pausing before her mirror, Sophie ensured her hair was presentable before emerging from her room.

Isobel leaned against the staircase, waiting like a hungry wolf ready to pounce on its prey. When Sophie's bedroom door opened, she pushed herself away from the railing. "So, who's the letter from?"

Since Owen would call on her within a few hours, revealing who had written the letter would squelch her sister's curiosity. "Laird Ramsey. He borrowed one of my books and is returning it. We are meeting to discuss it."

"Oh." Isobel watched her sister descend the staircase, suspicious that their meeting may be more than her sister let on.

Unwilling to face any more prying questions from her family, Sophie went to the kitchen and plopped onto a stool before the worktable.

Olivia looked up from the batter in a bowl she was stirring. "Hiding again?"

"Aye."

"So, who are the letters from?" The cook grinned.

Sophie tilted her head to one side. "Och, not you too." She glared at Vertie, who was enjoying a cup of tea at the small kitchen table. The guilty maid grinned, silently apologizing.

"Don't blame her." Olivia confessed. "I weaseled it out of her." She began stirring the batter again. "I'm just teasing. You don't have to tell me."

Sighing, Sophie resolved herself to confide in the cook. After all, he would soon be appearing on the doorstep. "Laird Ramsey."

The cook's hand stilled. "Thee Laird Ramsey?"

Nodding her head, she admitted. "Aye, thee Laird Ramsey."

The cook's eyebrows raised. She glanced at Vertie, who looked equally surprised.

Sophie scoffed. "It's nothing. We're meeting to discuss a book we both read."

"A meeting, you say." The cook shook her head as she continued to stir the batter. "Something tells me it's more than nothing."

Chapter 24

Owen shuffled the papers on his desk, filing each one appropriately. He hoped to finish business quickly, for he had other things on his mind. "Phoebe!"

The young maid hurried into the study. "Aye, Laird."

"I need a blanket, food, and wine packed for a picnic. Tell Isla to use the freshest bread, our best jam, and various kinds of cheese. Oh, and plates too."

"Aye, and you wish this to be packed in a basket?" Phoebe assumed by her laird's frazzled state that the meal was to impress whomever he was entertaining. "Any sweets?"

Owen looked at the maid. "Aye, good idea. Sweets are always needed."

"Anything else?"

"Have my coach readied. I plan to leave at 11:45," he filed another paper and paused as he looked at the clock on the mantel, "no, 11:30." Owen sat back in his chair, realizing he would be unable to clear his desk before leaving Hilltop.

"Aye." Phoebe curtsied before hurrying to the kitchen. "The Laird wants a picnic packed. He has requested the finest bread, jam, a variety of cheese, wine, and sweets. He seems a bit rattled."

Isla grinned, offering an assumption. "Maybe he is entertaining a lass?"

~

As noon approached, Sophie waited near her bedroom door, listening. She hoped to save Owen from the on-slot of her family inquiring about his intentions for their meeting.

A knock sounded on the front door as the hallway clock struck noon. Vertie opened it to see Laird Ramsey standing on the stoop. "May I help you?"

Grace and Isobel paused their chess game in the sitting room and entered the hallway.

"Good day. Miss Sophie is expecting me." Owen looked at the two young women with inquisitive expressions on their faces and touched his index finger to the brim of his hat. "Hello."

Grace and Isobel grinned like ninnies. They looked at the top of the stairs as Sophie appeared.

Isobel peered down the hallway to ensure their mother remained in the kitchen with Olivia. She nodded to Grace.

"Hurry. Mum is busy telling Olivia what she wants her to prepare for dinner." Grace whispered encouragingly with a wave of her hand, assisting in her sister's unescorted escape.

Sophie descended the stairs at a near run. "Good day, Mister Ramsey." She grabbed her overcoat from the wall and passed through the door, leaving Vertie to stare in disbelief at the most beautiful coach she had ever seen.

"Good day, Miss Sophie." Owen greeted as she passed him in a blur without making eye contact, stuffed her arms into the sleeves of her garment, and entered the awaiting coach. Uncertain of the reason for her erratic behavior, he joined Sophie cautiously and sat in the seat across from her. "Are you well today?"

The coach jerked forward.

"Aye, and you?" Sophie looked at the picture window to see Grace and Isobel grinning.

"Aye. You seem to be in a hurry. I hope I'm not imposing on your time."

"Not at all. I only wished to avoid my mum's humiliating inquisition." She changed the subject. "How was your trip? Successful, I hope."

"As well as to be expected." He grinned. "I arrived home late last night. I was unable to sleep, so I finished reading your book." He reached to his side, retrieved the hardcover trio of volumes from the seat, and handed them to her. "As you can see, I took excellent care of them."

"Ah, aye. Thank you." Sophie placed the books in her lap and glanced out the window. "Where are we going to have our discussion?"

"I thought Calton Hill would be quiet enough for us to discuss the book without interruption."

"It has a great view of the city." Sophie tilted her head to the side. "An excellent choice. It's been a while since I was there. I've forgotten about its advantages."

Owen was pleased that Sophie had agreed with his chosen location. He wanted their visit to be public, yet private, with his coachman as a chaperone. He hoped to keep their picnic out of the sight of prying eyes and whispering onlookers.

The coach rounded a corner. Before long, it stopped, and the door opened. Owen exited and turned to offer his hand to Sophie.

Even though she was awkward, she was equally agile. Sophie looked at the assistance he offered, knowing it was unwarranted. As not to insult him, she placed her fingertips in his hand and stepped out of the coach with the volumes tucked in the crook of her arm.

The coachman retrieved a leather strapped, wicker picnic basket and followed the couple until Owen chose a suitable spot overlooking Edinburgh's Old Town. After taking a blanket from the basket and spreading it on the ground, he placed two China plates, silverware, linen napkins, a plate of various cheese, smoked fish, fresh bread, rhubarb jam, and shortbread sprinkled with sugar in the center of the ground covering.

Sophie's attention was drawn from the view of the city and the lazy clouds that dotted the sky as she heard a slight pop and watched the coachman pour wine into a stemmed glass.

"Miss." He held a glass toward her.

Sophie accepted it with a nod.

Owen accepted his glass. "Thank you."

The coachmen propped the open bottle inside a corner of the basket before returning to the coach.

"Miss Sophie, shall we sit?" Owen offered his hand and helped her sit on the blanket.

She crossed her legs at the ankles. "The food looks delicious."

"I will relay your compliment to my cook." He sat across from her, with the food between them, casually removed his hat, and placed it on the blanket. Owen stared at her profile as she sipped wine. "Tell me, what is your opinion of Elizabeth Bennet?" He prompted.

Lowering her glass, she watched the curls of his hair shift in the breeze. His face appeared genuine, as if he were truly interested in what she had to say. "As the title suggests, I find Elizabeth is prejudiced, and Fitzwilliam Darcy is proud. I can agree with Elizabeth's first impression of him, though. After all, what he said was unkind, and it was her misfortune to overhear his comment. Nevertheless, she is quite headstrong and is the only sister with a sense of reason. Mister Darcy is clearly enthralled with her, but for someone so wealthy, he must overcome the difference in their ranks in society. He knows what his heart wants, yet he has difficulty communicating his affection without being offensive." Sophie took another sip of her wine. "Being a person with great responsibility, I believe Darcy is used to being in control and influences his friend, Bingley, thus ruining Jane's chances of marrying a higher social rank. So naturally, Lizzy holds this against him." She smiled. "It is interesting that Lizzy and Darcy both have arranged marriages to someone they despise." Sophie realized she had been prattling on. She looked at Owen. "What is your opinion?"

"I believe Darcy knows he is in love with her; his intentions, however destructive, were done in the interest of his friend, and he desires nothing more than for Lizzy to see past his mistakes and fall in love with him. He corrects his errors to win Lizzy's heart and refuses to marry his aunt's choice for a spouse. As you have stated, his lack of communication is a hindrance. He admires Lizzy for her intelligence and her beauty."

"Yet Jane's beauty outshines Lizzy's."

Owen grinned. "Not from Darcy's perspective."

Sophie took another sip of wine. "I was proud of Lizzy when she didn't buckle to her family's pressure to marry her cousin."

"Ah, aye, Mister Collins, an undesirable match just so the family could retain their home."

"Poor Charlotte, because of her age and her opinion of being a burden to her family, married him. Lizzy was quite upset to see her friend face such an undesirable future." A gentle breeze forced Sophie to pull a wayward strand of her hair away from her eye.

"Aye, since Charlotte had no previous offer of marriage, she assumed it would be her only chance to wed." Owen spread jam on a slice of bread and placed it on a plate. He added a selection of various foods to the serving before setting it on the blanket before Sophie. He clasped his hand over hers as he took her nearly empty glass of wine and refilled it.

The bread with rhubarb jam was too much to resist. Sophie bit into the slice and closed her eyes. "Mmmm. . ."

Owen smiled as he nudged her hand with the filled glass. "One of my favorite jams too."

She opened her eyes and accepted the glass. "Thank you." Sophie added. "Lizzy's ridiculous sisters remind me of my own. They are so silly when it comes to men. My oldest sister, Marjorie, is now courting a gentleman. At least my younger sisters can gossip about her instead of me." She ate another bite of bread, savoring its flavor.

Owen scowled. "You? Why would they gossip about you?"

Sophie chuckled. "I find myself similar to Mary Bennet. Much like her, I don't fit into my family. I would rather read a book than gossip about men or dream about who I will marry someday. As far as I'm concerned, it's a waste of time." She confessed more than she intended.

"I agree. Your perspective is sensible, not to be mocked."

"Thank you." She smiled as she drank her wine. Sophie suspected the drink may have loosened her tongue because she found it easy to converse with Owen.

Their discussion of the book continued. When they could not agree on the author's implication, Sophie would open the novel and find the exact paragraph as evidence to support her point. Not to be outdone, Owen also found other paragraphs to counter. Ultimately, they agreed the book was eloquently written with good perspectives from both protagonists.

"Darcy's love for Lizzy caused him to cast aside her lack of rank in society and correct his offenses to win her heart. She admitted she was wrong about her first impression of him." Sophie concluded.

"I admire his endurance in pursuing her until he wins her heart." Owen thought for a moment. "Do you believe Darcy changed, as a person, to win her heart?"

"That's a good question. Deep down, I believe Darcy will always be himself. However, he may be more conscious of his actions after learning what Lizzy has identified as distasteful behavior."

"But isn't that Darcy's willingness to change for Lizzy?" Owen assumed their discussion was coming to an end. He stood and extended his hand to help Sophie rise from the blanket. Owen removed the empty wine glass she held and placed it in the basket before retrieving the three volumes.

"Mister Ramsey, this is a deep conversation for a work of fiction."

"But doesn't it apply to real life?" He insisted.

Sophie considered his comment before nodding. "Aye. I imagine it does."

The coachman gathered the dishes, repacked the remaining food, and folded the blanket as the pair walked to the coach.

"I hope you enjoyed the picnic." Owen opened the door for her to enter.

Once seated inside, she replied. "Aye, the food was delicious, and it was most enjoyable discussing a book with you, a luxury I do not have with anyone in my family." She admitted as he handed her the novel.

Wishing to enjoy her company further, Owen ventured an idea. "Shall we go to the bookstore and purchase another book for us to read?"

"Perhaps another time. I didn't bring any money with me."

"Then I shall buy a book for us to share. After all, you purchased the one we just finished." Owen motioned toward the novel in her lap.

"Very well, but you must add it to your library after we read it." Sophie insisted.

As the coachman closed the door, Owen stated their destination. It was a short ride to the bookstore, where the coach came to a stop. He exited and helped Sophie step down onto the sidewalk. She froze as she spotted Marjorie with her arm entwined with Carson. Sophie stood staring, analyzing the couple as her sister stared up at Carson with besotted eyes. Trailing behind the couple were Grace and Isobel.

Owen looked over Sophie's shoulder into the distance. "What are you looking at?"

"More like who. My sister and Mister Hamilton."

Owen looked at the couple and made his assumption. "They appear to be happy."

Feeling a tap on his shoulder, Owen turned around and met the smiling faces of a mother and daughter.

"Laird Ramsey, may I introduce my daughter, Elizabeth."

Sophie turned to see who was speaking. She almost laughed at the woman, who smiled proudly and pushed her daughter forward. The silly girl grinned while fluttering her eyes as if she had been instructed to do so against her will.

"Aye, we met at the last ball. It's nice to see you again, Elizabeth. If you will excuse me." He motioned for Sophie to enter the bookstore before him.

Once they were both inside, she turned to Owen. "Such a burden to be the most eligible bachelor in Edinburgh." She jested.

"It is an annoyance I must tolerate without appearing rude."

"And you did it so eloquently." She complimented him and smiled.

"They fail to understand that I will choose my bride when I find a suitable one."

"Out of spite, I have addressed you as Mister, yet you have not corrected me."

As the door opened behind him, he stepped toward Sophie to allow the person to enter. He looked down into her pale blue eyes. "Because by addressing me incorrectly, you made me feel like I was like everyone else. It was nice to be considered as such."

They stood there a moment, spellbound.

Sophie spoke her mind. "Shall I continue to do so, or would you prefer to be addressed properly, Laird Ramsey?"

"Whichever endearment you wish to choose." He grinned. "Based on the past, when you address me, Mister, I'll assume you are cross with me."

"Not always." She confessed.

"Sophie, it's nice to see you again." Greeted the bookstore owner, interrupting the conversation between the two.

Sophie stepped away. "Hello, Mister Edwards. My friend and I are in search of a book that we can share and discuss. Do you have any recommendations?"

The bookstore owner looked at Owen. "It's nice of you to visit my bookstore, Laird Ramsey." He bowed.

"The pleasure is mine." Owen nodded.

Mister Edwards searched the titles on the shelves, pulled several he recommended, and placed them on a table. Owen and Sophie sorted through the stack of novels and narrowed their choice down to two.

As the bell above the door rang again, Mister Edwards excused himself to help an elderly lady.

"Oh, I can't decide." Sophie admitted. "Since you have offered to purchase the book, you choose."

"Then I say we shall get them both. You read one book, and I will read the other. Then we shall exchange them." Owen suggested.

"Aye." Sophie smiled, warming Owen's heart.

Mister Edwards joined the couple at the counter. "So, you have decided," he accepted the pair of books Owen presented, "on both."

"Aye," admitted Sophie. "It was too difficult for us to choose just one."

Owen paid for the books and instructed the bookstore owner to leave them unwrapped. He carried them as they went to the coach and entered. "Which one would you like to read first?" He held the books up for her to see. They rocked in their seats as the coach's wheels were set in motion.

Tapping her index finger on her chin, she looked from one book to the other. "I believe that one." Sophie pointed to the intended novel.

Owen grinned, unable to contain the pleasure the purchase had given Sophie.

The coach stopped in front of Sophie's house. She glanced at the picture window to ensure her mother was not waiting to reprimand her. The coachman opened the door for Sophie to exit. Owen followed.

"I have had the most enjoyable day." She admitted as she stood before him.

"As have I." He walked her to the door. "Have a pleasant evening, Miss Sophie."

"Aye, and you too, Mister Ramsey." She smiled devilishly, knowing he preferred the incorrect title.

He grinned as he nodded, reluctant to part from her company. Owen forced himself to turn away and enter the coach, vowing to read his book as quickly as possible, giving him the excuse to see her again.

Chapter 25

As a blanket of darkness fell upon Edinburgh, Phoebe entered the study. She stoked the fire, added several logs, and ensured the laird had enough candlelight to read his book. "Laird, I'm retiring for the evening. Is there anything you need before I do so?"

Owen sat in the upholstered chair, legs crossed at his ankles, and looked up from his book. "No, thank you."

The loyal maid curtsied, exited the room, and quietly left the house undetected. Fearing her lover might not wait for her, she borrowed the horse-drawn wagon from the stable and hurried to their usual meeting place, hoping to arrive at the appointed time.

~

Rising early after a restful night's sleep, Owen went to the dining room for breakfast and stood by his chair at the head of the table. He stared at the askew place setting. The meal had yet to be served. Instinct told him something was wrong as he pulled out his chair to sit.

Isla hurried into the dining room carrying several dishes filled with eggs, toast, sausage, and other items. "Sorry, Laird. I'm running late." The cook wore an apron over her dress. It was spotted with flour and grease and wrinkled from Isla wiping her damp hands on its bottom corner.

Owen sat, laid his napkin in his lap, and watched as the various food selections were placed before him. "Where's Phoebe?"

"I'm here, Laird." The maid tucked a loose strand of her blonde hair beneath her linen bonnet as she entered the room.

The expression on the cook's face was a combination of anger, shame, and disgust. She retreated to the kitchen, leaving Phoebe to scan the table for what was missing. "Salt, pepper, coffee. I'll be right back, Laird." She vanished from the room as if a magician had waved a magic wand.

Owen placed scrambled eggs, sausage, mushrooms, tomatoes, and toast onto his plate. He paused with his forkful of eggs in midair as raised voices echoed from the kitchen. As the conversation quieted, he heard footsteps from the hallway. The laird shoveled the eggs into his mouth, picked up his knife, and cut the sausage into several bitesize pieces.

Phoebe carried a tray into the room. She placed the salt and pepper before him.

Owen picked up the saltshaker and sprinkled it over his eggs. He watched the maid's hands shake while tilting the coffee pot and pouring the steaming beverage into a cup. She placed it before him with a small bowl of sugar and a pitcher of cream. Owen paused in eating and looked at the maid. "I assume Isla is not pleased with your tardiness."

There was no reason to lie. "Aye. I slept in. I take total responsibility." Phoebe confessed.

Owen simply nodded as he pushed his fork into the eggs. The maid was young, not more than twenty, only a few years younger than himself. It was apparent she was ashamed, so there was no reason to make her feel worse than she did. After all, Isla had given her a good tongue-lashing.

His silence was worse than being reprimanded. Phoebe looked at the floor, fearing she may be let go from her job, and meekly stated. "I'm sorry, Laird. It won't happen again."

Owen waved the maid off without looking in her direction. As he began planning his day, he recalled the stack of paperwork on his desk. Even though Laird Ramsey wished to spend his day otherwise, he would confine himself to his study and address his responsibilities of running the business and estate. That is, if he could keep his mind on his work.

~

By early afternoon, Sophie finished reading her book and placed it on the stack beside her chair. She assumed Laird Ramsey would need additional time to read his novel. It would allow her to reread the book to easily recall its details for their discussion.

"Enough sitting." A restlessness stirred within her. "I need to get out of this house." It had been a while since she had visited her friend, and the walk through Old Town was the perfect opportunity to stretch her legs.

Grabbing her overcoat on her way out the front door, Sophie stepped onto the stoop and pushed her arms through the sleeves. She looked at the overcast sky. Uncertain if it would rain, she cared little if it did.

Along her way through New Town, construction continued to meet the increasing population of Edinburgh. She looked down into the Princes Street

Gardens as she walked across the bridge. It continued to evolve with each planted tree and bush. As Sophie entered Old Town, its thick smoke lingered in the air, making her cough as she passed through a dense, acrid area. Several of the homeless stared at her as she walked by them. Their askance eyes conveyed their hope that she would throw them a coin or two. Not that Sophie was unsympathetic to their plight, but she had left the house without taking money with her once again.

Weaving her way through the ancient cobblestone streets, Sophie turned the corner and spied the town witch's cottage framed by the waist-high stone wall. She opened the rickety gate and walked up the flagstone pathway.

Haggadah foresaw who was on the other side of the door before hearing the knock. "Guess who is here, Barret?" She assumed Sophie was seeking a quiet place away from her family or had news to share.

The canine pranced to the door with his tail wagging. He looked back at Haggadah, his body curling to form the letter C, and waited for the town witch to join him. As he heard the latch click and a crack of daylight was revealed, Barret pushed his head forward, forcing the door to open wider.

"Sophie, I knew you would stop by today. Shall we have tea?" Haggadah turned and went to the kitchen without waiting for her friend's reply.

Sophie greeted Barret before stepping inside and closing the door behind her. "As long as you have biscuits." She teased.

"Other than getting out of the house, I ken you have something on your mind." Haggadah made the tea quickly and placed the steaming brew and a plate of biscuits on the table. She sat across from her friend, eager to hear what she had to say.

"Marjorie is courting a Mister Carson Hamilton." Sophie selected a biscuit and dunked it in her tea.

"Oh."

"He seems nice. They appear to be happy together. In fact, I've never seen Marjorie smile so much." She bit into the dripping sweet.

The town witch dug a bit deeper into her friend's true feelings. "Are you happy for her?" Haggadah peered at Sophie's face as she sipped her tea.

Sophie met the town witch's inquisitive gaze. "Aye. But there is just something about him. Maybe he is too perfect."

"Could you be jealous of your sister's happiness?" Haggadah pried.

"Me? No. I'm happy for her. Truly."

"Do you picture yourself as a better partner for Mister Hamilton?" It was a simple question, and Haggadah hoped to understand her friend's heart.

Sophie scrunched her face. "Och! Definitely not." She helped herself to another biscuit. "He insists I dance with him at the next ball. You ken how I'm awkward and clumsy. I can't say I'm looking forward to it."

Haggadah chuckled. "I ken you will someday enjoy attending a ball when you are in the arms of the person you love, and he is whirling you about the dance floor."

Sophie laughed. "Ah, but I don't whirl, I stumble. And I doubt there is a man who will ever love me for who I am. So, I'm considering a life as a spinster, either a teacher or a nun."

The town witch shook her head, hoping her friend's future would be brighter than the solitary one she led. She glanced over Sophie's shoulder at the flat cap and purple ribbon hanging on a peg. Haggadah had never planned to grow old by herself. Even though she was a healer to many, she was often lonely. The town witch grinned at the possibility of rekindling her romance with Tavish, but was she being foolish? He was so determined to discover who killed Flora. She assumed the thought of them finally being together had yet to enter his mind. She looked away from the hat.

Haggadah sighed, determined to open Sophie's mind to the possibility of marriage by strategically diverting her friend with a task while approaching the subject. "Would you mind helping me restock the apothecary while you are here?"

"If you don't mind explaining their properties while we work." She negotiated as she finished her tea.

The town witch stood and opened the apothecary doors, revealing the many jars and drawers containing various herbs.

Scanning its interior, Sophie stated her observation. "Some of the jars are nearly empty. There must have been a lot of requests for your remedies lately."

"Aye. The illness has spread from person to person, so many have become sick in Old Town." Haggadah began pulling jars and handed them to Sophie, who turned and put them on the table. The town witch selected another bottle. "This one too." She gave the jar to her friend as she looked up at the dried herbs hanging from the beams in the ceiling and pointed to a bundle. "We will start with that one."

Sophie moved a chair from the table, stepped onto the seat, and took the bound herb from the nail where it hung. Then, as Haggadah pointed to each desired herb, Sophie retrieved it and placed it on the worktable.

Haggadah placed her hands on her hips and looked at the stacks of dried herbs and bottles on the table. "This may take a while." She matched a dried herb with its vessel, beginning with the one on the table.

Sophie looked at the jar as she sat to work. "Lavender, one of my favorites."

Sitting across from Sophie, Haggadah uncorked the jar before her. "Aye, it is a powerful herb and can be used for many remedies. It has calming properties and helps one sleep. It can also relieve achy joints, headaches, and a woman's painful courses."

Sophie removed the cork, crumbled the stalk of the herb into tiny pieces, and added it to the jar. "What herb do you have?" She looked across to Haggadah at the dried plant with large leaves.

"This is mullein. It is used to help clear the lungs and help one breathe. A tea is made from it." The town witch changed the subject. "When is the next ball?"

"Hopefully, never, but I doubt I can be that lucky. The last ball Archie Pringle stepped on my foot." Sophie crumbled another stalk. "It gave me the excuse not to dance the remainder of the night. Laird Ramsey kindly escorted me to the garden and away from my mum, who was certain to force me to dance anyway."

"Laird Ramsey, you say." Haggadah crumbled a large leaf.

"Aye, we have discovered common ground. We both like to read. Laird Ramsey is one of the few men I ken who does." Sophie confided.

"Does he have any other redeeming qualities?" Haggadah prompted.

"He is polite, punctual, and communicates well. Some say he is handsome." Sophie placed the cork into the jar.

"Do you think he is handsome?" The town witch pressed.

"Haggadah, not you too?" Sophie accused. "Laird Ramsey and I are merely friends. Besides, I'm no beauty. I'm much too plain for him." She returned the jar to the apothecary.

The town witch thought Sophie was beautiful. "Maybe he likes plain." She whispered to herself.

Chapter 26

Over the next few days, Owen remained at his desk while sifting through paperwork. With his mind distracted by the thoughts of Sophie, it had taken him longer to accomplish the task. Each evening, to help calm his racing mind, he read the novel they purchased together before retiring. However, his sleep was often restless.

As the sun announced another day, he rose and sent a note and the finished novel to Sophie. "Phoebe, have a servant deliver this right away." Owen instructed as he gave the book and letter to his maid before leaving the mansion to address an issue brought to his attention by a tenant.

Phoebe met her laird at the door as he returned in the afternoon. She picked up a book with an attached letter from the foyer table. "Laird, this arrived moments ago."

Owen noticed the maid's face was quite pale. "Are you well?" He accepted the book from the maid's outstretched hand and looked at the letter held securely to the book cover by a tied ribbon.

Phoebe tried to smile. "Aye."

He removed the letter, broke the seal, and unfolded the paper.

> *Mister Ramsey,*
> *Thank you for the novel. I have*
> *sent my book in exchange.*
> *Miss Sophie*

He grinned, knowing she purposely addressed him as Mister Ramsey. "That's all, Phoebe."

The maid curtsied and returned to her duties. Phoebe placed her hand at the base of her neck as if drawing strength from the gift she hid under her uniform. She entered the kitchen and collapsed on a stool.

Isla put her hand on her hip and tilted her head from side to side as she scrutinized the maid. "You look sick, a bit pale."

Phoebe took a deep breath to squelch her queasiness. "I've got an upset stomach."

Squinting her eyes, the cook suspected the maid suffered from another ailment. She cut off the end of a freshly baked loaf of bread and gave it to the maid. "This may help settle it. I'll make you some peppermint tea."

~

Owen woke the following day, sat on the edge of his oak four-poster bed, and yawned. He stood, stretched, and pulled his auburn curly locks away from his eyes as he waited for the cobwebs to clear his mind. Peering out the bedroom window, he saw the glowing sun filtered by a blanket of fog and could barely identify the ghostly pathways in the garden below. "It should clear away by noon."

Eager to see Sophie again, Owen read until early in the morning. In his opinion, he enjoyed the book more than the first. He pushed his legs through a pair of pants and put on a shirt before leaving his bedroom.

Phoebe saw her laird descend the grand marble staircase. "Good morning, Laird. Shall I serve your breakfast?"

"I'll have coffee in my study. Hold my breakfast for now." He ordered as he went directly to his desk and scribbled a note to send to Sophie. Hearing footsteps on the hardwood floor, he looked at the doorway to see Phoebe carrying a tray with a pot of coffee, a cup, a small pitcher of cream, and sugar. "Set it on the table." Owen pointed to the small table before the window.

The maid placed the tray on the table. She poured a cup of coffee and turned to serve her laird when her vision turned to darkness, and a wave of dizziness forced her to drop the cup and swoon.

The cup shattered on the floor, drawing Owen's attention. He watched as the maid's eyes rolled back in her head. Realizing Phoebe was about to fall, he rushed forward and caught her before she collapsed.

"Och! Phoebe." Owen lifted the maid, carried her to an upholstered chair before the fireplace, and gently lowered her to the seat. "You're ill."

Phoebe took several deep breaths as the darkness dissipated from her vision. "I'm fine. I just had a dizzy spell."

Noting the maid's face was as pale as a sheet, Owen ordered, "Stay seated." He left the room, lengthened his strides, and entered the kitchen. "Isla, I need a glass of water."

The cook's eyes widened. Her laird's presence in the kitchen was seldom seen, especially during the day. "Laird, you seem flustered." She wiped her flour-covered hands on her apron, retrieved a glass, and filled it with water.

"Aye, Phoebe nearly fainted. I fear she is ill."

She handed Owen the glass. It was not her place to convey her suspicion, yet he must know the truth or risk tarnishing his reputation. "She isn't ill, Laird."

"Och, she is. She nearly collapsed onto the floor."

Isla shook her head. "My guess is she is expecting a bairn."

Owen's eyebrows raised. "A bairn?"

"Aye. Phoebe has been sneaking out at night. I suspect she's been meeting a gentleman and gotten herself with a bairn."

Dumbfounded, Owen stared at the cook's face, hoping she was telling the truth. "How long have you suspected her condition?"

"A month, maybe more."

"Why didn't you tell me?"

"Laird, I'm not a tattler. You would have sacked her. It's what happens to unmarried women in her condition. I wasn't going to be the one to condemn her and her babe to life on the streets or in the vaults with little chance of either of them surviving."

Owen ran his hand through his hair, pulling it over the back of his head. If she was carrying a bairn, protocol called for the maid to be dismissed; otherwise, many would suspect he had relations with a staff member. Images of the woman with her infant child by the vaults pulled at his conscience. As Isla indicated, if he cast Phoebe out, he would condemn her and her child to live in filth with little means of supporting themselves. He was faced with a delicate situation in which he had no answer. Owen pried. "Who is the father?"

Isla shook her head. "She keeps the secret close to her heart. I fear it is a gentleman who will deny his involvement."

"Most do." Owen began to think out loud as he scratched his chin. "A month, maybe more." He hoped there was time to create a viable solution before her pregnancy became apparent.

Childless, Isla could only relay what women in her family had experienced. "I suspect two months at most. The sickness she is experiencing usually goes away after the third month."

Owen looked at the floor. "How many months does a woman carry a child before giving birth?"

"Nine, usually. Some give birth sooner."

"So, there's time." He mumbled, thinking to himself.

"Laird?"

Looking up at the cook, he sighed. "I need you to come with me."

Isla followed as Owen entered his study and handed Phoebe the glass of water. "Drink this, and then I want the truth."

Phoebe did as ordered and lowered the glass from her lips to her lap.

"Now, I've noticed you have been unwell lately. Isla believes you have left the estate at night, met up with a gentleman, and could be with bairn. For your sake, I demand you tell me the truth. Are you with bairn?"

Looking at the floor, Phoebe hid the shame on her face. "Aye." She nodded as she anticipated her dismissal. "I'll pack my belongings and be on my way."

Owen crossed his arms over his chest. "You will remain employed and confined to Hilltop until I can solve the predicament you've gotten yourself in. Is that clear?"

The maid and cook looked at their laird, unable to fathom his reasoning.

"Who is the father?" Owen pressed.

Phoebe instinctively reached for the base of her neck, feeling the gift beneath her uniform. "I do not wish to say."

"If it is a gentleman, you have been played the fool. Does he ken of your condition?"

Phoebe shook her head.

"If you reveal to him that you carry his bairn, he will only cast you aside. Therefore, I warn you; you must keep your pregnancy a secret. I need your word, or I will change my mind about helping you."

The sternness of her laird's voice conveyed the severity of his threat. Fearing he would throw her out of the house and force her to live among the homeless in Old Town, she looked him in the eye. "Aye. You have my word. I'll not see or contact him in any way or leave Hilltop."

"Very well." He picked up the letter to Sophie. "Now, if you are feeling well enough, have this letter delivered."

"Aye." Phoebe looked at the shattered cup and puddle of coffee. "And I'll clean the mess I made. Thank you, Laird." She clasped the letter and left the room.

Owen stared at the retreating cook, who was leaving the room without his permission. "Isla."

She turned toward her laird. "Aye?"

"You must never tell anyone of her condition, or I will have to sack you." Owen's stern face confirmed his threat.

"Aye, Laird. My lips are sealed." She waited. "Did you need anything else?"

"Another coffee cup and my breakfast." Owen glanced at the clock on the mantel as the cook left the study. He had a few hours before hoping to visit Sophie.

Chapter 27

A knock sounded on the Conway door as the hallway clock struck one.

Vertie went to the front door while Grace and Isobel rushed toward the foyer. They pushed and shoved each other, vying to be the first to see the caller.

Marjorie stilled her needle in her embroidery, looked heavenward, and huffed. "You two stop. You look like a pair of cats with your tails tied together. It's most unbecoming."

The silly girls stopped their antics and glared at their oldest sister, who sat on the sofa, returning their stare.

Owen stood on the stoop looking skyward while he waited for the maid to answer the Conway door. As he predicted, the fog had lifted, and a cloudless sky was overhead. Hearing the door open, he looked at the round-faced maid standing before him.

"May I help you?"

"Aye, Miss Sophie is expecting me."

"And who shall I say is calling?"

Sophie descended the stairs with the borrowed book in her hand. "Never mind, Vertie. I ken who is calling." She looked at the handsome laird standing on the stoop. "Good day, Mister Ramsey."

Owen tipped his top hat as he grinned at the intentionally incorrect endearment, confident she was not cross with him because she was smiling. "Good day, Miss Sophie."

Donning her overcoat, Sophie dashed out the door before her mother could question her reason for leaving the house and joined Laird Ramsey on the stoop. She turned and pulled the door shut as her nosy sisters tried to peer through it.

"I hope you are well." Owen walked beside her as they descended the steps in unison.

"Very well. And you?" Sophie peeked over her shoulder at the picture window to see her younger sisters staring like a pair of peeping toms.

"Much better now that I'm in your company. Our talk is a welcomed break from the past few days where I have been burdened with responsibility." They paused before the coach with its door held open by the coachman. Owen waited for Sophie to enter first. "Where would you like to discuss the books?"

Sophie glanced at the interior of the coach. "If you don't mind, I would like to walk. It's a nice day, and sitting on a bench in Princes Street Garden is the most relaxing. Shall we go there to discuss the books? She handed him the book from the crook of her arm, which he placed on the coach seat with the other book.

Even though their destination was only a few blocks away, Owen preferred the isolation of the coach rather than being accosted by eager mothers trying to entice his interest in their daughters. He wished, however, to appease Sophie. "Very well." With his walking stick keeping time with each step, they soon reached Princes Street. Seeing a familiar smiling woman towing her daughter in his direction, Owen looked about and suggested, "Let's stop in here for a treat before we sit."

Sophie looked at the posted sign above her head and peered into the window at the delicious sweets on display. "Looks tempting."

"Shall we?" Owen held the door open for Sophie to enter. He glanced at the mother and daughter rushing toward him and ducked inside the shop.

Sophie scanned the treats on display in jars on the shelf and trays in the display case. "Oh, there is so much to choose from."

"Take your time to select what you want." Owen looked out the window, hoping the overzealous woman would avoid following him into the establishment.

After making their purchase, Owen opened the door for Sophie to exit. As they stepped onto the sidewalk, the pushy woman waited just steps away to reacquaint Owen with her daughter.

"Laird Ramsey. You remember my daughter, Elizabeth." The woman nudged her daughter forward, who curtsied.

Owen nodded politely. "How can I forget. If you will excuse me." He placed his hand on the small of Sophie's back, encouraging her to walk forward.

Sophie looked over her shoulder at the pair of women. "Quite forward and determined, isn't she?"

"Aye, like a headstrong mule." He emphasized.

Even though Sophie sympathized with his plight, she chuckled at his comparison.

The pair dodged horse-drawn wagons as they crossed the street and found an empty bench overlooking the transformed Nor Loch.

Owen untied the string on the makeshift brown paper envelope and offered Sophie her choice of sweet.

She selected a small piece of tablet. "Mmmmm, it's been a while since I've eaten tablet. I'll have to ask Olivia to make some." She put the candy in her mouth, eager to learn Owen's opinion on each book. Sophie cared little for appearing mannerly before him and spoke while she ate the treat. "Which novel was your favorite?

Owen selected a chunk of tablet himself. He looked up as a shadow blocked the sun before popping it into his mouth.

"Laird, may I introduce my daughter, Daisy."

Sophie devoured the candy in her mouth and stood abruptly. "No, you may not. We are trying to have a conversation."

The women glared at Sophie and back to Owen, who shrugged his shoulder. They scurried away like a pair of scared mice.

Plopping down on the bench, Sophie selected another piece of tablet, popped it in her mouth, and mumbled under her breath, expressing her distaste for the rudeness of the women.

Owen could not understand what she had said, or perhaps, he assumed, what she said was not for his ears to hear. "What?"

She pushed the candy to one side of her mouth. "I'm sorry. It's impolite for me to talk with food in my mouth. I said the women were being rude. Can't they see we are conversing?" She scowled. "How often do you get approached by women such as them?"

"More than you care to know. It's another reason I avoid appearing in public." He confessed.

Sophie remained silent. She was aware of the rumors that Laird Ramsey was a womanizer. Maybe it was a reputation he had obtained in his younger years before his parents' death. But what Sophie perceived of the man sitting beside her was quite the opposite. His confession gave her a glimpse into his life as a single, wealthy laird pestered by shallow women who wished to increase their social rank and live in luxury. "May I speak freely, as your friend?"

"Aye, as my friend." He nodded.

"Perhaps the day will come when a desperate mum pushes her daughter forward, and you will accept her as your wife." Sophie scanned the nearby benches with women in whispered conversations as they looked at Owen. "I see no other solution to your problem than to marry."

"I believe you're correct, but I will choose a wife without the influence of others." He grinned, eager to change the subject. "Now, our discussion about the books." He ate the bite of confection he had held between his fingers.

They brought up valid points in both novels but agreed they liked one book more than the other. With their discussion concluded, they decided to walk the entire length of the gardens and observe the change in landscaping. Unfortunately, within a few steps, a woman pushed her daughter forward and made an introduction. Owen was polite in dismissing himself without engaging in conversation.

"I fear you will be bombarded by every mum with a single daughter while we stroll." Sophie scanned the people walking toward them in search of women with their sights set on talking with Owen.

"Would it be too bold for you to take my arm?" Owen bent his arm, presenting the offered escort. "They may be less inclined to interrupt our conversation."

Glancing at his offered arm, Sophie looked up into the piercing ocean-blue eyes staring at her. She grinned. "Not at all." She threaded her arm with his, knowing their deception would soon be the talk of the town. She did not care. After all, they were just friends.

Chapter 28

Owen and Sophie stopped at the bookstore before returning to the Conway house. The Laird of Hilltop selected a book and went to the counter while Sophie continued to scan the titles.

"Hello, Mister Edwards." Owen placed his book on the counter. He peered over his shoulder to ensure Sophie was occupied before reaching across the counter for a pen and paper and jotted down his request. He touched his fingertip to his lips, indicating silence.

The bookstore owner read the note, nodded, and whispered. "I will notify you when your order arrives."

"I finally decided on one." Sophie placed her book on the counter as Mister Edwards put the laird's order under the counter out of sight. She withdrew her purse from her pocket, but Owen insisted on paying for both books.

With their novels in hand, Sophie entwined her arm within his, and they continued to stroll down Princes Street. As they rounded the corner onto a side street, Sophie unthreaded her arm. "I believe you are safe now."

Her arm entwined with his was comforting, as if it should always remain there. "I hope to call on you whenever I need protection."

She chuckled. "Mister Ramsey, you are strong enough to fend off overzealous females on your own, and politely so, I must add."

"But I feel more at ease with you by my side." He chuckled, recalling her scolding the persistent woman. "You do have a way of speaking your mind. The horrified look on the women's faces . . ." He laughed.

Sophie grinned at his laughter, then joined him in doing so. "I'm guilty of acting most unladylike. If Mum knew, she would reprimand me for sure."

They climbed the stairs to the front door of the Conway House.

Owen opened his mouth to speak when the door flew open.

Grace and Isobel appeared. "Laird Ramsey, when will you be hosting a ball? Of course, we are most eager to attend." Grace grinned from ear to ear.

"He doesn't host balls." Sophie retorted.

Owen imagined his arms around Sophie's delicate body, waltzing her around the room while staring into her pale blue eyes. "Miss Sophie is correct." He watched the smiles on the girls' faces turn into frowns, then added, "But if Miss Sophie promises to dance with me throughout the evening, I will gladly host a ball."

Almost offended by the contradiction of her statement, Sophie stared at him. "Dance with you?" Worry lines appeared on her face.

"Aye." He smiled.

"Oh, please, Sophie." Isobel begged.

"Please, Soph." Grace clasped her hands as if praying.

Sophie looked at her sisters, who were ready to pounce onto the stoop. She turned toward Owen. "I'm much too clumsy."

He stared down at her, his expression sincere. "I pray you will consider allowing me at least one dance."

She looked at the sisters, who awaited her reply, then back to Owen. "Very well, one dance."

The girls shrieked and ran to tell Marjorie.

Owen smiled, displaying his pearly white teeth.

Sophie was unsure if he was amused by her sisters or pleased that she had agreed to dance with him. "I suggest you wear heavy boots. Your feet will surely suffer from me stomping on them." She teased.

"With you in my arms, I doubt I'll notice the pain." He touched his index finger to the brim of his hat. "I look forward to our next book discussion. Good day, Miss Sophie."

"Good day, Mister Ramsey." She recognized a lightness in his step as he walked away and entered his awaiting coach. Sophie looked at the book in her hand, passed through the open front door, and secretly regretted her promise to dance with the Laird of Hilltop.

~

Haggadah wrapped a cloth around a freshly baked loaf of bread and put it in a basket with a small jar of jam, several biscuits, and a bit of dried beef. With Barret by her side, she walked the streets of Old Town, searching every close for the handsome face she longed to see.

Tavish saw her from across the street. He grinned, confident he knew she was looking for him. He crossed the street and began walking behind her.

Barret stopped, raised his nose in the air, and sniffed. He turned around and began wagging his tail.

Noticing her dog was no longer beside her, Haggadah turned around to see Tavish smiling as he gave the dog a good patting on his shoulder.

"Are you looking for me, love?" He teased.

"Aye, I thought you would like something to eat." Haggadah held the basket aloft.

The couple settled on a nearby step to share the meager meal.

"Have you learned anything yet?" Haggadah pressed as she spread a slice of bread with jam and gave it to Tavish.

"Aye, I learned of a common place where the wealthy men meet with lasses, but too many men go there to determine which one beat Flora."

"Should you report it to a constable?"

"I went to the station house to make them aware of it. I met an old friend, McLeary. He was glad to see me. He's a good man, fair, and it's nice he has advanced to chief inspector. He knew of the place but told me it's only one of many." Tavish bit into the warm bread. "You always could make a good loaf of bread."

~

The city was a buzz as invitations were delivered to households for the ball of the season at Hilltop. It had been nearly a decade since one was held in the highly acclaimed mansion. Poor Miss Jaymiee and her staff sewed their fingers to the bone to keep up with the demand for new dresses and alterations.

Sophie slept very little, her appetite had nearly halted, and she became more jittery as the gala event neared. The thought of everyone watching her stumble on the dance floor while dancing with Laird Ramsey tied her stomach in knots. Her sisters' incessant chattering about the ball, dancing, and an evening with certain gentlemen only added to her distress.

Sophie tried to ignore her sisters' continued conversation about men and the ball as she read her book in the sitting room after supper.

"You ken it won't be him," Grace taunted Isobel, "your walnut didn't pop off the hearth."

"Aye, but yours didn't either." Isobel retorted. She looked at Marjorie. "Come to think of it, did you see Mister Hamilton's face in your chemise?"

Marjorie shook her head. "No, but maybe it's because I didn't whisper his name into the walnut."

Sophie glanced at her sisters before turning the page. She wished their nonsensical chatter would cease.

Isobel needed a reasonable opinion. "What do you think, Sophie? Do you believe the predictions of Saint Mark's Eve to be true?"

Sophie lowered her book to see her three sisters on the edge of their seats, genuinely interested in her answer. She doubted the wives' tale of determining one's soulmate or true love by merely imagining the wrinkles in an undergarment to simulate a face or a walnut popping away from the fire to be accurate predictors. Unfortunately, the predictions of Saint Mark's Eve were far from fictional. The parade of souls had foretold of those who would soon meet their demise. "Do you ken anyone who has determined their true love by seeing their future husband's face in a chemise or whispered his name into a walnut and had it pop off the hearth?"

Her sisters shook their heads.

Not wanting to discourage their belief in the romantic fantasy, Sophie chose a logical clarification. "So, it has yet to be proven. However, that doesn't mean it isn't possible." Sophie watched as her sisters, who unknowingly held their breaths, exhaled. They seemed pleased by her answer, so she hid behind her open book, pretended to read, and grinned with satisfaction. The memory of her whispering Laird Ramsey's name into the walnut and hearing it pop off the hearth caused her smile to fade. She lowered her book and looked at the clock on the mantel. It had been well past the hour of one when the nut rolled toward her feet. Reasonably confident that the spell of Saint Mark's Eve would have been null and void, Sophie returned to her reading.

Chapter 29

The days until the Hilltop ball passed slower than the Conway sisters wished. Except for Sophie, who hoped it would never come. The sisters occupied their time by trying on their dresses, adding embellishments, and deciding how they wanted their hair pinned up. Sophie secluded herself in her bedroom, paced the floor, and practiced the footwork she imagined Owen would select for them to dance.

On the morning of the ball, the household was in a flutter. The Conway sisters' anticipation grew with each hour that rang on the hallway clock, knowing they would soon put on their gowns and ride in a carriage to the Hilltop ball.

Vertie darted from one sister to the other, helping them dress and pinning their hair in place. Then, with only one sister left to prepare for the ball, the maid stepped into Sophie's room to see her pacing the floor dressed only in her chemise. Her golden gown lay on her bed.

"Your sisters are ready. Time to get you dressed, Miss Sophie."

Sophie looked at the maid. Her eyes were wide as saucers. "I don't think I can go through with it."

"Och! Such nonsense. Of course, you can." The maid watched as Sophie wrung her hands. "You have nothing to be nervous about." She picked up the lovely gown from the bed.

"Vertie, you don't understand. I promised the laird I would dance with him. I'm so awkward. Everyone will be watching us dance. They will be staring at me and laughing when I stumble." Sophie sat on the edge of her bed and wiped her sweaty palms on her chemise.

"No need to trouble yourself. That handsome laird will take you into his arms and guide you around the floor. They may be looking at you, but that is because they wish they were you. I guarantee you, envy will mask their eyes, especially when you are dressed in this gown." The maid readied the dress to slip over Sophie's head.

Sophie refused to raise her arms.

Vertie lowered the gown. "Miss Sophie, I fear if you don't show up at the ball, the laird may come, pick you up in his arms, and carry you there. So, come now, put on a brave face, and let's get you dressed."

Sophie was indeed acting cowardly. She looked at the maid, who held the gown over her head, slipped her arms into the puffy golden sheer sleeves, and stood as the dress was guided to the floor. Sophie turned, presenting her back, and waited for it to be fastened.

"Now, sit, and I'll do your hair."

Encouraged by the maid's positive attitude, Sophie sat in her desk chair and stared at the gloves, hairpins, and ribbon she put on the desk hours ago. Vertie brushed the young lady's brunette locks, pinned them in place, and added a ribbon. Sophie put on her gloves, pulling them over each elbow, stood, and looked at the maid, who smiled approvingly.

"Miss Sophie, as elegant as you look, your father should have you sit for a portrait."

Sophie shook her head. "You're just being kind." She gripped the sides of her skirt and lifted it away from her body to ease any wrinkles.

The maid took Sophie by the hand and ushered her to stand before the mirror. "Now, you listen to me. You are beautiful. You are going to be the envy of everyone tonight. You walk into that ball with your head held high and have a grand time."

Sophie nodded, appreciating the maid's kind words. "Thank you, Vertie."

The maid noticed the embroidered wrap lying on the bed. "Oh, don't forget this."

Sophie held out her arms as the maid draped the shawl on each and across her back.

"Lovely." Vertie grinned. "And I want a full report in the morning."

Understanding the maid would never attend a ball in all its grandness, Sophie smiled. "Aye, and hope it will be worth listening to."

"Sophie, the coach is here!" Grace called from the bottom of the staircase.

Taking one last look at herself in the mirror, Sophie emerged from her room and grasped the railing as she descended the stairs, careful not to trip. Waiting at the bottom were her parents and sisters.

Marjorie's mouth fell agape. "Sophie, you are absolutely radiant." She admired the details of the dress.

Kendrick smiled. "My dear, you have never looked more beautiful."

"Thank you." Sophie glanced back at the top of the stairs as her family went to board the coach.

Vertie stared down at Sophie. She waved her hands as if shooing her out the open door. "Go, have fun."

~

A knock sounded. Haggadah looked at the door and saw Barret standing before it with his tail wagging. "A familiar face?" Opening it, she steadied herself with her cane and looked into Tavish's chestnut eyes.

"There's a ball tonight. I thought you may want to watch the parade of coaches and share something to eat with me." He took a step to the side and motioned at the awaiting coach.

Haggadah's mouth dropped open. "You got a coach?"

"Aye. It wasn't easy. Many are taking guests to the ball." He held out his hand. "We must hurry. They are most likely taking guests now."

"Let me put together something for us to eat." She offered and turned away.

"No need. I've got a basket of food." Tavish tilted his head toward their awaiting transportation.

Haggadah looked back at Tavish, who grinned proudly. "You aim to spoil me tonight." She took her overcoat from the peg on the wall as Nero awoke from his nap, stood on her bed, and stretched. Seeing the open door, the feline trotted through it before Haggadah joined Tavish and closed it. Barret raced to the carriage and jumped inside.

Tavish offered his hand to assist the town witch into the coach, entered, and sat beside her.

The coachman drove to the Princes Street Garden, where they sat on the closest bench to the street. Barret sat before them, anticipating his share of the food within the basket.

"We should be able to see the coaches well enough from here." Tavish sat beside Haggadah and set the basket of food on his lap. "I had the basket packed by several shops. I guess we will both be surprised to see what's inside." He grinned.

"That's very thoughtful of you. Thank you." Haggadah wondered where Tavish got the money to pay for the coach and food. She assumed he used funds he saved from over the years. She lifted the cloth cover of the basket to reveal scones, sweets, and a bottle of wine with glasses. Haggadah recalled years ago when they watched the wealthy leave for a ball. "This is much nicer than sitting on the ground in the close to watch them go by. However, it's one of my fondest memories."

The couple sipped wine and enjoyed the delicious sweets as the parade passed by them.

"It seems to get grander every year. Perhaps we will recognize someone." Haggadah hoped to catch a glimpse of Sophie, quite certain the Laird of Hilltop would invite her young friend.

~

Sophie stepped onto the stoop and glanced up and down the street lined with coaches. The coach, before their house, seated only four.

Isobel stated the obvious. "We can't possibly all fit in there."

Grace and Isobel looked at each other before trying to see who could squeeze through the small doorway first. Marjorie sat between them. Kendrick and Elspeth took their place across from their daughters, leaving Sophie to stand alone on the sidewalk, staring inside the coach. Her sisters sat uncomfortably squished together, and her parents filled the opposite seat, leaving no room for her to sit. "Am I to stand?"

"Miss Sophie." A man called.

She looked at the coachman who called her name.

"Laird Ramsey wishes for you to ride in his private coach." He opened the door for her to enter.

Sophie tilted her head and smirked at her sisters. "It seems as if I have other transportation to the ball."

Isobel leaned out the coach window as Sophie walked away.

The Hilltop coachman offered his hand to help her enter and waited for her to sit before closing the door.

"Well, this ought to be an interesting evening." Isobel scowled.

"Let me see." Grace leaned over Isobel and poked her head out the window as the coach jerked forward. She plopped back into her seat. "Laird Ramsey sent a coach for Sophie?"

"Aye." Isobel grinned devilishly, causing Grace to giggle.

The ride to Hilltop was long and winding. Even though the solitude of a private coach allowed Sophie to escape the usual criticism from her family, it did not calm her rapidly thumping heart.

The coach turned onto the loose gravel of the majestic mansion. It seemed aglow, with lit torches throughout the garden and a candlelight interior welcoming guests inside. Countless coaches stopped before the stone-pillared entry just long enough for their passengers to disembark before moving on.

Sophie was the first to arrive in her family. As the coach door opened and a hand was presented to assist her exit, she glanced down at her foot to ensure she did not twist her ankle on the loose gravel. Lifting the hem of her gown, she climbed the stone steps and waited under the overhang of the majestic porch as her family stepped out of their coach. A servant accepted the family's wraps and overcoats as they entered the foyer. Another offered them a beverage from a silver tray.

Sophie admired the marble floor, the oversized paintings on the walls, and the vases of fresh flower arrangements on every side table lining the foyer. Her breath was nearly taken away by the sight of the grand staircase. She looked upward at the high ceiling and admired the architectural embellishments of the crown molding.

The Conway family followed the incoming crowd like herded cattle. Sophie took a deep breath, trying to control the rapid beat of her heart. As she passed through the richly embellished oak doorway of the ballroom, she wondered where the Laird of Hilltop may be.

Chapter 30

Owen stood on the balcony overlooking the ballroom with his hands clasped behind his back. As expected, the room was filled near capacity with curious visitors wanting to see Hilltop's interior. The unwed young women looked up at him flirtatiously as if making fools of themselves made them more appealing.

The Laird of Hilltop was smartly dressed in black slacks and a jacket with tails. His wool vest proudly displayed the Ramsey tartan colors of blue, black, and white. Beneath his vest, he wore a white high-collared shirt and ascot pinned with a silver brooch embellished with a large sapphire.

The musicians' music filled the air with a welcoming melody. Several women swayed to the tune. Dancing had yet to begin, giving patrons time for introductions, reserving dances, and consuming a beverage.

Keeping a watchful eye on the guests as they entered the ballroom, Owen stood slightly taller as he saw Sophie enter the room.

~

Sophie's breath was taken away by the vastness of the ballroom. The ceiling was at least two stories high, equal to the foyer, and beautifully painted like a famous cathedral. Various plants resembling different types of trees were placed strategically around the room's perimeter to allow the large oil paintings to be seen in all their beauty. Candelabras, with their multiple branches, and sparkling crystal chandeliers, showered the room with a golden glow.

Sophie saw Archie walking toward her. He was grinning like a slobbering idiot. She groaned inwardly. Since she promised to reserve a dance for the host, she could not risk him stomping on her foot and causing her to become lame. Sophie turned away, hoping to escape his invitation. A hand reached for her glass of wine before she bumped into Owen's chest. He placed the stemmed crystal vessel on a tray as the servant passed by them.

Owen clasped her upper arm and steadied Sophie before bowing to greet her. "Miss Sophie."

Sophie curtsied. "Mister Ramsey."

"May I have the first dance?"

"Only if you are willing to risk becoming lame for the remainder of the evening." Sophie warned.

"It's a chance I'm willing to take." He raised his hand, and she hesitantly placed hers upon it.

He tilted his head toward her. "It is customary for the host to begin the dancing for the evening." He explained.

Sophie glanced about the room. "Many other women are quite willing and more capable than I." Butterflies fluttered in her stomach as they stepped to the center of the floor. "I'm sure any of them would be honored to lead off the evening of dancing with you."

Owen turned to face her. "Aye, but I wish to only dance with you."

The expression on Sophie's face questioned his implication. Their dislike for each other had turned to friendship. Did he imply that his feelings for her had deepened to something more?

A slow and sensual tune began. Sophie recognized the song. Unfortunately, she had only practiced the steps once. Whether she could perform them correctly was another matter. The knot in her stomach tightened.

Owen bowed as Sophie curtsied. Then, as if on cue, they stepped toward each other, their eyes locking, unsmiling.

"Relax, Sophie. If you stumble, I'll catch you." He stared into her eyes, conveying his sincerity.

The intensity of his stare forced her to look away. Instead, Sophie focused on his sapphire brooch, suddenly self-conscious of their closeness. Taking a step backward, they stepped forward with their right shoulders touching and circled once, staring into each other's eyes.

"And I put on my heaviest boots." He added, causing her to grin and relax just a bit. They separated once again.

Owen held out his left hand and waited. Sophie looked toward it and placed her right hand within his. It fitted perfectly. He gently clasped his protective fingers over her dainty hand. She stared into his eyes as she curled her left hand over his shoulder, drawing her body near him. As a couple, they swayed forward and backward several times before rotating and parting again. They grasped each other's right hands and then their left, crossing their arms between them. Owen raised their clasped hands above Sophie's head, forcing her to step forward until their bodies nearly touched. Releasing her left hand, he wrapped his arm around her slim waist. Sophie hesitantly put her free arm around his waist. Owen raised their clasped hands, forming an arch over Sophie's head. They rotated in a circle before releasing their right hands. Sophie twirled several times with her arm above her head like her father used to do when she was a little girl. Coming out of the twirl, Sophie smiled, as did Owen.

The tempo of the tune quickened. Owen and Sophie twirled, waltzed around the dance floor, separated, and came together. They laughed, smiled, and danced as if they were the only people in the room.

"Do you see that?" Isobel elbowed Grace, whose mouth fell agape.

Elspeth and Kendrick looked on approvingly.

"I told you something was happening between them, Kendrick." Elspeth boasted. "A mum can always tell." She sipped her drink.

Kendrick scowled. "Now, dear, they are just dancing."

As the song slowed to completion, Owen held Sophie close to his body as the waltz ended. He stared into her nearly gray eyes, his face so close to hers, wishing to kiss her and never let go. Sophie became aware of the silent guests watching them. She took a step backward, breaking the spell between them.

Caught up in the moment, Owen realized he must do the same and stepped back. He respectfully bowed as she curtsied as the song ended. Standing frozen, staring into each other's eyes. Owen wondered if she sensed his fondness for her, and he prayed she would open her heart to his affection.

The applause from the guests jarred Sophie and Owen back to reality. They turned toward the musicians and clapped in appreciation.

Sophie exhaled. A smile spread across her face as she realized she had not stumbled. Instead, she had been held securely in the arms of the Laird of Hilltop, glided across the floor, and enjoyed the dance. She turned and looked at Owen. The smile on his face indicated he was equally as pleased.

"Shall we step out onto the veranda?" Owen guided Sophie from the dance floor.

Looking about the room, her parents, inquisitive sisters, and Archie, licking his lips, were staring at her. To escape from her family and the repulsive suitor was much to her liking. She assumed Owen wished to avoid the persistent females in the room too. "Aye, please."

~

Arriving late, Carson entered the foyer and took two fluted glasses from a tray. He stepped through the ballroom doorway and grinned as he spotted Marjorie across the room. Weaving his way between guests, he went to her side. "You look lovely tonight."

Marjorie smiled as she accepted a glass. "Thank you."

Carson took a step back and glanced at her from head to toe. "Something is missing, though."

Worried his observation may be a cause for alarm, she glanced down at her dress. "What?"

He pulled a necklace from his pocket and dangled it before her. "This."

Marjorie's heart skipped a beat as she reached for the pendant. It lay against the palm of her hand as she examined it. "It's beautiful."

He handed her his glass before tying the trinket around her neck and ensuring the bow was secure. Carson stood before her. "Aye, it fits you well. A lovely embellishment for a lovely woman."

Marjorie gave him his glass before touching the necklace at the base of her neck. "I'll have to find a mirror to see how it looks on me. I believe there is one in the foyer. Excuse me." She left the ballroom.

Quite satisfied with himself, Carson drank the contents of his glass in celebration, placed it on a passing tray, and helped himself to another. He watched the dancing couples as he waited for Marjorie to return.

~

Marjorie wove her way through the crowd of elegantly dressed guests. She saw the floor-to-ceiling mirror at the end of the foyer, stood before it, and admired the necklace.

"Drink, Miss?" Phoebe presented a tray.

Marjorie held up her drink, indicating she had one. She touched her necklace and lifted her chin so the maid could see it. "I just received this as a gift. Isn't it lovely?"

Phoebe stared at the necklace. "Aye, quite." The maid turned and went directly to the kitchen.

Isla looked up from the tray she was filling with various hors d'oeuvres. She watched the maid plop down on a stool and place the tray of drinks on the worktable. Her face was absent of color. "Are you well?"

Phoebe shook her head, trying to breathe deeply. "I believe he is here."

The cook continued to fill the tray. "Who?"

The maid pulled the necklace from beneath her uniform. "A woman is standing in the foyer with this same necklace on. She said she just received it as a gift."

"Could be a coincidence. Jewelers make copies of the same necklace, especially when they sell well."

Phoebe entertained a risky idea. "Dare I follow her to see if it is him?" She began to quiver. Tears well in her eyes.

Isla filled the tray, wiped her hands on her apron, and looked at the maid. "From the color of your face, you must sit a spell." Isla shook her head. "The laird should be notified. He may want you to stay out of sight for the rest of the evening." The cook sent a servant to fetch Owen.

~

Sophie looked at the countless stars dotting the indigo sky. "I'm surprised I didn't step on your foot while we danced."

Owen leaned against the stone railing, staring at her profile. "Aye, we dance quite well together. Do you agree?"

Looking at him, Sophie opened her mouth to reply when a servant approached them.

"Laird, you are needed in the kitchen immediately." The servant stood like a statue and waited to ensure the urgency of his request was understood.

"Very well." Owen disliked leaving Sophie vulnerable to unwanted requests to dance from gentlemen. "I'll return soon." He followed the servant.

Marjorie was walking past the doorway when the Laird of Hilltop passed her. She saw her sister on the veranda and hurried to share the news of the gift she received. "Sophie, look what Carson gave me. I think he really likes me, maybe even loves me." Marjorie beamed with happiness as she proudly displayed the trinket around her neck.

Sophie's stomach became queasy. She was unable to speak as she stared at the necklace. It was the identical dainty gold Celtic knot and ruby pendant that Flora had treasured. Sophie forced herself to grin. "It's lovely. I think we should share your news with Laird Ramsey." She grabbed Marjorie's hand, pulled her forward, and asked a servant to point her toward the kitchen.

"Why would Laird Ramsey be interested in my necklace?" Marjorie forced her feet to keep up with the rapid pace of her sister.

Chapter 31

Phoebe looked at her laird as she heard commanding strides announcing his entry into the kitchen. She tried to wipe away the rivulets of tears that stained her cheeks.

Owen looked from the upset maid to Isla and placed his hands on his hips. "What is the trouble?"

Phoebe perceived his perturbed mood. "I think he's here."

Confused, he needed clarification. "You think? Who's here?"

Isla answered. "The man she had an affair with. She believes he is at the ball."

The last thing Owen wanted was a disruptive scene at his gala gathering. The man, whoever he was, had been a perfect guest thus far. Owen turned to the maid. "I can't throw him out of my house for an affair you had with him. Phoebe, you entered the arrangement willingly." He reasoned. "What is his name?"

The maid shrugged her shoulders. "He told me his name was Sam."

"His name is Carson Hamilton." Sophie stated as she marched into the kitchen.

Owen turned to see Sophie with Marjorie in tow.

Phoebe stared at the necklace around Marjorie's neck. Tears cascaded down her cheeks as she realized she had been played a fool. She looked at the floor in shame.

Sophie walked forward, placed the palm of her hand beneath the maid's necklace, and examined it. It was the same necklace Marjorie had around her neck and identical to the one owned by Flora. Letting the necklace fall to the maid's uniform, Sophie looked at Owen to explain the pieces of the murderous puzzle. "On the Eve of Saint Mark, after our chance meeting, I encountered my family's maid and watched as she collapsed to the street. When I went to her, Flora was unconscious and badly beaten." She glanced from Marjorie to the maid. "She later died. Her journal revealed she was seeing a gentleman and was with bairn."

Marjorie looked at Phoebe. "Och, we have the same necklace. How nice."

Phoebe looked at her laird and hoped he would keep her pregnancy a secret.

Sophie continued. "My maid was wearing the same necklace as she has on," motioning to Phoebe, "and as my sister." She motioned to Marjorie. "Chief Inspector Rodger McLeary has Flora's necklace at the station house as evidence."

Owen scowled. "Are you accusing this Carson Hamilton of your maid's death?"

Marjorie's breath was taken away. "My Carson? Killed someone?"

Sophie ignored her sister's ignorance. "The evidence is circumstantial and rather weak unless a jeweler can confirm Mister Hamilton purchased all three identical necklaces." She opened her mouth to continue.

Owen held up his hand as he scanned the concerned faces of his staff in the room. He understood how quickly rumors spread. The less the servants heard, the better. "Let's get out of the way of my loyal staff and go to my study to discuss this further." Everyone seemed frozen in place. "Marjorie, Phoebe, this way, please." He motioned for the women to exit the room.

Sophie stepped beside him as they went to the door. She kept the volume of her voice for his ears only.

"Until this scandalous situation can be resolved, I don't want my sister anywhere near Mister Hamilton."

Owen nodded and motioned for her to exit the room before him.

~

With the trio of women secured behind the pocket doors of his study, Owen scribbled a note, slid open a door, and stood in the doorway. He called aside a servant. "Have Thomas saddle a horse. I need you to ride to the station house and deliver this to Chief Inspector McLeary. When you return with him and his constables, enter through the servant's door. I don't want to alarm the guests that something is amiss."

"Aye, Laird."

Owen turned to enter the study and nearly bumped into Sophie, who tried to peek around him. He clasped her arm to steady her and rubbed it tenderly as he closed the door behind him.

She looked up at him. "I think my father should join us. I promise to be discreet in retrieving him."

He looked at Marjorie's worrisome face. "Aye." Opening the door wide enough for her to pass, he placed his hand on the small of Sophie's back and ushered her forward.

Sophie went to the ballroom entrance and scanned the countless people for her father. She saw Carson talking to a rather pretty woman. She looked for Isobel and Grace, hoping they did not notice Carson with someone other than their sister.

"There you are, Miss Sophie. May I have this dance?" Archie bowed before her as the previous dance ended.

Unwilling to appear rude, she nodded in agreement, praying he would not stomp on her foot. Sophie placed her hand upon his and was led to the dance floor. She kept a watchful eye on Carson's flirtatious behavior as he, too, escorted a woman to the dance floor.

Lining up directly across from Archie, Sophie spotted her mother and father standing behind him. The music began. The lively tune allowed Sophie to keep her distance from her partner. As she entered the space between them, she rotated in a circle with Archie and stepped into his former starting place. She turned to her father behind her. "Laird Ramsey would like to see you in his study."

She repeated the steps and returned across the floor to her starting place. She repeated the same steps, stopping before her father.

Kendrick leaned toward his daughter. "Where is the study?"

"Ask a servant. They will escort you," Sophie said over her shoulder before stepping away and continuing the dance.

Curious why the Laird of Hilltop would want to speak to him, Kendrick turned to his wife. "I'll return shortly." He left the ballroom, assuming someone at the gala event was ill. He asked a servant for directions to the laird's study and was escorted to the room instead.

~

Owen turned around at the sound of the door sliding open. "Doctor Conway, thank you for joining us." He watched the servant close the door, wondering what was keeping Sophie from returning with her father. "Welcome, and thank you for honoring my request to visit with me during the ball." Owen extended his hand and shook Kendrick's.

Marjorie, in tears, ran to her father and threw her arms around him. Kendrick patted her daughter's back. "Calm yourself." He looked at the host in question of their meeting.

"May I speak with you in private?" Owen requested.

Kendrick looked down into the eyes of his distraught daughter. "Go and sit before the fire. I will be with you in a moment."

Owen led his guest toward two chairs and a small table on the other side of the room. He offered a chair to the doctor before sitting on the opposite side of the table.

"Sophie has informed me that your maid, Flora, was murdered." Owen began.

"Aye."

"She also informed me that your maid was with bairn."

Kendrick's eyebrows drew together. "I was unaware and had no hint of the maid's condition. How did Sophie know Flora was with bairn?"

"She discovered the maid's journal in her room and read it in an entry. Chief Inspector McLeary has the journal as evidence. He also has a necklace that your maid wore on the night she was beaten. Unbeknownst to me, my maid was seeing a gentleman who gifted her an identical necklace. She is also with bairn. Your daughter, Marjorie, was given the same necklace tonight by the gentleman she is courting. Sophie saw the necklace your maid received as a gift from the gentleman she was seeing. She recognized the same necklace on her sister and, later, on my maid." He paused so the doctor could absorb the implication.

Kendrick glanced at his upset daughter, noticing the addition of a gold pendant around her neck that was absent during the ride to Hilltop. "So, Sophie believes the gentleman Marjorie is courting is the same person your maid and my maid . . ."

"Aye." Owen interrupted. "The case is weak, but if the evidence proves Carson Hamilton purchased all three necklaces, Sophie may have saved your family from embarrassment," he glanced at Marjorie, "in more ways than one. Once I learned of my maid's pregnancy, I forbade her from seeing him again, possibly saving her life." Owen stood, went to a side table, and picked up a crystal decanter. "Care for a whisky?"

"Please."

"I've sent for Chief Inspector McLeary. He should arrive soon." Owen poured whisky into two crystal glasses and gave one to the doctor. He glanced at the study doors, concerned about Sophie's delay.

Kendrick read his mind. "I believe Sophie is keeping an eye on Mister Hamilton while risking her toes of being stepped on by Mister Pringle." He grinned before sipping the caramel-colored beverage.

"If I may ask you to remain in the study with your daughter and my maid, I will ensure that Sophie's feet aren't suffering too badly."

Kendrick nodded as he motioned toward the doors.

Owen grinned before downing the last of his whisky and leaving the room.

Chapter 32

Owen entered the ballroom and stood among his guests on the edge of the dance floor. He scanned the twirling couples in search of Sophie. When he saw her dancing with a familiar gentleman, he scowled, recalling Mister Hamilton asking Sophie to dance at the previous ball. Acutely aware of the man's alleged crime, Owen was thankful Archie Pringle had injured her foot that night. Owen assumed the awkward man must have improved his dancing skills because Sophie appeared unscathed from her latest dance with him. As he watched Carson wrap his arm around Sophie's waist, Owen clenched his teeth and balled his hand into a fist, wishing the music would end.

Sophie saw Owen as she twirled by him. She smiled and winked.

He pulled aside a servant, pointed out Carson, and instructed him to keep a watchful eye on the gentleman for the remainder of the evening. If Carson left the mansion, the servant should notify him.

"Laird Ramsey?"

He turned around to see a familiar, overzealous mother and her daughter smiling from ear to ear. Owen forced himself to be polite and nodded as they curtsied.

The woman pushed her daughter forward. "May I introduce my daughter, Elizabeth, to you?"

"As I recall, I've met you twice before." The music was ending. "I hope you are enjoying the evening."

"Very much so." Elizabeth began. "I have many amiable qualities. I can sing and play the . . ."

"I'm certain you are quite talented. It's nice to see both of you again. If you will excuse me." Owen turned his back toward them.

Sophie curtsied to Carson, unable to look him in the eye. "It may have taken a while, Mister Hamilton, but I finally fulfilled my obligation to dance with you."

"Aye, as promised and appreciated." He glanced about the room. "Do you ken where Marjorie could be? She has been absent from my side for quite a while."

Sophie pretended to look about the room. "She seems to have disappeared." She offered a suggestion. "Maybe she is getting some punch."

He looked at the table in the corner of the room, where a large crystal bowl contained a red fruity beverage. "Aye, I'll search for her there."

Relieved to be rid of Carson, Sophie turned as Owen went to her side and escorted her from the dance floor. "When I went to fetch my father, Archie asked me to dance." She explained.

"Aye, he said as much."

"And then Carson followed through with my promise to dance with him. He asked if I had seen Marjorie. I sent him on a wayward trip to the punchbowl. Has Chief Inspector McLeary arrived?"

"No. He and his officers should be here soon, though." Owen clasped her hand as they wove through the crowded room and returned to the study.

~

Kendrick stood as Owen and Sophie entered the study. "My wife and youngest daughters may be wondering where I am. Please send word when the constable arrives, and I will return for his questioning."

Owen nodded and opened the door to allow Kendrick to leave. After securing the door, he turned to see Sophie standing in the center of the room, gazing at his vast library. He stepped beside her. "It may take you a lifetime to read them all."

She chuckled. "Och, probably not a lifetime. You have no idea how quickly I can read."

The study door opened. Everyone watched as Chief Inspector McLeary and a handful of constables entered the room.

"Chief Inspector, thank you for coming." Owen stepped forward and shook the officer's hand.

"Laird Ramsey." McLeary nodded at the doctor's daughter as she stepped beside Owen. "Miss Sophie."

"Hello, Chief Inspector." She glanced at Marjorie, who scooted to the edge of her seat. "Perhaps you should begin by interviewing me." Sophie suggested.

Owen motioned for the officer to sit at the small table with Sophie. "I'll go retrieve your father." He pulled the chair out for her to sit before leaving the room.

Sophie entwined her fingers and placed her clasped hand on the top of the table. "Thank you for coming, Chief Inspector. What I am about to share with you is only speculation. I'm certain you recall the necklace Haggadah gave to the constable for evidence, which belonged to Flora."

"Aye."

"My sister received an identical necklace from Carson Hamilton tonight. It was also revealed that Laird Ramsey's maid had an affair with a gentleman and received the same necklace."

"So, you're implying that Carson Hamilton may be the gentleman who beat your maid and caused her death."

"Aye."

Phoebe's broken heart had hardened into anger. She lifted her chin, stood from the chair, and approached the officer. "He told me his name was Sam, and like Flora, I too am with child, his child." She removed the necklace from around her neck and dropped it onto the table, ridding herself of the tainted trinket.

Overhearing the maid, Marjorie untied the ribbon from around her neck and took it to the Chief Inspector. "Here is the necklace Carson gave to me tonight." She laid it on the table.

Picking up the necklaces. They were both indeed a gold Celtic knot embellished with a ruby. McLeary concurred it was the same necklace found on the deceased maid. "To prove Carson Hamilton is possibly the murderer, we must discover where the necklaces were bought and verify if he purchased all three. Plus," he looked at Phoebe, "since you knew him as Sam, we must verify the man you were involved with is Carson Hamilton."

The study door slid open once again. Kendrick entered, followed by Owen.

Chief Inspector McLeary stood. "Doctor Kendrick, it is good to see you again." He turned to Owen. "Laird Ramsey. Would it be possible for you to have Mister Hamilton discreetly brought to the study?"

"Aye." Owen looked at Sophie and winked before leaving once again. He entered the ballroom and spotted Carson across the room. As expected, Hamilton was entertaining a lovely woman. Owen approached him, causing Carson to take notice and halt his conversation.

"Laird Ramsey, the ball is grand."

Owen refrained from showing his displeasure with his guest. "Thank you. If you come with me, Miss Conway is with Miss Sophie in my study."

Carson whispered to his female acquaintance. "Save a dance for me." He followed the Laird of Hilltop. "I have been searching for Miss Conway for nearly an hour. I'm pleased to hear she has been found."

~

Phoebe sat in the vacant chair across from Sophie and began wringing her hands. The minutes ticked by on the mantel clock, making it seem like an eternity. She stared at the door, anticipating the moment of truth, vowing to remain strong and do what must be done if Sam was indeed Carson.

As the door opened, Marjorie turned and stared into Carson's questioning eyes.

"There you are, Miss Conway. I have been searching for you." He smiled until he saw Phoebe stand and face him. His smile faded. He noted the officers in the room and heard the door shut behind him. "What's this?"

McLeary looked at Phoebe. "Well, is it him? Is he Sam?"

The maid lifted her chin before nodding. "Aye, it's Sam. He is the gentleman who gave me the necklace." Phoebe looked away, unable to withstand his deceitful face any longer. She was thankful Carson was unaware of her pregnancy and that the laird had forbidden her to see him, thus possibly saving her and her bairn's life.

Marjorie's heart ached. Her hopes instantly evaporated with the maid's identification of her former lover.

"Mister Hamilton, we have a few questions to ask you, but we will do so at the station house." McLeary nodded to his men, who escorted Carson out of the mansion.

Owen stepped forward. "What happens now?"

"We'll hold Mister Hamilton in a cell until we can interview the city's jewelers. If they hadn't sold him the necklaces, perhaps they would ken where he purchased them. Those in this room must go to the station house tomorrow and give their statement. You may be asked to testify in the future. Laird Ramsey, thank you for bringing this matter to our attention. I bid you all goodnight."

"Thank you." Owen shook the officer's hand and escorted him to the door. He sighed, pleased the matter was behind him. He turned and looked at his maid, determined for the evening to continue as planned. "Phoebe, you can return to your duties."

"Aye, and thank you, Laird." The maid curtsied and left the room.

Kendrick looked at Marjorie, reasonably sure she was ready to retire for the night. "Laird Ramsey, it has been an interesting evening, but it's time for me to collect my family and escort them home."

Owen looked at Sophie. The corners of her mouth turned upward slightly before she looked down at the floor.

Noticing her sister's disappointment, Marjorie stated. "I doubt Isobel and Grace will come willingly. You ken how much they like to dance. After all, this is the ball of the season."

"Then, if I may be so bold as to offer an escort for Isobel, Grace, and," Owen looked at the woman he had become quite taken with, "Sophie in my coach and deliver them home safely whenever they are ready to leave the ball?"

The expression on Owen's face confirmed Kendrick's suspicion of the laird's fondness for his favorite daughter. However, he wondered if she felt the same. "Sophie, is that agreeable with you?"

Sophie looked at Owen, appreciating his generosity. "Aye. I would like to stay, and I'm certain Isobel and Grace would like to do so too."

"Very well." Kendrick motioned for Marjorie to accompany him. "Goodnight, Sophie, Laird Ramsey. As I stated, it's been an interesting evening and one we shall always remember."

"Goodnight, Doctor Conway." Owen smiled at Sophie. "With your parents departing, we should keep a watchful eye on your sisters." He presented his bent arm.

She went to him and wrapped her gloved hand around his bicep.

Owen guided Sophie out the study door. At the entrance to the ballroom, he paused and looked at her. "Do you care to take another spin around the dance floor?'

Sophie grinned. "Only if you dare to risk me stomping on your feet?"

"Och! With you in my arms, I'm willing to take the chance. But as a precaution, I'm still wearing my heaviest boots." He smiled.

Chapter 33

Grace and Isobel giggled as they turned away from the punchbowl, sipped the spiked drink from their cups, and stood on the edge of the dance floor. They watched as their sister and the Laird of Hilltop stepped to its center.

The couple faced each other as the music began. Owen bowed, and Sophie curtsied. She looked up into his ocean-blue eyes, placed her hand in his palm, and her left hand on his shoulder. He stared intensely into her nearly gray eyes, desire masking his face. As they waltzed around the room, the strength of his arms and the security they offered made her smile. He smiled in return. She did not stumble nor step on his foot. He was indeed the right dance partner for her.

When the music faded, Owen delayed releasing Sophie from his embrace. With a regretful grin, he took a step backward. She curtsied as Owen bowed. When he stood, he noticed Sophie's sisters on the edge of the dance floor. "Shall we share the events of this evening with your sisters?" He nodded in the onlooker's direction.

Sophie turned to see Grace and Isobel. By their flushed faces and silly grins, she assumed they had indulged in the beverage more than they should. "Aye. I think it is wise to eliminate the drama of the evening and only inform them that we will be escorting them home. It looks as if they could use some air to clear their heads. May I suggest the veranda? We can speak to them out of the earshot of others."

The girls giggled and pointed at Sophie as she approached.

With her face intensifying to a vivid shade of red, Sophie grabbed her sisters by their hands and led them to the open door and out to the veranda. "The two of you are making fools of yourselves." She grabbed the cups from their hands and dumped the contents over the stone railing.

"Och!" Grace objected.

"Marjorie became ill, so Mum and Dad took her home to rest. Laird Ramsey has offered to accompany us in his carriage whenever we wish to leave the ball." She extended her index finger to emphasize her sternness. "No more punch. If I see you drink another glass, we will leave immediately. Do you understand?"

The girls nodded.

"Go and enjoy the rest of the evening, and remember, no more punch." Sophie sighed as her intoxicated sisters disappeared into the crowded ballroom. She sighed and turned to Owen.

He was impressed by Sophie's handling of her sisters and quite happy they were out of the way. Finally, alone with her, he offered his bent arm. "Shall we take a stroll in the garden?"

Sophie threaded her arm within his. "Sounds lovely."

They descended the front stairs and walked to the torchlit garden. With the merriment of the guests and the music serenading them in the background, they entered the pathway and strolled among the trimmed hedges and shrubs. The fragrance of blooming flowers lingering in the air caused Sophie to inhale and momentarily close her eyes.

Owen admired the profile of her face. "May I affirm once again that I don't like hosting balls, but in your company, it's at least tolerable."

Sophie chuckled. "I ken the circumstances of this night have been quite unusual."

"Aye." He placed his hand on her dainty fingers wrapped around his arm. "Miss Sophie, since meeting you, my perspective on life has changed greatly."

She looked into his ocean-blue eyes, curious about what he might say next.

"After visiting the vaults and observing the plight of those within it, I have decided not to cast Phoebe out." He stopped walking, unthreaded her arm, and held her hands within his as he faced her. "I would like to help alleviate the situation that women, such as Phoebe, face. Their bairns are innocent and should not be condemned for a mistake or a moment of lust by their mums."

"Aye. What do you propose?"

Giving himself a moment to think, Owen watched a couple walk past them. "I don't rightly know. I cannot cast my maid and her bairn to a destitute life."

"They need a place to live," Sophie began, "and a way to make a respectable living to provide for themselves and their bairns."

Owen looked up at the sparkling stars splattered across the night sky like an abstract painting. "Aye."

Sophie looked skyward too. "I don't think you will find the answer among the stars." She looked at his profile. "But I'm confident you will think of something."

He stared into her eyes as he brought her hands near his heart, forcing her to step toward him. "I often think about the first time I saw you in the kirkyard and bless the day our paths crossed. You helped me realize that I no longer want a life of solitude. I've discovered I feel whole in your company and incomplete when you are away from me."

Sophie's stomach fluttered as if tiny butterflies flew within it. Then, she recalled Haggadah's words and grinned. "I must admit, you are the perfect partner to guide me around the dance floor, preventing me from looking like an awkward fool or stepping on your toes."

He smiled. "Sophie, I hope I can be more to you than a dance partner." Owen took a deep breath and exhaled before revealing his heart's desire. "I promise to prevent you from falling and pick you up if you do. You mean everything to me, and I love you dearly. My fondest desire is to share my life with you and be by your side when you wake every morning."

Sophie's grin faded at his serious tone.

"Will you do me the honor of becoming my wife?" With hope, Owen waited for her reply.

Sophie scanned the handsome features of his face as she searched her heart. She had believed society's prejudiced rumors of the Laird of Hilltop, only to have them dissipate like a fog as she grew to know his true character. She enjoyed being in his company, admired his intellect, and his willingness to truly listen to her perspective on all matters, including books. He was kind and thoughtful. Did she love him? The corners of her mouth turned upward, and she smiled. "Aye."

Owen lifted her hands to his lips and kissed them. He kissed her forehead before touching his forehead to hers. "I suppose asking your father for your hand in marriage is in order."

Chapter 34

The sun peeked over the horizon. Sophie woke, rolled onto her back, and smiled as she stared at the ceiling. Even though Owen had escorted her and her sisters home in the early morning hours, Sophie was too excited to remain in bed any longer. As she rose and put on an everyday muslin dress, she wondered when Owen would ask her father for her hand in marriage. Until then, their engagement would remain a secret. She picked up her golden gown from the back of her desk chair, held it before her body, and stared at herself in the full-length mirror. Sophie smiled, recalling the heartfelt proposal from her future husband.

With her joyous news bottled up inside her, she left the house while her family was still in bed.

The sun's rays peeked through the scattered clouds, shining on the sidewalk as if illuminating Sophie's way through Old Town.

~

Barret's ears lifted upward, and he tilted his head as quickened footsteps on the flagstone walkway announced a visitor. He stood from his favorite spot near the fireplace and went to the door.

Tavish arrived moments ago to join Haggadah for breakfast. He stirred the glowing embers and placed a log on the fire. He looked toward the canine, assuming Barret heard the footfalls of an ill person in need of a remedy.

The town witch entered the house through the back door. She placed a basket of eggs on the worktable and noticed Barret at the door. "A visitor? So, early in the morning." Haggadah arrived at the door as a knock sounded. She looked down at her canine companion, his tail wagging like a loose shutter. "Ah, you ken who it is." The town witch opened the door to see Sophie's smiling face. "You bring us good news, I see."

"Aye." Sophie entered and petted Barret. "Hello, Tavish."

"Good morning, Lass." He swung the kettle over the fire to heat the water.

Haggadah closed the door. "I assume the news has to do with the ball."

Inhaling deeply at the thought of conveying the drama, Sophie nodded. "We'll need to make tea before I tell of the evening's events."

~

Owen returned to Hilltop after escorting the Conway sisters home, only to toss and turn in his bed the remainder of the night. As the sun announced the new day, he left his bedroom, unrested. After several cups of coffee to clear the cobwebs from his mind, Owen sat at his desk and found it impossible to concentrate on business matters.

Phoebe entered the study. "Laird, would you be wanting your breakfast now?" She looked inside the coffee pot to ensure some remained.

"No, have my horse saddled." He tossed the paper in his hand onto the stack to his right, went to his bedroom, and made himself presentable for his future father-in-law. He heard his maid call from the bottom of the stairs when his horse was saddled and awaited him. Descending the staircase, he thanked Phoebe, climbed atop his awaiting ebony stallion, and rode to the Conway house while rehearsing his request in his head.

~

Vertie placed a bowl of fried potatoes on the table for the family's late breakfast. The maid left the dining room and stood in the hallway to eavesdrop on their discussion of the previous night's ball.

"There isn't much to tell. I was feeling unwell and needed to come home." Marjorie informed her nosy sisters.

"Where did Mister Hamilton go? He seemed to disappear too." Grace pried.

"I believe he left for the evening about the same time." Kendrick added as he sipped his coffee.

"Didn't Laird Ramsey and Sophie look magnificent on the dance floor?" Isobel prompted.

A knock sounded on the front door. Vertie silently cursed as she fisted her hand and went to answer it. The maid was surprised to see the very gentleman, who was the topic of discussion, at the front door. "Laird Ramsey. If you wish to see Sophie, she is not here. I believe I heard her leave the house just after sunrise." The maid noticed his ebony horse tied to the post in the street.

"Good, because I wish to speak to Doctor Conway, privately." Owen requested.

"Please come inside, and I will announce your arrival." She stood aside for Owen to enter. The maid left him standing in the foyer while she stepped away.

Overhearing the maid, Grace, Isobel, and Marjorie left the dining room, went to the hallway, and curtsied.

"Good morning." Owen removed his hat.

"Good morning, Laird Ramsey." Marjorie greeted. "I want to thank you for your assistance last night."

"You're welcome, Miss Conway."

"The ball was splendid. When will you host another?" Grace encouraged.

Vertie returned before Owen could reply. "Laird Ramsey, follow me, please." She escorted Owen to the doctor's study, waited for him to enter, and closed the door.

Kendrick stepped from behind his desk. "Good day, Laird Ramsey." He shook the gentleman's hand and motioned toward the vacant chair in front of his desk before sitting in his chair. "Thank you, again, for all of your help last night and for escorting my daughters safely home."

"It was my pleasure." Owen placed his hat in his lap as he sat.

"Is there something you need?" The doctor inquired, wondering the reason for Owen's visit.

"Aye. With your permission, I would like to marry Miss Sophie."

Kendrick sat back in his chair. "I see." He inhaled in thought. "She is my favorite daughter, you ken. To part with her will be difficult."

Owen admitted. "To part with one so dear is indeed difficult."

"I've vowed to never arrange a marriage for my daughters. So, does Sophie's heart feel as deeply as yours does?"

"I proposed to her last night. She accepted, knowing we cannot proceed with the ceremony without your permission."

Kendrick could think of no finer gentleman than the Laird of Hilltop to become Sophie's husband. She would be well cared for and live in luxury. However, knowing her best, she would not have agreed unless she truly loved the man sitting before him. "Then, I give you my permission to wed Sophie."

Squeals of excitement echoed from behind the closed door.

Owen and Kendrick looked in its direction.

"Snooping daughters." Kendrick chuckled. "I'm certain you have realized Sophie has a mind of her own. Thankfully. I would have it no other way."

Owen smiled. "Aye, nor I. It's what I admire about her most."

"Have you set a date for the wedding?"

"No, not yet."

"I think August is a lovely month for a wedding." Kendrick suggested.

"Aye, then August it will be." As both men stood, Owen shook the doctor's extended hand. "Thank you." He put on his hat and opened the door. Grace and Isobel, whose ears were pressed against it, nearly fell into his arms.

"Do any of you ken where I may find Sophie?"

Marjorie smiled. "This early in the morning, she could only be in two places. Either the Princes Street Garden or Haggadah's cottage."

"Most likely the town witch's cottage." Isobel confirmed.

"Then I shall look for her there. Thank you. Good day." Owen left the house, eager to share the news with his bride-to-be.

~

Haggadah lowered her teacup to the saucer. She shook her head. "Och, that poor maid. At least she didn't suffer the same fate as Flora."

"Laird Ramsey said he won't sack her. He didn't want to condemn her to the vaults. I'm not certain what he has planned for her, but it's only a matter of time before her bairn begins to make its presence known."

Tavish looked at his cap and the purple ribbon on the peg. Knowing the criminal who killed the poor maid was captured, there was little reason to remain sleeping on the street. He ate the last of his buttered bread as an idea formed in his mind.

Barret stood from his resting spot by the fireplace. His ears perked, and his head tilted to the side. Nero opened his eyes to watch the dog, twisted his body into an awkward position, and returned to napping on Haggadah's bed.

Haggadah looked at the front door. "A guest is arriving for you, Sophie."

As a knock sounded, Sophie opened the door to see Owen's smiling face. "I see you tracked me down."

"Aye." He stepped inside and nodded to Haggadah and Tavish before petting Barret.

"I assume you bring us good news, Laird Ramsey." The town witch prompted.

"Aye." Owen turned to Sophie. "I spoke to your father. He has granted us permission to marry. We are to wed in August."

"August? That's next month." Plans for the wedding swirled in Sophie's mind.

"Congratulations." Tavish stepped forward and shook the laird's hand.

Haggadah stood from her chair. "An August wedding will be lovely. Congratulations." She began clearing the dishes. "The two of you have plans to make. Run along now."

Chapter 35

With Sophie busy with wedding plans over the following weeks, Owen tried to devise a solution to Phoebe's predicament. He often rode to New Town, met with advisors, and hoped to find a way for single mothers to live and provide for themselves and their children.

He was pacing the floor of his study when Phoebe entered and presented a letter that had been delivered. Breaking the seal, Owen smiled. "Phoebe, have my horse saddled."

"Aye."

After riding into the heart of the city, Owen arrived at the bookstore and entered. "Mister Edwards, I understand my order has arrived."

The bookstore owner looked over the rim of his glasses at his customer. "Aye, Laird Ramsey."

"Perfect, it is a wedding gift for Miss Sophie." Owen grinned.

"Congratulations on your upcoming nuptials. For the happy occasion, allow me the time to wrap it in some special paper." Mister Edwards did so quickly and wrapped it a second time in brown paper to protect it on the journey to Hilltop. He presented the package to Owen.

"Thank you. I'm sure Miss Sophie will thoroughly enjoy this gift." Touching his index finger to the brim of his hat, Owen set off on another errand with the package in hand.

~

The warm sunny day was cooled by a gentle breeze that made the leaves on the trees appear to wave in celebration. A pair of the finest coaches waited outside the Conway house. Laird Ramsey stood at the open door of the first coach. His stomach was in a nervous knot as he awaited his bride. He wiped his damp palms on his dress kilt of blue, black, and white.

"Now, Soph, remember, you must step out of the house with your right foot," Grace lectured, "your right foot. Otherwise, you will have bad luck. Oh, and I put a sixpence in your shoe too."

Sophie emerged from her bedroom, followed by her sisters and mother. She paused at the top of the staircase dressed in her Conway tartan gown of steel blue, black, accented with gold, light blue, and the prettiest shade of heather stripes. The skirt with a split in the center allowed a second ivory skirt to show. In her hand was a small bouquet of heather that contained a white rose and a single sprig of white heather for good luck. A strip of her family's tartan was tied in a bow at the base of the flowers. She tilted her head to the side as she descended the stairs. "Another one of your silly superstitions, Grace." Secretly, she prayed she would not trip down the stairs.

Vertie, who seldom spoke unless spoken to, watched from the bottom of the staircase as Sophie descended. "Best not tempt fate, Miss Sophie."

Over the past few months, Sophie's perspective on the superstitions practiced by those who lived long ago had changed. They knew of the evil in the world and had no way of fending it off other than to perform and believe in their rituals for protection. Were their beliefs far-fetched? Did she not see those who would die in the parade of souls? Was the belief that a walnut could predict a woman's husband so terrible?

Sophie glanced at Vertie as the maid opened the front door. She stared into the ocean-blue eyes of the man who stood before her, counted her blessings, and heeded everyone's warnings before stepping onto the stoop with her right foot.

Grace sighed in relief.

Owen stepped forward, presented his hand, and escorted his bride to the coach. Once inside, Sophie took her usual place, and Owen sat across from her.

"You look lovely." His smile was genuine.

"I must admit, your full dress is impressive. However, I feel I pale in comparison." She grinned, staring at his exposed knee below his kilt.

"Pale in comparison? My dear, I think of you as the most beautiful woman today and will forevermore think so. I'm so proud to call you as my wife."

They decided on a private ceremony and, going against tradition, not walk the distance with a piper or fiddler leading the way. The coach jerked forward and drove the short distance to Saint Cuthbert. As it came to a stop before the kirk and the coachman opened the door, Owen exited and helped his bride disembark to join him. They waited momentarily for the family to exit from their coach.

Owen looked at his bride. "Ready?"

Sophie was never more certain of herself. "Aye."

The bride and groom led the procession into the kirk. Haggadah, Tavish, and Wiley were already seated. Barret, whose tail beat like a drum against the pew, seemed to smile when he saw Sophie.

The priest began the sermon. His monotoned voice droned on like the reverberating clang of a church bell echoing over the city. However, the bride and groom were deaf to his words as they stared into each other's eyes.

". . . the tying of the knot." The priest's words registered in their minds.

Sophie untied the Conway strip of fabric from her bouquet and handed her flowers to Marjorie, who sat in the front row. She faced the groom as Owen pulled the Ramsey strip of material from his sporran.

Grace had made her sister practice this vital part of the ceremony. Sophie glanced at her youngest sister, who nodded her encouragement.

The bride and groom held each end of both strips of fabric.

"The bride will tie her tartan around the groom's tartan as a sign of her loyalty and devotion." The priest paused while she did so. "The groom will tie his tartan around the bride's tartan as a sign of his loyalty and devotion." The priest paused while it was done. Finally, the clergyman explained, "With each tartan representing the families, these two knots will join as one."

Sophie and Owen pulled the end of their spouse's tartan, forcing the knots to slide along the fabric until they joined as one in the center.

The priest went on to clarify. "The tighter the fabric is pulled, the stronger the knot is joined. Owen and Sophie, this knot represents your marriage today and always."

Owen put the knotted fabrics in his sporran. As in tradition, it would be displayed for guests to see when they visit Hilltop.

"And now the lighting of the unity candle." The priest stepped aside for the couple to approach the three candles. The outer two candles were lit. Sophie clasped one while Owen took the other from its holder.

The priest went on to explain. "Each candle in their hand represents their clan. As they light the center candle, it represents the two families coming together."

The bride and groom lit the center candle's wick, put each candle in its holder, and returned to their place before the altar.

After they exchanged vows, Owen placed a wedding ring on Sophie's finger.

The priest poured whisky from a decorative pitcher into a quaich. He handed the silver dish to Owen, who grasped both handles and sipped the warming liquid. The groom looked into his bride's eyes, lifted the vessel to her lips, and tilted it for her to drink the last of the whisky before giving the quaich back to the priest.

After a final blessing of the couple, the bride and groom held hands as they faced their guests. The priest announced, "May I present the Laird and Lady of Hilltop!"

The newlyweds faced each other to seal their commitment with a tradition they anticipated. Owen stepped toward his wife until their bodies were nearly touching, lifted her chin with the knuckle of his index finger, and reverently kissed her. Sophie flung her arms around his neck, deepening their kiss as her husband wrapped his arms around her waist and lifted her off the floor. The guests' laughter was accompanied by their applause.

Marjorie handed the bouquet to Sophie as the couple walked down the aisle, and the guests rang bells provided by the kirk. Once outside, Owen kissed his wife again.

The children living in the surrounding area began to gather at the entrance of the kirk, anticipating the wedding tradition.

Kendrick was the first to hug his newly married daughter. "Congratulations, Sophie. I wish you every happiness."

"Thank you, Father."

"I'm so happy for you, Soph." Grace hugged her sister, as did Marjorie, Isobel, and Elspeth, while Kendrick shook his new son-in-law's hand, welcoming him to the family.

Owen clasped his wife's hand and led her to a small table with a beautiful wedding cake in the center. Isla stood proudly behind it. Sophie turned to her husband, who explained. "I thought it would be nice for all our guests," he looked at Haggadah, Tavish, Wiley, and Barret as they exited the kirk, "to partake in the celebration too."

Sophie's heart burst with happiness. "Thank you for including them." She admired the two-tiered cake. "It looks delicious. Thank you for making it."

"Let me remove the top layer. It must be saved for the celebration of the firstborn." Isla winked. After transferring it to a plate, Isla presented the knife to the bride, who made the initial cut of the fruit cake flavored with brandy. Sophie handed the knife to Isla, who cut and placed a piece on a plate for each guest.

The bride and groom approached Haggadah, who awaited her turn to speak to the newlyweds. "Thank you for attending the ceremony."

Haggadah hugged Sophie, foreseeing only happiness in the young couple's future. "I appreciate the invitation to witness your vows. After you settle in at

Hilltop, please come visit me," she said, looking at Owen, "both of you, whenever you have a chance."

"We promise." Sophie squatted and petted Barret. "And I'll come and see you too." The canine wagged his tail. "Please, have a piece of cake. Make sure Barret gets a piece too." She grinned, patting the dog's head again.

The Laird of Hilltop shook Tavish and Wiley's hands, thanking them for attending and encouraging them to enjoy a piece of cake.

Owen kissed his bride's hand. "Come with me." He led her to his parents' grave. "Mum, Dad, I have searched long for the perfect woman to share my life with. I love her dearly, and I believe you would approve of my choice. I would like to introduce my wife, Sophie Ramsey, Lady of Hilltop."

A breeze whistled through the leaves of the trees as if his parents whispered their approval.

Sophie curtsied and bowed her head respectfully. "As you look down upon us from above, I'm sure your hearts swell with pride as Owen carries forth the legacy of the Ramsey name. He is a proper and respected laird, and I hope to fulfill the role of his wife and the Lady of Hilltop and that you will be proud to call me your daughter-in-law. I love Owen wholeheartedly and promise to remain steadfast by his side."

The newlyweds stopped by Flora and Jack's graves. Sophie glanced from one headstone to the other, taken back by what she saw.

Owen confessed. "I didn't want their graves to remain unmarked. Haggadah told me their names." He looked at the small, engraved headstones. "Their lives had significance, and they should be remembered."

Sophie wrapped her hand around her husband's arm and nodded, holding back her tears. "Aye."

They returned to their quaint reception, visited with their guests, and enjoyed a piece of cake. As the Laird and Lady of Hilltop stepped inside their coach to depart, Kendrick threw coins into the air and watched the children scurry to gather them. Sophie could hear Grace and Isobel arguing over who would get her vacant bedroom.

The husband and wife sat arm-in-arm on the seat.

"I received a note from Chief Inspector McLeary this morning. He said they found the jeweler who sold Mister Hamilton the necklaces. He will testify as a witness during the trial, accusing Carson of Flora's death. It will be up to a magistrate to determine his fate."

"I'm pleased to see justice will be done. Flora can rest peacefully now." Sophie looked out the window. "Where are we going?"

"We have one stop before going home," Owen announced.

"I like the sound of that. Home." Sophie grinned. "Where are we stopping?"

"It's a surprise, a wedding gift."

The grin faded on Sophie's face. "A wedding gift? But I didn't get you a gift."

"My dear, you have given me the greatest gift of all, your heart."

~

Haggadah chuckled. "I've yet to eat a second bite of cake, and Barret has already finished his piece."

Tavish glanced at the dog, licking the crumbs from the plate. He finished his piece of the tasty dessert and waited patiently for Haggadah to do the same. A servant collected their empty plates and silverware as she ate the last bite.

"Well, I think it's time to fulfill my long overdue promise to you." Tavish stated as he clasped the fingertips of Haggadah's hand, brought it to his lips, and kissed it. "After all these years, my heart still belongs to you."

Haggadah watched as Tavish pulled the purple ribbon from his pocket.

"Will you do me the honor of becoming my wife?"

Haggadah stared at the ribbon in his hand, unaware Tavish had taken it from the peg. She had dreamed of his returning, to be held in his arms once again, and live with him as husband and wife in her tiny, aged cottage. Much to her disappointment, her dream faded over the years and became a nightmare of loneliness. Now, the possibility of sharing her life with the man she loved was about to come true. She looked into Tavish's sincere, chestnut eyes. "What took you so long?" She grinned. "Aye, with all my heart, I will wed you."

They returned inside the kirk to see the priest sitting in a pew, waiting. He turned toward the sound of footsteps and took his place on the altar. Noting only the pair who stood before him, he ventured a question. "Do you have a witness?"

"Aye." Came a reply from the back of the kirk.

The couple turned to see Wiley and Barret walking up the aisle.

The gravedigger smiled. "We'll be their witness."

The priest raised an eyebrow at the canine as he sat before the couple and took a deep breath. "Let's begin." He motioned for the bride and groom to face each other.

"No need to make this a long ceremony, Father. After all, we've just attended a wedding and don't need it repeated." Tavish stated as he clasped Haggadah's hand and gave the purple ribbon to the priest, who entwined it around their hands.

"Very well, then. Tavish, do you take Haggadah to be your wife, to love and cherish until parted by death?"

"Aye." Tavish smiled.

"And Haggadah, do you take Tavish to be your husband to love and cherish until parted by death?"

"Aye."

"The ring." The priest looked at Tavish.

With a smile on his face, Tavish pulled a small box from his pocket, opened it, and proudly showed Haggadah the golden wedding band engraved with a Celtic knot. At its center was a detailed thistle with an amethyst stone for its blossom.

Haggadah's mouth dropped open.

The priest removed the ribbon from the couple's clasped hands and watched Tavish place the wedding ring on his bride's finger.

"By the power invested in me by our Lord above, I pronounce you husband and wife. You may kiss."

Tavish placed the palm of his hand on his wife's cheek and lowered his lips to meet hers.

Haggadah put her hand atop his as their lips met. As the couple lingered in the moment, Barret stood and barked. Parting, the newlyweds looked at the canine and grinned.

The priest handed Tavish the ribbon keepsake and waited for him to put it in his pocket before shaking the groom's hand and congratulating the couple.

Wiley stepped forward. "Finally, after all these years. Congratulations and best wishes."

"Thank you, Wiley." Haggadah looked up at her husband as he shook the gravedigger's hand. "Well, I got work to do. Good day."

As the couple left the kirk, Haggadah threaded her arm through Tavish's bent elbow. "Do you mind if we stop at my mum's grave?"

Her husband nodded before they walked the short distance and stood before Freya's resting place.

"Mum, I finally married Tavish, but I'm certain you ken that as you watch over me from above. I'm happy, quite happy. He's a good man." Haggadah looked up at the kind face of her husband. "Let's go home."

They exited through the iron gate of the kirk and stepped onto the sidewalk.

"Och, my husband, I forgot to tell you. I still have my mum's tin with the coins you gave me for our future."

Tavish grinned. "You didn't spend them over the years?"

"No. I knew you would return, someday." Haggadah smiled.

~

The coach stopped before a building, and the coachman opened the door. Owen stepped out and helped his wife step onto the sidewalk. She looked up and saw a sign that read 'Flora's Place' in bold letters on the building. Peeking through the large picture window, she saw a display of pastries and various loaves of bread. Turning to her husband, Sophie scowled. "I don't understand."

"You will. Let's go inside." He encouraged her as he placed his hand on the small of her back and opened the door.

Phoebe greeted them as the couple entered. "Congratulations, Laird and Lady Ramsey. I'm pleased to welcome you and give you a tour."

Sophie saw tables with chairs, a counter with a register, a display case with pastries, racks with loaves of bread, and several women working to create the delicious delicacies. She looked at Phoebe with an askance expression.

The former maid proudly explained. "Through the kindness of Laird Ramsey, he has provided a way for homeless, unwed, or widowed women, some with bairns, to work and provide for themselves. The upper floors are used for housing, and we have a teacher who comes to educate the children. Isla has shared her recipes and taught the women how to make them. Together, we women operate the shop, and our bairns are safe," she smiled and placed the palm of her hand on her abdomen. "Or will soon be, and we have a roof over our heads. We are eternally grateful for Laird Ramsey's generosity."

Sophie cupped her hand over her mouth as she scanned the shop's interior. Her eyes welled with tears and cascaded down her cheeks.

"Hey, I thought this would make you happy." Owen took her in her arms and drew her into his chest.

She could hardly speak the words. "It has made me happier than I thought I ever could be. I just wish Flora . . ."

He looked down into her tear-streaked face and gently brushed away the falling droplets with his thumbs. "We can't change the past, but we have honored her memory in a way that will help others like her."

Sophie nodded.

"I can't save all the women, but this place is a start." He kissed her forehead. "Hush now. This is our wedding day. You are supposed to be happy."

"I am. These are happy tears." Sophie went to the display window and gazed at the delicious pastries. "I have never seen such thick scones. They must be two inches tall." She turned toward her husband. "Promise me, we will eat here at least once a week."

Owen laughed. "Aye, once a week." He extended his hand toward her. "Come, I have another gift for you at home."

"Honestly, I don't think you can top this one."

"Probably not, but I feel you may like it all the same."

Bidding Phoebe and the women farewell, the newlyweds returned to their coach and headed to Hilltop.

Sophie was going home, home to Hilltop. She imagined the many happy years they would share as husband and wife and, if blessed, fill the mansion with children.

As the coach stopped before the steps of the front door, Owen swooped his bride into his arms and carried her over the threshold. He gently lowered her to the floor of the foyer before kissing her. "Now, as promised, your other wedding gift." He guided her toward his study and motioned for her to sit in an upholstered chair before the fireplace. He retrieved a wrapped package from his desk and placed it in her lap.

Sophie giggled as she carefully unwrapped the gift, read each spine, and opened each book to the title page. She counted them. "Six?" She looked up at her husband, who stood before her with his arm crossed over his chest.

"Aye, every book written by the anonymous author."

"Mister Ramsey, you certainly ken how to win my heart."

"As you have won mine, Missus Ramsey." Owen grasped both arms of the chair, leaned forward, and kissed his wife gently.

If you enjoyed reading

The Parade Of Souls

please post your review on Amazon.

For additional information about the author, signings, and her books, please visit

www.BrendaHasseBooks.com